THE UNSEEN GODDESS

The Unseen Goddess

A novel

Sangeetha Shinde

Contact Information:

Villa Magna Publishing, LLC
4705 Columbus Street
Suite 300
Virginia Beach, VA 23462

www.villamagnapublishing.com

ISBN: 978-1-940178-74-5 (pbk)
ISBN: 978-1-940178-75-2 (ebook)

For Ammachi, my paternal grandmother,
a woman who was almost a century ahead of her time,
and Kardelen Azazi, for all that she is, and all that she is to me.

About the Author

Sangeetha Shinde began her writing career at the age of 14 when she won first prize for her essay on world peace. She has since published four books with The Unseen Goddess being her fifth. She has a successful journalism career that has included Principal Correspondent, Contributing Editor, Publishing Director and Managing Editor for publications such as The times of India, Living Well Magazine, I Magazine, The Capital Magazine, The Business Innovator and Aspire Magazine. Her 2017 manifesto 'I am an Indian woman', went viral on the Internet and was published by Vidura, The Press Institute of India, and by Mind's Journal. She is currently Managing Director of Incubation Worldwide and Managing Editor of Inside43 Magazine.

Sangeetha has been working with women and men from different parts of the world for many years, helping them overcome the trauma of abuse and oppression, having lived through the same herself. She has conducted workshops on creative writing and women's empowerment in India and spoken on women's issues at European conferences. Her work won her the award of The South Indian 'Most Inspirational Woman of the Year 2019' and a place on the Haut Monde judging panel for the Mrs India Worldwide contest, 2019. She has coached the Ethnic Queen

2022 contestants in Malaysia and lectured at the Defense Services Staff College in India in 2020.

She delivered the keynote address at the Women's Day celebrations at IYTE, one of Turkey's largest universities in 2022, and addressed the University Women's Association of the Nilgiris for Women's Day, 2023. Sangeetha was a professor at IYTE teaching creative writing and spoken English in 2023.

She is a passionate advocate for animal rights and injustice in all its forms. She has single-handedly rescued and rehabilitated 57 stray animals, including a Brahmini Kite, a Bulbul, three parrots, and an assortment of dogs and cats around the world. She has also volunteered and fundraised at/for animal charities in the Middle East and India.

Sangeetha is currently working on several books relating to the cause of women's rights in India. She has lived and worked in 7 countries, to date. She is fascinated by the paranormal and Tudor England history, is absurdly fond of dogs, and is a die-hard Trekkie. Her ultimate aim is to leave the planet a kinder and fairer place than she entered it.

Other Books by Sangeetha Shinde

The Naked Indian Woman

The Book of Anglo Indian Tales

A Moral Murder and Other Tales from the Blue Hills

Amman: Story

Table of Contents

Prologue

Today Amma left and I don't know what will happen to me from this point onward. For the last two years she has sustained me, keeping me alive and well in this misery that is my life. How will I bear this loss? As her car drove away, I wanted to run after it and scream at her for abandoning me. But she had already explained to me in her broken Tamil, that she could not take me with her, for she was going to a faraway place, out of India. I know it is a really big world - at least I think it is. But even going to the T Nagar market is a big adventure for me. What do I know of far-flung places when I have not even visited the other side of this crowded, dusty city? All I know are my little area, my slum, my little one-room house and the neighbours there. But as I think these bleak thoughts I realise that, without Amma, my life has changed forever and I am suddenly angry that she showed me a different world, and then left taking that world with her. Perhaps it is better never to know better things, for then you never miss them.

Even as a child who was sold into misery I never felt such a keen sense of loss. Perhaps as an adult, a grown woman with three children - no, two children, for I must never think of the other one - one feels things more deeply.

I am still standing at the side of the road, staring down the busy, smoggy road, hoping that I will see Amma's car coming back to take me away from this life. All the security men at Amma's old building are laughing and smirking at me; they are delighted I no longer have her protection. My husband is among those men, and he is perhaps the happiest of them all now that

Amma has gone away leaving me without the support that has kept me safe these last two years.

I suppose now my life goes back to what it was always meant to be – an unceasing flow of time where one weary day blends into the next, while I struggle to survive this world I wish I had never been born into.

I turn around and walk home with slow and measured steps, ignoring the jubilant gaze of the clutch of watchmen at the building and it seems to me the dust clings a little more stubbornly to my feet today. As I near the slum, that is my neighbourhood, people come out to stare at me as I pass by. Kalyani, then Prema, and Lakshmi, then the others trickle out to see me walk home, staring silently at me, willing me to break down and cry. But I refuse to give them that satisfaction.

"Let them stare. Let them laugh. Let them mock. I will overcome this too. Somewhere inside of me, I will find the strength to find another life for myself."

The fish stall next to my house is buzzing with flies. The sound they make seems even louder than usual. The smell is really bad – Prema must be selling older fish than usual. How I hate living next door to her shop. The smell of her fish clings to my clothes and those of my children, no matter how much I wash them. If I hang them to dry elsewhere, maybe they would smell of the precious soap I spend so much money on, but in this dangerous slum, I cannot leave my clothes to dry anywhere except at the front of my house, or else they will be stolen.

It is dark and stuffy inside the house. I look around the tiny room, that serves me as kitchen, bedroom, living room, dining room and bathing room and a fresh longing comes over me to be back in Amma's house, with its cream curtains and beautiful furniture and delicate scents. Amma's house was beautiful and people envied that I worked there. But I know what they really envied was how Amma treated me. With kindness and courtesy. She always said thank you and please to me and always offered to share her food with me and used to make me cups of tea if she thought I had worked too hard. The first time she did it, I was too embarrassed to accept it for it was my job, not hers, to make the tea. She offered it to me in one of her own mugs, and I was also too embarrassed to accept such an offering. I suggested she bring a cheap mug and plate for me to use, but she laughed and said it was silly to buy more things and she expected me to use the same things that she did. I really thought she was quite mad and to this day my neighbours at the slum refuse to believe me thinking I made it up to make myself seem grander than them.

Amma rarely shouted but whenever she did, it felt like my world had ended. But afterwards, she always came and put an arm around me and said sorry, and then the sun would shine for me once again. I loved working for her and the prestige of being her servant lifted my life out of a routine of daily survival and struggle.

My children are not at home and my husband is on the day shift of his security guard duties. I have this tiny 50 square-foot concrete room with its asbestos roofing to myself - what a luxury. I sit down and open the bag Amma gave me before she left. In it I find a picture of her and me standing in her kitchen and an envelope filled with - one, two, three - thousand rupees. This last act of kindness and the sight of Amma's smiling face finally breaks the dam that has been welling up inside me. The tears pour down my face as I put Amma's picture on the little shelf where I keep the pictures of all the Goddesses I have worshipped my whole life, and yet have never seen. The memories of my good times with her only serve to remind me that I have, once again, fallen back to my old life.

PART I

Chapter One

THE CHILDHOOD

My memories of childhood are fragmented. I have heard that one can normally remember right back to the time one is three or four, but my recollections are hazy. Prema, the woman who keeps the smelly fish stall next door to my house, says she can remember being born, but all of us in the slum know that she is a liar. She lies about the freshness of her fish all the time, even though we know from the smell they are three days old, at the very least. But this is not about Prema, but my early years. I have some clear memories of my childhood, but it can be argued that I never really had a childhood, not the way they show it on television these days. I keep telling my children how lucky they are since all they have to do is go to school and come home and play and eat the food I make for them.

I recollect playing with some marbles I had found in a dustbin. They were two of them, one blue with red cloudy stripes running through it, and the other a wonderful transparent green. I remember looking through the green marble, with one eye tightly shut. Through the marble the world looked wonderfully distorted and blurred, and all of it seemed to be bathed in a green light. That's when green became my favourite colour I think. I rolled them around enjoying seeing the bright spheres against the sandy whiteness of the roadside. Then my two brothers came and pushed me away, grabbing the marbles for themselves.

The eldest one, Mani, grinned and shoved me aside saying, "Little girls don't play with marbles. Are you a boy or a girl? Go be a girl and cook with mother."

My other brother, Senthil, also older than me, stuck his tongue out at me mockingly. They were both several years older than me, almost grown up to my little eyes. I must have only been about five, but even then I knew it was pointless to cry. I grabbed a nearby stick and began tracing designs in the dust instead, ignoring them quite magnificently. I wished inside my head I was my little sister instead. She was just a little over a year old and my parents had named her Radhi. In Tamil it means *beautiful woman*, and she was a beautiful baby, with wheat-coloured skin and the softest, downiest curls on her head.

We used to live in an area called *Thousand Lights* in Chennai. It was just a small room at the top of a grimy, rickety building. I had to climb four flights of stairs to get there and by the end of that journey I was always tired. When I got a little older, if my mother needed something, down I would have to go again, to buy onions or tomatoes or whatever she needed and make the arduous journey up the stairs once more. My brothers were never asked to run errands, as they had their jobs after school, acting as delivery boys for the dïosa kadai down the road. My father was never at home, working at a nearby garage fixing scooters from ten in the morning until whatever hour he chose to return home.

One day I was so tired. It was summer, and the hot sun had made me dizzy and sweaty. I had waited to be served at the little corner store for what seemed like an age, to buy a handful of tamarind for our evening meal. Bigger people kept pushing past me and by the time the store clerk noticed me it had been quite a while. I walked home slowly, feeling droopy and lethargic, my poor limbs aching for rest as this was my fourth trip to the corner shop today. I reached my building and slowly began the tortuous ascent. The stairs were steep and narrow and dark and at the second flight I decided to sit down and rest for a minute to catch my breath. I sat on the topmost tread and stuck my finger into the little wedge of tamarind and sucked at the dark gob smeared on it. The sour, tart taste was delicious and made my eyes water. I put the tamarind down and leaned against the wall wearily, hoping I would not be sent out again. The wall was cool against my head, and the next thing I knew I was being shaken and slapped by Mani, while my mother was hurling abuse at me for falling asleep on the stairs. I had delayed our evening meal by falling asleep on the landing still clutching the tamarind that was to go into our evening meal. She was in a complete rage.

"Wait till your father comes home. You are a curse to be sure. There was never a more unruly daughter in the world. What sort of example will you be for your younger sister?" she hissed at me, brandishing a wooden ladle angrily. I could hear my baby sister's wails carrying down into the stairwell.

I said nothing, as it was not my way to argue. I had to go without dinner that night as a punishment and never again made the mistake of falling asleep anywhere, even if every last muscle in my body was crying out in exhaustion.

I remember when I was seven years old I was finally admitted into a school. My father was very much against it, but this was one of the few times my mother was able to prevail against him. She said it was free, and education for me would result in better marriage prospects which seemed to convince him of the wisdom of allowing me to acquire an education. I was packed off to the local Government school where I was given a new dress, a slate and two pieces of chalk.

There were a lot of new children in my class, and we all stared at each other curiously. We spent the first half of the morning learning how to write the English alphabet. I was able to write up to E by the end of that first morning without looking at the board. My class teacher was a grim-faced woman, with a big, heavy hand that frequently came down on the heads and backs of students who were unable to copy properly. We were to call her Teacher she informed us sternly. She passed by my slate and nodded at my scribbling and I felt my first thrill of receiving a compliment, unspoken though it was. I hungered to make her nod at me like that again so I slaved over my work and was rewarded with a small smile a bit later.

At 1 pm we were taken to a large shed where a man stood over steaming vats of food. We had to form a long line and as each of us came up to him we were given a plate onto which he slopped some rice and thick curry. The food was tasteless and my neighbour in class found a cockroach in her food. She fished it out and continued to eat the meal as if nothing were amiss. When she noticed me staring in horror, she shrugged her shoulders and answered my unspoken question.

"This happens all the time and if we complain they will throw the food away and won't give us anymore," she said in a monotone. "Cockroaches are not so bad, you can take them out; it's when the little worms are in the food, that we have problems, because we will be seen fishing them out as there are so many. The teachers then get angry and accuse us of being ungrateful."

I lost my appetite and asked if she wanted to eat the rest of my food. She took my plate silently and slopped the food onto her plate, and continued her meal. I was disgusted. In my home, even though we were poor, our food was always fresh and hot. I realised how lucky I was and felt an overwhelming need to go home. I felt sorry for another person for the first time in my life as I watched her, with pity, as she wolfed down the disgusting meal, and wondered what sort of home she came from. Eventually the bell rang to signal that school was over for the day. I went to meet my brothers at the school gate and they walked ahead of me, glancing back every now and then to make sure I was still following them. Back home my mother had prepared dinner and I ate ravenously, not even noticing that my brothers had finished their meal and had gone off to work.

"What an appetite you have! Don't eat so fast," said my mother cuffing me on the side of the head.

But it was not ill-intentioned I knew, for she had hit me playfully, and from the tone of her voice, I knew she was quite proud that she had a daughter who was attending school.

My days continued in this fashion uninterrupted by nothing more than the scolding of my mother and the drunken shouting of my father when he returned home each night. I was always unhappy when he returned home. I think I might have even hated him, but I knew it was wrong to hate one's parents. I did my homework on the stairs outside as there was a hall light there that was bright and for which we did not pay electricity bills. When it got dark, my mother would open the front door and let this hall light brighten up our gloomy room.

I remember this room so well. Compared to my home now, that rooftop house was luxurious. We had a fan that creaked heavily through the summer months, a small balcony with a washing stone and tap where my mother beat our clothes to get them clean and then hung them out to dry, and a bed for my mother and father. My brothers shared a mattress on the floor next to their bed, and I had a smaller dhurrie next to the balcony. My baby sister slept in a little cradle type affair my mother had fashioned out of an old saree and that hung like a hammock from nails off two walls.

A cast-off lungi of my father became a screen around the bed and we used this as a little room, climbing onto the rusty old metal bed, pulling shut the lungi like a curtain, and using the privacy to change our clothes. The kitchen was off to one side, and a faded bedcover separated it from the rest of the house. There was a little tap as well, and so we also used the kitchen as our bathing area.. The most important place in the home was the altar on the narrow kitchen table. Here my mother had placed a gold-coloured frame with a picture of the goddess our family worshipped every morning before leaving the house. I used to stare at her for hours marvelling at her beauty and the brilliant red saree she wore. I once asked my mother why we only ever saw her picture or her statue at the temple we visited occasionally. She shushed me immediately. "The goddess is something we see only in our dreams and prayers," she said. "Otherwise we do not see her." And even at that young age I wondered if I was a goddess. Because even though I existed, it felt like no one ever really saw me.

We had no bathroom or toilet to call our own. The whole building used the two toilets on the second floor. In fact, it was through using these facilities that we got to know our neighbours. I cannot remember any of them with much clarity now, however. But our house on top of the building, with the window that looked down on the rumble of Thousand Lights and Anna Salai and its flow of never-ending traffic, along with the goddess who prevailed over it all – those I remember well.

In later years, this was where I fled in my mind when the world became too uncomfortable for me. A time and place where all I worried about was climbing four flights of stairs and hoping the lights would not go out so that the fan continued to offer its creaky wafts of warm wind.

This routine continued for five years. My baby sister, who was just this wailing noise in the background of my youth, began to toddle and then walk around and started talking. I enjoyed bathing her and playing with her and the memory of her baby talk and innocent smiles always makes me feel warm. How terribly her poor little life turned out. I think perhaps life was even crueler to her than me. My father's drinking grew more and more pronounced and he would often come stumbling home, drunk and incoherent. The fights he and my mother had became more vehement and they often came to blows. Once he hit her so badly that he broke open the skin around the corner of her mouth and chipped two of her teeth rather badly. Mani and I had to take her to the Government hospital in an auto. It was my first time in an auto and I was really excited. I stuck my head out feeling the air rushing past me quickly and it was absolutely exhilarating. I watched buses go past belching thick grey fumes in their wake, and cars whizzed by in a flash of colour, and wondered at motorcyclists wearing helmets with their women draped daintily across the pillion – it was a wonderful feeling to be part of this big and busy world.

The Government hospital was a huge building. Lit by tube lights that cast a harsh white light on the oily looking green walls, it was busy… busier even than the road we had travelled on. My eldest brother ran around trying to sort out some forms and I sat in a crowded waiting room holding my mother's hand. She had a rag stuffed against her mouth which was red with the blood that continued to seep, and she had tears pouring down her face. It reminded me of the red vermillion that my mother adorned the parting of her hair with every morning to reflect her married state. It was also the colour of the goddess's saree in the picture at our altar at home. I stared around me. The room was filled with crying babies and their mothers who tried to hush them noisily. Men stood around in groups and the elderly sat in chairs, hunched and shaking, silently awaiting their turn. Little children, some older, some younger than me, ran about making a tremendous racket. And every now and then, unsmiling nurses in white sarees and little stiff white caps would scurry about looking very important. The room went very silent when a man in a white coat came out. All these white-coated men were stern-looking and some of them seemed to have a perpetual scowl etched into their faces. The waiting men would bow their head deferentially to this man and even the babies seemed to know they needed to stop crying. I learned from my mother that these men in white coats were doctors, beings that were only next to God in status and commanding as much reverence. It was four hours before we were seen by one of these great men.

We went into a room with whitewashed walls that held a desk and a small, very high bed and a nasty smell. A nurse was standing beside the doctor and she glared at me and my mother as if we were an unwanted interruption in her busy schedule. They made my mother sit on a small stool and performed a very quick general examination. I was almost half asleep, and I don't remember the conversation exactly, but I do remember the doctor asking my mother how she had come to be so badly hurt.

"Doctor sahab, I fell down the stairs and cut myself," my mother answered humbly. The nurse sniffed disbelievingly, and the doctor turned around to look at me.

"Is that true? Is that what happened?" he asked me loudly. I was about to respond and say my father had hit her, when I felt the warning pressure of my mother's hand on my arm. So I stopped just in time and instead nodded mutely.

"What's the point? They're all the same," the doctor said wearily, and he pushed a piece of paper at the nurse.

She glanced at it and then nodded curtly at my mother, indicating that she wanted my mother and me to follow her. We walked down a long corridor and were taken into a room that had badly stained floors with plaster peeling off the walls. The nurse swiftly filled an injection and then stabbed it roughly into my mother's arm. My mother whimpered as she yanked it out and I clutched her hand firmly trying to comfort her. A big fat tear rolled out from the corner of her eye and she used her free hand to grab her saree pallu and wipe it away. The nurse took no notice of her distress. She was busy threading a wicked-looking curved needle with thread. I wondered what she would do with it and a second later she jabbed it into my mother's face sewing up the still seeping wound. It took only a few minutes, but it felt like hours as I watched my mother being stitched up like some hessian sack.

My brother was waiting outside in the reception area. His eyes were swollen, from crying or lack of sleep... I am not sure which. Maybe it was both. Later, many years later, when we were both grown up with children of our own, he reminded me of this night – when he had cried from the humiliation of not having enough money to buy all the drugs written on our mother's prescription. We went out into the night and it was welcomingly cool after the stuffy air inside the hospital. I must confess I was glad to get away from that place – it seemed, to my childish mind, a wicked place filled with cruel, rude nurses and doctors, and a crush of humanity that filled my every pore with the sight and smell and taste of disease.

We had to walk some way before we were able to find an auto to take us home. Dust rose up in clouds by the roadside as vehicles overtook and swerved onto the dusty sidewalk, making me cover my face with one hand, as I breathed through a filter I made with my fingers. Eventually one stopped for us and the driver, with red-rimmed eyes, smelling strongly of sweat and alcohol, allowed us in, after we haggled a fare home. Even so it was twenty rupees and I could tell this was the most distressing aspect of the whole affair for my mother. I was so sleepy and the sight of the flashing lights, and brightly lit billboards were barely enough to keep me awake. I must have fallen asleep, for the next thing I knew was my brother shaking me trying to wake me up. I was about to start crying and complaining, but something in his tired, weary eyes told me this was not the time for it. I clambered out and waited while he paid the auto driver and then trudged up the stairs with him, my mother having gone ahead of us. She was curled up in a tight, silent ball, covered completely with a thin bed sheet under which I could see her shoulders shaking. It only struck me then that this was the first time I had seen her in tears. In the hustle and bustle of the hospital it had not quite registered. This was my mother who never cried, who carried on no matter what life brought her way. I went to her and gently touched her arm.

"Ma, what happened? Are you okay? Is your mouth hurting? What shall I do?"

She said nothing, but her shoulders continued to move jerkily under the sheet and after a few minutes I left her and went to my place by the balcony, and lay on my side. Trails of ants were making their way up the wall to the roof, and I wondered where they were going. Then I wondered where my father was. It was my last thought before I fell asleep.

The following morning I awoke and the room was silent. The usual noise of the morning was missing. My mother saw that I was awake and nodded her head in acknowledgment of the fact.

"It's late. Get up and get ready for school. Your brothers have already left."

She took me to school herself, covering the dressing on her face with her saree pallu. She left me at my class door telling my teacher there had been a problem at my home in the morning. My teacher looked at the bandage covering half her lower face and nodded and gestured me to my seat. That evening I went home and helped my mother with the cooking and washing of clothes. We did not speak but worked together in silent companionship. My brothers came up for the evening meal and then went out to work again without mentioning the previous evening. My father came home at his usual time and I could tell he had been drinking as usual. He stared belligerently at my mother for a minute then very loudly asked for his food. He yanked at the screen around their bed and went in shutting himself off to change into the pajamas and vest he wore at nights. When he finished he swept the fabric back and settled himself cross-legged on the bed. My mother took a plate heaped with the food we had made that evening and laid it before him. He did not look at her and dived into the steaming sambhar and rice with relish. When he had finished he handed the plate back to my mother who stood by the side of the bed, silently, as he ate.

"It was good food," he said gruffly, and went out the door to have his nightly round of beedies with the rest of the men who congregated at the bottom of the building each night, to exchange news and complain about their lot in life.

Life continued much in this fashion mostly. I lost track of time I suppose, but I had started speaking a little English at school and knew how to count and write my name and a few other words in Tamil. You might think that this is not very much to brag about, but for a girl of my social standing this was a huge achievement. A foreign man came somewhere between those years to visit my little shack of a slum school and left clothing for all the children. I got to wear a new pavada and blouse and was pleased as could be. I even went to look at myself in the neighbour's mirror. The skirt was a bright blue and green with a matching top. With the red ribbons in my hair I thought I looked rather nice, until my neighbour, a fat, cheerful woman, the wife of a vegetable-seller, gave me a friendly slap and said,

"What a shame you are dark. If you had been fair those colours would have looked better on you."

It wasn't the first time I had heard remarks like this, but I was not going to let her know I had been hurt by her thoughtless words. I stuck my tongue out at her and flounced out of her house and back into mine with my head held high. My little world was my school with the dusty, playground and the lunch I took with me every day, the chores at home and my school work and friends in the building. Or I should say friend. There was just another little girl in the building and she was a few years younger than me. We played together, but after a while I would always get bored and wander back home as her childish prattle bored me. She could not even count till ten and refused to learn, despite my efforts to teach her. She was a dull, placid thing wanting nothing more than food and the chance to play with a rag doll her mother had made her from some old pieces of cloth. I told her grandly that one day when I was very rich and educated I would buy her a real doll. In any case, I always preferred the company of Radhi, who I loved to pet and cosset and treat like a precious toy.

Then one day at school in the middle of class, the principal came in and called me out. My brothers were waiting outside and she told us to go home immediately as our mother needed us. My brothers set off at a quick trot, wondering why they had been called home at this hour and I had to run to keep pace with them and was quite out of breath by the time we reached home.

At the bottom of the stairwell we found a group of men standing and talking in hushed whispers. My neighbour, the vegetable seller's wife appeared beside us as if by magic, and led the way up to our top floor house where I found my mother sitting on the floor and staring blankly at the wall before her. Around her a group of women had gathered, some of them stroking her arms and her hair and reassuring her that it would be alright. It was unbearably hot and stuffy in the room and the smell of incense was overwhelming. My father was lying on the bed in a gleaming white shirt and pajama, new ones; his eyes were closed, his hair neatly brushed and his beard and moustache were neatly trimmed. I was surprised at how good he looked.

At first I thought he was sleeping and wondered if we were performing some sort of religious ceremony and why we hadn't been told before about it. I was about to go up to our mother and demand an explanation as to why we had not been involved in the preparations for this gathering, when my mother caught sight of the three of us, and burst out into loud wails. She got up and ran to us, grabbing my brothers to her and crying uncontrollably.

"He left us, he left us," she screamed, tears pouring down her face. My brothers too broke into loud cries and my elder brother ran to where my father was lying and shook him roughly, begging him to get up. And that was when it registered on me finally. While the sun was shining brightly and while I was learning to spell the months of the year in English, my father had died of a heart attack in the middle of repairing a motorcycle tyre that had been punctured.

Chapter Two
THE ASHRAM

In the days that followed my father's cremation none of us said a word to each other. The house was filled with sadness and uncertainty and my mother did not get up from bed at all except to use the communal toilets. The vegetable seller's wife cooked food for us once a day which we ate gratefully. I realised then that despite his drunken ways and surly behaviour at home, my father had very much been the central figure around which our lives revolved. We cooked meals for him, my brothers gave him the money they earned and his salary paid for most things in the house. The feeble little rent, the food at home, all these flowed from him. It wasn't much, but it kept a body together, I suppose.

I realized all this dimly at the back of my eleven-year-old mind as I made the food and tried to keep the household together in place of my mother. I used to sit and comb her hair for her every morning, an activity she used to do for me, before I left for school, in the days before my father died. She no longer wore the red vermillion streak in her hair, and this wounded me terribly for reasons I could not quite comprehend. Even though less than a month had passed since that dreadful day, it felt like a year and I knew my life would never be the same again. I had not gone back to school as I was needed at home to help around the house and look after my baby sister. She was starting to look very much like my father with skin that was lighter than mine – how I envied her this. She was a sunny little thing and clung to me every chance that she got. Now that she was bigger, she slept next to me and I loved the feel of her lying close to me, the smell of her hair oil spilling into my nostrils as we drifted into slumber. The other big change was that my mother started sleeping on the floor, giving up her bed to my brothers. When I asked her why, she shrugged her shoulders.

"They are the bread-winners, the men in the family now. I am just a poor widow," she said, when I asked her why she had given up her sleeping space in this fashion.

I did not quite see the logic to her argument; after all she was our mother and should get prime place in our household. But like many things in my life, I learned to accept what I was told and carry on without questioning the whys and wherefores of the situations that life presented to me.

My brothers continued to go to school; being boys an education was deemed necessary for them. It did not last, however, as finances became even more strained and the paltry monthly school fees became impossible to pay. One day, a few weeks after my father's funeral, a man came around in the evening. He was wearing a fine cotton shirt and dark green trousers. He was a tall thin man and carried an air of authority about him. He knocked on the door as mother and I were starting to make the evening meal. My mother wrapped her sari pallu closely around her head and stood up looking at him questioningly. He nodded curtly and told her he was the owner of the building we lived in. The little one-room apartment we dwelt in belonged to him. He curtly told my mother that we owed rent. My mother looked down at the floor, and softly told him of our circumstances.

"We have no money. My husband died a few weeks back and we have no way to pay anything at all, with all the recent funeral expenses," she said softly, looking at the floor.

He answered sharply, "That is your problem, not mine. But seeing as you are a widow, I will give you one month. By which time you and your family have to clear out." And he turned on his heel and left.

That evening the vegetable seller and his wife came to see my mother. I was sent out of the house while they talked in hushed whispers. Had I known what their discussions meant, I would have run away from home then and there. The vegetable seller was helpful I suppose, and I should have been grateful, but to this day I feel an unaccountable anger towards this man. In my childish head, it seemed he was the one responsible for all our problems. He went and spoke to my late father's employers and it was arranged that my brothers would work in place of my father at the motorcycle repair shop, and live in the little room at the back, for which they would earn a stipend and learn the trade. This was an additional blow to my mother as she had always hoped her sons would finish their schooling, at the very least.

The day my brothers left was a truly sad one. While I had only been at the receiving end of their teasing and cuffing and smacks, their presence had somehow served as protection - a steadying presence in an unknown world. We all got up early that morning. The sun was already blisteringly hot, a dusty orange ball that pierced through the haze that lay over the city like a cloying cloud. The water from the tap ran warm and offered no cooling against this shimmering heat.

Mani and Senthil packed their worldly possessions into two plastic carry bags; a couple of ragged T-shirts and shorts and a pair of long trousers and a white shirt to wear to the temple. Mother fed them breakfast silently, which they wolfed down. I think they knew it would be a long time before they would get another decent meal. I stared at them silently, memorising their faces. The unruly coil of hair on Senthil's forehead that no amount of hair oil could keep down, the downy moustache on Mani's rangy face, a face that was lengthening into manhood, these things flooded into my head and heart. But what I remember the most is the look in their eyes. For all their advanced years in comparison to mine, their eyes were filled with terror for what the world now held for them. I wished with all my heart they did not have to leave, but they did, going down the stairs a step at a time, instead of running down them, leaping, and trying to see who could jump the most stairs, which was their normal mode of departure. Their footsteps died away and my mother, Radhi and I were left alone. Outside the hum of traffic continued as if nothing in our lives had changed.

My mother bade me go bathe, and I did so my tears mixing with the warm water from the tap. She then told me to put on my new clothes, given by the foreign man. They were not so new by this time and quite small for me. My ankles poked out like two thin sticks from the bottom and my arms sprouted awkwardly from the little puffed sleeves that were just a little too tight. Bundling little Radhi who had been hastily washed and dressed, my mother grabbed me by the arm and set off down the stairs. She did not lock the door as there was no need for we had nothing of value that anyone could want. What little jewellery my mother owned had been sold to pay for my father's funeral expenses. I got quite excited and tugged impatiently at my mother's saree, asking her where we were going. Mother did not respond. But at the bottom of the stairs she stopped and knelt down.

"Madhuri!" she said sternly. "Today you are going to go to a new school. I want you to be very good there and do exactly as you are told. I don't want to hear any complaints. You must always remember this is a very good opportunity for you and you are very lucky to be there."

I stood as if turned to stone from the shock and excitement. School! I was going to continue studying… I could not believe my ears. I could not wait to get started and jumped up and down, a happy little dance and tugged at my mother again trying to pull her along to make her move faster. Once again we took an auto and this time because it was daytime I could see everything clearly. Seeing the enormous buildings of Anna Salai and the big curving river that ran alongside, stinking and sluggish, these thrilled my very soul. I saw women driving little cars and riding scooters, and huge lorries and vans belching their way through the traffic that moved ever so slowly. One woman especially caught my eye. She was driving a red car and our auto came to stand next to her vehicle at a traffic light. I could see her through her car window. She was wearing a pale pink saree and a deeper pink blouse with a shiny trim. Her long black hair flowed down her back like a cascade of black silk and fell over one shoulder artistically. Dark sunglasses perched on her dainty head and everything about her was unlike anything I had ever seen before. Not even the women in the big film posters lining the road could compare to her and I could not stop staring for she was the most beautiful woman I had ever seen. She must have sensed me looking at her, for as the lights changed, and before she zoomed off in her car, she turned to look at me and gave me a dazzling smile that has stayed with me all the years. The memory of it served to remind me of beauty in life even when everything else around me was ugly and sad.

The journey seemed to go on forever and I was surprised at how big the city was. I had only ever seen Anna Salai that wound on a fair distance before it was blocked by towering buildings and then one could see no further, and I had only known my immediate neighbourhood - the corner shop and my school, all these were a ten-minute walk from my rooftop home. But it seemed that Chennai was a grand city, and one could traverse in autos for more than half an hour and still not see the end of it. We went through an area filled with beauti-ful houses, with tall gates and walls protecting them. Through these gates I glimpsed white buildings with high roofs and lush green lawns in the front, some with security guards out in the front of the buildings. I was overwhelmed. Unschooled as I was about the larger world, I knew we were in a land inhabited by very rich people. Why one of those houses alone would have been bigger than the dusty building we lived in. I wondered for the first time why we were poor and other people were rich. While I was pondering this mystery the auto drew up to a pair of iron gates painted brown and green. My mother got out with Radhi straddled on her hip and helped me out with her free hand. She asked the auto driver to wait and went up to the gate and knocked. Looking up at this large, cream and brown structure I had a sudden sense of foreboding and I pulled away from my mother's arm.

"I don't want to go there. Let's go home and I'll stay with you," I said feebly.

My mother gave me a harsh look and would have said something stern to me, but at that moment an old man came out of the gate. He looked at my mother questioningly and my mother asked humbly if she could see Madam Shanthi. The man looked at us disparagingly for a moment, and then shrugged and gestured for us to follow him, as he shuffled across the cement drive that led up to a large building with huge glass windows in the front. We walked up the stone steps into a large reception hall that was sparklingly clean and smelled of something that reminded me of the hospital visit two years ago. I later learned this was bleach. The man disappeared into a door at the side and we waited outside in this large hall. There were rows of benches along one side, but we remained standing. After what seemed like an age, the man reappeared with a very large woman dressed in a dull cream saree. She was a large woman, with protruding eyes and a gruff way about her. The man left silently, walking through the door into the deep recesses of the building and I stared after him wondering what lay beyond the door he had just gone through. My mother introduced me.

"Madam, this is Madhuri. I was told to bring her here today," she said timidly.

"Yes, yes!" said this giant figure snappily.

She looked at my mother sharply, and then taking the end of her saree pallu, she untied it and took out a wad of notes and handed it to my mother. My mother counted it out, nodded and then tucked the money into her blouse for safekeeping. I watched the whole transaction wonderingly, as I could not imagine why this strange, bad-tempered looking woman was giving my mother this money. And then I found out.

"Well come along now," she said beckoning me with a fat finger. "We don't have time to waste."

My mother who was holding my hand clutched it tightly for a moment, and then let go and gave me a push towards this alarming woman who had appeared so suddenly in my life. I knew then that she meant to leave me here with this scary person, and the realisation shocked me into a scream that was dragged out from the depths of my soul.

"Noooooooooo!" I screamed and grabbed at my mother. "Take me home with you."

But my wails fell on deaf ears and my mother was already walking towards the large front door and then she was out and gone, while this large woman in the cream saree, this Madam Shanthi, held my arm in a vice-like grip refusing to let me run after my mother.

I continued to scream for a while, pulling against this lady's vice-like grip on my arm, straining to go out and after my mother.

Madam Shanthi had no patience with me and after a second of tugging at me, she shook me roughly and told me to shut up. Her harsh tones silenced me instantly and I stared up at her angry face wishing I were dead. She then dragged me behind her like a limp doll, going through the door she had entered from. It led to a narrow dark corridor, with rooms running down either side along the length of it. She pulled me along, and I stumbled after her till we reached the end of the corridor and went through a door at the end. It led onto an enormous room painted an oily-looking white and green that had many mattresses on the floor, thin soiled affairs most of them, all laid out symmetrically in rows on the floor. There were three other women in the room, but they were not what caught my attention. I was transfixed by the crowd of children that were lying on these mattresses. These were no ordinary children and it was like a scene from a nightmare. They were grotesquely twisted, some of them, with arms and legs bent askew, others had huge heads and tiny bodies and lay looking up at the ceiling, another had his arms wound around the table next to his mattress and was biting at one of the legs, others were screaming and drooling and making strange sounds … I was petrified. Was I to be turned into one of these creatures?

Madam Shanthi hauled me across to one of the other women and spoke to her curtly.

"Nalini, she is your charge for now. Make sure you do what is needed."

Turning to me she said, "Do whatever Madam Nalini tells you to." And with that she turned on her heel and marched out of the room.

My legs could not hold me up anymore and I sat down with a thump on the floor and started crying again, this time great silent, shuddering sobs that dragged the breath out of me in painful, tattered gasps. I desperately wanted to stop but could not. Madam Nalini knelt down and looked at my face. I looked back at her, still gasping out sobs and wondered what fresh terror this new woman would have for me. But to my utter surprise she bent down and stroked my head gently and then pulled me up to make me stand again. I fell against her weeping and I must have stayed like that for a long time, until my tears finally began to subside.

When I was finally spent and silent, she took me to a corner of the room where a stack of plastic glasses stood next to a huge stainless steel container with a tap on it. She took a glass and filled it with water and gave it to me to drink. The water refreshed my parched throat and mouth and I drank it down in several heaving gulps. Madam Nalini put her hand on my shoulders and propelled me back down the corridor and into one of the rooms off the side. It was a large room with a row of beds down one length of it. The paint on the walls were chipped and patches of dark mould spoke of many a leaking monsoon. She told me to sit quietly and she would return in a few moments. I sat down gratefully on one of the beds as my legs were still weak from the shock of what had happened and I waited, taking in the austere white surroundings.

The mattress on the bed was lumpy and stained, and the pillow when I tested it, was as hard as a rock. Madam Nalini returned a few minutes later armed with a towel and a pair of scissors. She took me across the hall to the opposite door and opened the creaking metal door. It led into a huge room partitioned off to provide bathing and toilet cubicles. She took me into one of the bathing spaces and opened up a tap to fill the bucket lying there. Then without another word she began to pull off my clothes. I started screaming again at that, and she stopped and looked at me wearily.

"Child, you have to bathe and dress in the clothes we give you. If you don't do as I say I will have to call Madam Shanthi."

I went limp immediately and let her bathe me. She scrubbed my hair with some strong, horrible smelling liquid that burnt my scalp a little.

"Lice medicine," she explained shortly, washing it off.

She dried me off and then told me to get into the clothes she had left next to the cubicle. It was a dark blue pavadai and top with long sleeves, made from a thick coarse material. I wore it wincing as the heat of the clothing added to the heat of the Chennai summer. Madam Nalini combed my hair through and knotted it into two tight plaits which she twisted back to make as short as possible, Securing this with a black ribbon, she inspected me and then nodded in a satisfied manner.

"At least we won't have to cut your hair off as you seem to have no lice," she said dryly, putting the scissors away on a small shelf in the bathroom.

She then took me back to the room where all the children were. This time, even though I was prepared for the sight, it still shocked me. What was wrong with these children? There were five new additions to the room from last time. Young girls, perhaps a little older than me wearing the same dark blue clothing, were standing and ladling out food into bowls and stacking them on a table. Madam Nalini pushed me towards them and I went forward, my fear a sour taste in my mouth. More strangers to meet … When would this day end? The girls looked up at me as I came close to the table and then the tallest, oldest-looking one pushed one of the bowls out at me. I took it from her gratefully and sticking my hand into the bowl scooped up some of the daal and rice and started to eat but before I could so much as get a mouthful in, the elder girl slapped my hand away and the food spilled out, and onto the floor. The shock of it made me spill the entire bowl on the floor and the food in it splashed out – a yellow viscous mess that stuck to the floor in a glutinous, sickly-looking puddle. I stared at it blankly, my mind empty and incapable of coherent thought. I looked up at the girl like a dumb animal staring at its killer.

"Feed the children first," she spat out at me, stabbing her ladle in the air and pointing at the children who were lying around making a horrific racket.

I continued to stare, my brain unable to register the horror of what she was asking me to do. I could not bear to look at them, leave alone feed them and I stayed rooted to the ground. One of the younger girls, in the meantime, delved into a basket of towels lying by the table and scooped up the spilled food. She dropped the dirty towel into plastic tub that was filled with an assortment of soiled clothing and material, and then taking a bowl she went up to the nearest child. He was a tiny, twisted thing, with a head that seemed to be blown out like a balloon on the left side. He was lying on his side and his left eye stared at me challengingly. His legs moved in uncoordinated jerks as if he were trying to run away from himself and as the younger girl sat down next to him, he began to keen, a high-pitched whining sound that went through my very soul. The younger girl took a plastic spoon, dipped it into the food and raised it to his mouth.

"Come on Thanga. Eat your food, it's your favourite, rice and daal," she said softly.

Thanga resolutely turned his face away and with that his eye was no longer fixed on me. Gently she took his head with her free hand and pushed his face back into position closer to the food. Thanga opened his mouth, a tiny slit in his head and in that instant she slipped the spoon in. He snapped his mouth shut and half the food came spilling out. But some did go in and he swallowed reluctantly, making a strange gulping sound. The sound brought me back to my surroundings and looking around I saw that there were several other women in the room, feeding these strange children, most whom did not seem to relish the idea of being fed.

"I'd rather not eat if I looked like these children," I thought rebelliously, feeling a glimmer of sympathy for these beings for the first time.

The elder girl interrupted my thoughts.

"There! You've seen Kalpa do it. Now go do some work, we're not around here to serve you," she said sharply and handed me a bowl of food.

Taking one herself she went off to feed a child at the other corner of the room from us. Carrying the bowl I looked around and spotted a boy of about four, lying peacefully against a bolster, quite close to Kalpa and Thanga. I walked up and sat down next to him. He had curly, dark hair and wide open eyes. He seemed to be absolutely normal and for the first time during the day I actually felt lucky. I dipped the spoon into the bowl and as I brought it close to his face, I saw the change, but did not have time to react… a fleeting shadow that chased across his face and a glaze that frosted his eyes into two searing points of fire.

He launched himself at me in a fluid motion, like a snake that had been coiled up, in readiness to strike. His hands came out claw-like and wound around my hair wildly, tiny sharp fingernails digging into my scalp, while he used his head as a weapon to butt me painfully in the chest. I don't know which one of us was screaming louder. Our screaming set off some of the other children and within seconds the room was filled with the crying and wailing of what seemed like a thousand demented demons.

I pushed at the boy, dimly aware of the bowl of food lying spilled somewhere behind me, trying to untangle his hands from my hair. Tears were pouring down my face and my own body was so racked by sobbing that I thought I would suffocate from the lack of air. After what felt like an eternity, someone pulled the boy off me and took me back to the dormitory where I had sat earlier during the day. I have no idea who it was who led me away or brought me back here. I was made to sit on a bed and I stayed there unmoving, the tears gushing down my face, feeling utterly alone and abandoned.

The walls were still white with their grimy damp stains, the beds were still rusty, the mattress still hard and lumpy, and this surprised me. The incident had changed me profoundly and I thought that the whole world should look different now. I no longer felt like I was eleven years old. I felt even older than my ammachi who had died when I was just five. I don't know what made me think of her now. Perhaps it was the love that I remembered her giving me, which I so needed to feel in the starkness and grimness of my new-found situation. I had stopped weeping by now and rubbed at my sore head gingerly and it came away wet; looking at my fingers I saw that it was smeared with blood. The sight of it brought on a flood of self-pity and I began to cry again. I was longing for my mother and my brothers and the loss of my father was suddenly more profound than ever before.

I felt someone slipping an arm around my shoulders – it was a gentle touch, a mere caress and that little gesture made me cry even harder. The arm stayed on my shoulders till I had calmed down and when the tears cleared, I looked up to see Kalpa sitting next to me. She had said nothing the whole time and looking at her seated close I could now see she was probably the same age as me. I realised now that she was the one who had lifted the boy off me and taken me into this room. She was looking at me now and she smiled – a sweet compassionate smile that immediately lifted the terrible feeling of loneliness. I smiled back at her, a watery, shaky smile.

She nodded sympathetically and said, "Don't worry. I know how it can be. When I came here two years ago, I had a lot of difficulty adjusting. But you will get used to it and I will help you as much as I can."

I looked at her as she said this. She had rough patches on her cheek and her dark, compassionate eyes were red-rimmed above a neat straight nose, while her hair was thick and coarse with little tendrils that escaped the tight plaits and spread untidily around her face. But to me, her most striking quality was her voice which was gentle, and her touch which was warm and loving. She had a grown-up air to her which I found immensely comforting and reassuring.

"Why did you come here? Where is this place? And what is wrong with those children?" I asked shakily, my words spilling over each other. "Will my mother come back for me?"

She answered just two questions. "This is the Anni Ashram for children with mental disabilities. The ayahs look after the older ones mostly, and we help them care for the smaller ones. You'll learn to do it soon enough and it will become easier as you get used to it."

I tried digesting this piece of information, but the burning question I had was now repeated. "Will my mother come for me?"

"I have no idea," answered Kalpa gently. "But rest now. I'll tell Madam Nalini your head was hurting and bleeding so you stayed back."

And with that she was gone.

I went back to the bathroom and bathed my head, and then returning to the dormitory, I went and lay down on the cot nearest to the door. It was very uncomfortable, the pillow was hard and felt like it had been stuffed with rocks so I threw it to the bottom of the bed and lay down on my side, resting my face against my hands. I was used to sleeping on the floor and this sensation of being raised above the ground felt alien and uncomfortable. My neck started to hurt, but after a while, the events of the day caught up with me and I fell into a deep sleep. I was woken several hours late by the loud clanging of a bell.

I got up with a start at the noise and realised that darkness had fallen. Kalpa poked her head through the door and came in with a bowl of food, as I sat up on the bed and looked around me wondering what to do.

"Madam Nalini asked me to give you this. She thought it would be better if you ate in the dorm today."

I took the bowl and nodding, accepted the food handed to me. I found myself ravenous and put heaped mouthfuls in; it was a tasteless vegetable curry, with rice and some pickle. Kalpa stared at me for a few seconds, smiled her gentle smile and then silently withdrew.

I look back now on that time and realize how resilient children are; I see that quality in my own children today. Despite the trauma of being abandoned, then being attacked the way I was, all it took was the smile of another girl my own age to bring in a small ray of hope and lift me out of the despair I had been feeling. This changes for us as we grow older, I think. I don't think we become more resilient; we just become more resigned to terrible things happening. As children we bounce back, but as adults we just tie up our emotions into tight, unfeeling bundles and carry on. But for that terrible afternoon, Kalpa's smile brought in a little ray of sunshine into what was possibly the worst day of my short life.

I sat curled on the bed and ate the rice that was on the plate and after I had finished I put the plate under the bed, I looked around to see if I could spot a toilet. There was another door at the other end of the long room and I got off the cot, and walked towards it. The door was ajar, and I peered in tentatively to see a cracked, stained toilet next to which stood a scratched bucket and mug, with some water in it. I went in, leaving the door slightly ajar to let some light in, hoping no one would come back as I was using it. I finished as quickly as I could and walked back wearily to the cot I had been sleeping on and lay down again, on my back, staring at the stained ceiling. I thought one of the stains looked like the shape of my brother Senthil's head and as I was trying to remember the last thing he said to me, I fell into an exhausted sleep. One filled with confused, unsettling dreams, with strange images of my grandmother and the boy that I had tried to feed, all jangling and colliding with memories of the little rooftop house in Thousand Lights and the sound of my brothers calling to me.

Chapter Three
THE LEARNING

I woke up with a start, wondering where I was. I had no idea what time it was, but I could tell it was that funny time between night and daybreak when everything is very still and all you can hear is the sound of traffic outside. Here it was muted and far away, a dull hum that resonated inside my head and mind making me painfully aware of a hollow feeling in the pit of my stomach. The distant rumble reminded me acutely of the roar and thrum of the traffic at Thousand Lights and with it came a new and bewildering sensation.

My first thought was that I was ill, and I pressed my hand down on my stomach to try and ease the aching, gnawing feeling that I was experiencing. It took me a few seconds to realise that I was not in physical, but emotional pain. I was missing my mother and my siblings and my home, and the anguish was so intense that it was a physical sensation. I sat up in bed, my hand still pressed to my stomach, and I let wave after wave of homesickness wash over me. I had never ever experienced such emotional agony and the sudden realisation that I really was all alone and completely abandoned hit me with a renewed force that cannot be expressed in mere words.

Every nerve ending seemed to be tuned into this new emotion, and it was all so profoundly painful that even crying was an impossibility. I sat dry-eyed, rocking backwards and forwards longing for all I had lost, the anguish of separation searing through my heart and mind. I then sat up with a jerk, hoping the movement would dislodge the pain I was feeling but it stayed with me, keeping me locked in its soul-crushing grip. Around me I could see the outline of the row of cots, with figures huddled under sheets, sleeping, and the hush of their breathing in slumber was oddly peaceful against the agony that was within me.

A light was streaming in through the large window at the end of the room, and overhead, two large fans hung, silent and motionless, like large birds waiting to swoop down on the unsuspecting sleepers below. I was wide awake now and I sat up in my bed, realising as I did, that this was the first time I had ever slept on a bed for an entire night. I got off, the floor meeting my feet in a cool, muffled thump as I slid off the lumpy mattress. I stood by the side of my bed and wondered what I should do.

All my senses were alert and the sound of someone turning over in their sleep, almost made me jump out of my skin. I padded across to the door and tried the handle. It gave, but the door would not budge and after a few more tries I gave up. I walked silently to the window. There was a ventilator above it, which was partially open, but the window seemed as locked as the door. I tried the latch hoping it would open, and I must confess, I did not know what I would have done if it had. But as it was, it stayed firmly shut and I ended up staring out the window at the courtyard that lay beyond the glass pane. It was quite large, cemented over around the edges, with dusty earth at the centre, in which stood some drooping coconut trees. There was a wall around, with barbed wire and glass shards running around the top. Even the faded moonlight could not make it seem anything other than what it was… a grim and forbidding prison, and the scene was, I realised, the perfect setting for all I was feeling. This place was harsh, filled with strange, distorted children and unfeeling women who did not care for me at all and I believed I had died and gone to hell. At the very least, I wished I was dead.

I turned around, and went back to my bed and crawled back in, and lay there under the sheet, dry-eyed and miserable, staring at the ceiling above me wide-eyed, wide awake. The pale fingers of moonlight lightened into bright hot shards of sunlight, and as the shadows got shorter, a bell rang, clanging furiously, jangling through my head and rousing the others in the dormitory out of their slumber. Next to me, I saw Kalpa getting up, stretching and yawning and then as if she sensed me looking at her, she turned around and smiled at me.

"That's the wake-up bell. It rings at 6:00 am every morning, and we have to be ready by 6:30 am to go and help feed the children breakfast. After that, we have to eat at 8:00 am, so hurry up and get dressed."

I was still in the pavadai from the previous day, and I looked at it, wondering what I should change into. Kalpa saw me looking at my clothes and got up, and came up to me.

"Have a wash and wear that again. Afterwards Madam Nalini will show you everything, and give you other clothes, as well."

She turned back and began making her bed, swiftly smoothing the sheets down and I copied her, fumbling to get the sheets straight and tucked in. I then followed her like a puppy into the bathing room, which was filled with the sounds of splashing water. Kalpa entered a cubicle as soon as it was empty, and I stood outside, feeling forlorn, wondering what this day would bring. She emerged five minutes later, and handed me her damp towel and her bar of soap and nodded to me to go inside. I washed and dried myself the best I could, and put on the same clothes I had slept in; they felt gritty and unclean against my freshly bathed skin. At home, my mother gave me fresh clothes every morning and the memory brought on a fresh attack of sadness.

Kalpa was waiting for me. She took the damp towel outside the room and went back into the dorm. She hung the towel over the bottom of her bed, and then reaching under, pulled out a small cardboard box. She put the soap into a small plastic dish there, replaced the box, and stood up.

Smiling at me, she said, "Let's go!"

I trotted behind her faithfully, and within a minute we were back in the same hall where I saw her for the first time yesterday. It was emptier than yesterday and the same long table was there, this morning stacked with large plastic bowls, a huge steel container piled high with idlis and a steaming vat of sambhar. My mouth watered at the sight, and it dawned on me that I was suddenly ravenous. The older girl was there from the previous day, and she glared at me, as if angry at my intrusion into her world. Kalpa tugged at my hand and nudged me towards the table.

"This is Revathi," she said, and pointing at me she said, "This is Madhuri!"

I smiled tentatively at Revathi, who looked me up and down and then looked away dismissively, and began ladling out the idlis and sambhar into the plastic bowls. Three other girls trooped in, and I recognised them all from the dorm. And behind them came the children from yesterday… Stumbling, shambling, and moving in jerky motions, they were led by Madam Nalini, and some other ladies who I did not recognise, some who must have been the ayahs that Kalpa mentioned. My revulsion to them was as extreme as it had been yesterday and when I caught sight of the boy who had attacked me yesterday, I shrank behind the huge idli container, fearful that he would launch himself at me again. Revathi prodded me in the back with the end of her ladle, and I turned around to face her. I looked at her closely this time, and recoiled from the look of utter dislike I saw in her eyes. Her hair was knotted into two plaits as well, and she wore the same uniform as I did. Her thin pinched-up features, were that of an older woman, though she could not have been much more than two or three years older than me, and I was only twelve. She gestured with her head towards the bowls and then the children, and I grabbed a bowl and went to the child who was now closest to the table, on the straw mat on the floor. It was a girl, maybe half my age and her legs were splayed at an uncomfortable angle under her, while her head tilted to one side, and a bit of drool rolled out of the corner of her mouth. Her eyes were expressionless and she looked around her constantly as if trying to make sense of her surroundings. In that, I felt she and

I had something in common and feeling a strange, unwilling sympathy for this strange scrap of life, I sat down in front of her with the plastic bowl and scooped up some food. To my utter relief, she opened her mouth and swallowed the mouthful and then looked up blankly at the ceiling. I spooned another mouthful in and the same thing happened. In a few minutes, the entire bowl was finished and I was filled with a sense of real accomplishment. I laid her down gently on the straw mat and went to return the bowl. Kalpa was standing by the table getting another bowl, as well.

"After the food, you have to make them drink water, as well," she said pointing to the end of the table where a large brass container with a tap affixed to it, was being used by one of the ayahs.

I walked up to the water container and grabbing a steel tumbler waited my turn. The ayah finished filling two glasses and gave me a little smile as she turned around to leave. I smiled back, suddenly feeling quite cheerful. I filled the glass and went back to my charge, who drank half the glass, and then turned her head away stubbornly, refusing any more. I looked around for help and caught Kalpa's eye. She waved her hand to me, as if to say I was not to worry, and gestured to me to move to the next child. This was a very young boy, no more than two years old who continually shook his head as if he were dancing to some secret music inside his mind. It was harder to feed him because of this, but I eventually managed to get some food into him and move on to the next.

The room was incredibly noisy, with the howling and moaning of the children, the voices of the ayahs and young girls who were trying to feed them … I counted 41 children, six ayahs, Madam Nalini, and the five other girls from my dormitory. Of Madam Shanthi there was no sign, and I was glad, as her harsh demeanor and stern voice filled me with dread.

An hour later, all the children were fed, and the six girls congregated near the table silently. Madam Nalini came up to us, and she smiled at me, and then looking at all of us, she said, "Good job, girls. Now time for your breakfast."

She laid out six bowls and ladled the sambhar in and put three idlis into each bowl and handed them to us. We were all hungry, I knew I certainly was, and gobbled up the food quickly. Revathi was the first to finish and went to the water container and swiftly filled up glasses of water and brought them to us on a plate. She looked at Madam Nalini, who smiled at her, and patted her gently on the head. I saw a quick smile glance over Revathi's features but it was almost instantly replaced by her habitual scowl. We each had a long drink of water, and then we walked across the large hall, heading for the door. I was about to follow them when I felt Madam Nalini's touch on my shoulder.

"Not you! You follow me! We have to settle you in, and I will explain how everything works to you."

She swept out the room, which was now a bit quieter, the children a little more silent on full stomachs and the ayahs were moving around with damp rags cleaning their faces and wiping their clothes where food had spilled down them. I trailed after Madam Nalini, wondering what was going to happen next. She led me back into the main outer foyer, where I had last seen my mother, and the sight of the room was enough to once again bring back the painful sense of loss with renewed force.

I let out a little gurgle of pain, and Madam Nalini must have heard me, for she turned around and asked, "What's the matter?"

I shook my head, and said nothing, and she must have sensed my unspoken pain, for she put her arm around my shoulders and guided me into an airless room off the side. There were three desks in there, with some chairs, and at the end of one wall was a row of steel cupboards. The room was painted a sickly green, and lit by two naked bulbs that hung from wires on the high ceiling.

"Sit here," said Madam Nalini, propelling me into one of the chairs and I sat down with a thump.

Madam Nalini pulled out a large set of keys which were hanging from nail on the wall and she went to the largest steel cupboard and opened it. She turned around, looked at me again, and then nodding her head, reached in and pulled out some clothing. Holding these under her arms, she moved to the next cupboard, and opening it, she started shuffling around inside. The clothing under her arm fell out and she tutted with annoyance.

"Damn it!" she said loudly, and picked them up again.

I had never heard those words before, and I liked the sound of it and immediately practiced it inside my head, wondering what they meant. She then turned around, her arms filled with a few other things and she brought them over to me and sat them all on a desk.

"Pull your chair closer," she urged and I dragged my chair across to the desk she was standing at. Madam Nalini sat down, across the desk from me, and sorted the little pile out.

There were two sets of dark blue pavadais, one printed nightie, a bar of soap, a rough cloth towel, a set of elastic hair bands, a toothbrush, toothpaste, three sets of shorts, a bottle of hair oil, and one of talcum powder, two sheets, a pillow case, and comb.

"Okay Madhuri, now listen carefully. You will change your pavadai every two days and the shorts everyday. You will wash the used ones yourself when you bathe, and hang it out to dry at the bottom of your bed. You will dry your towel there every day. You must wear the nightie when you sleep, and you must put powder under your arms after washing. You can oil your hair twice a week, but you can only wash your hair once a week as we have a water problem and you must always be careful about how much water you use. Do you understand?"

I nodded at her, blinking rapidly, as I tried to remember all the instructions. Madam Nalini continued, satisfied that I was clear about what had been said so far,

"You will change your sheets every Sunday morning and wash the soiled ones yourself, in the taps in the courtyard outside, and then hang them to dry on the big line. Everything must always be folded neatly and placed inside this box and kept under your bed," she said, pulling out a large cardboard box, from under the table.

She put all the things into it, and pushed the box towards me. I stood up, and lifted the box, which felt heavy. In fact, my arms felt heavy with the weight of ownership, as I had never had things that had belonged exclusively to me before, except for my toothbrush. Even my clothes I had eventually had to share with Radhi. This treasure trove in my arms felt incredible, and the thought crossed my mind that this was what it probably felt like to be wealthy.

I clutched the box close to me, my feelings of being homesick replaced with the pride of ownership. Madam Nalini, seemed to know what I was feeling, and as I smiled my gratitude at her, she smiled back, a wide lovely smile, that suffused her face with warmth and gentleness. I learned over the course of the years how rare this smile was.

"Look after them carefully," she said kindly, "and now you must start your classes, but first let's put all this away under your bed."

She went back to lock the cupboards, replaced the keys on the nail and walked swiftly back through the foyer, down the corridor and into the dorm. I put the box under my bed, and promised myself I would come back and look at it all in closer detail as soon as I had the time. Hugging myself with delight at the prospect, I followed Madam Nalini like a faithful slave, which I must confess I already was, down the corridor to another room that led off it. I walked in, and stopped short.

There was Madam Shanthi, large as life, sitting at a big desk in the front of the room, while two rows of wooden tables and benches held the six girls from my dorm. There was a free space at the end of one of the rows, and as Madam Nalini led me to it, Madam Shanthi stopped her.

"No need to spoil the girl, Nalini … she can walk to the empty place herself. You're always too soft with them," she said crisply.

I looked up nervously at Madam Nalini whose colour was suddenly high, but she smiled at me reassuringly, and pushed me towards the empty spot. By the time I reached the desk and had sat down Madam Nalini had left the room.

I sat down, and looked around me diffidently. Kalpa was sitting in the row behind me, and Revathi was next to me, unfortunately, and I could feel the waves of antagonism from her wash over me like a gritty deluge. I tried to ignore it, and tried smiling at her, but she stared back at me, her face frozen into a mask of dislike for the newcomer that was me.

Madam Shanthi clapped her hands loudly.

"Come here!" she said to me loudly, and I shuffled out of my seat and walked up to her, seated at the desk.

It felt like I had walked a mile by the time I reached her, and my legs were wobbly. It was hot in this room, and a trickle of sweat ran down my back as I stood before Madam Shanthi like a prisoner awaiting a death sentence. She pushed a notebook and a pencil and eraser towards me, and said,

"That is for your writing practice. Keep it clean and do not tear pages out of it."

I nodded and turned around to go, when she barked,

"Say thank you, you ungrateful clod."

I turned around and tears filled my eyes.

"Thank you, Madam," I said, and she nodded grimly at me, and waved me back to my place.

I slid back into my seat and stared wide-eyed at the board on the opposite wall. It was filled with writing in English and I could only make out some of the words.

"Copy the passage on the board," said Madam Shanthi, and we all obediently took our pencils and bending our heads began to laboriously copy out the passage.

She got up every now and then, and walked up and down the two rows, to see how we were doing, and I heard a dull whack, as one of the girls in the row behind me got a smack for some error. I hoped it was not Kalpa. As she walked past me, she looked at my well-formed script and nodded, and despite my fear of her, I felt a thrill of pleasure.

I loved learning and school had always been a joy to me. Learning new words, studying how numbers worked together, these had been of my greatest joys in my old life. We had mostly studied in Tamil at my old municipal school, but even then my teachers had always praised my handwriting in English. So I wrote on furiously, determined to be the best in this class. 'Jack goes to the market to buy vegetables.' I had no idea what vegetables were, but the words looked beautiful on the paper.

After half an hour of intense concentration, Madam Shanthi, made us stop and asked us to read from our papers. She had a little cane on her table and she now picked this up and came towards us. She pointed at the girl furthest from me, in the back row.

"Sindhu, you start!"

Sindhu stood up and began reading nervously, in a high voice. She seemed to have managed it correctly, for after two sentences, Madam Shanthi moved to Kalpa. Kalpa stood up and read out,

"Look ow heavy the box is!"

Madam Shanthi walked over to her and said,

"How, not ow."

Kalpa tried again,

"Ow!" she said.

"I'll show you ow" said Madam Shanthi and brought down the cane against Kalpa's arm.

I was craning around to see what was going on, and I saw Kalpa flinch, even though she did not make a sound, and I knew the blow must have hurt considerably. Madam Shanthi moved onto the next girl, who read in a low voice and must have got it all right as well. It was then my turn, and I stood up, my legs shaking, my palms sweaty.

"Jack has to go home before it gets dark."

I read very slowly, hoping I was forming the words correctly. It was not a bad effort, but Madam Shanthi, made me say the words, 'Jack' and 'before' slightly differently. I repeated them after her, and she seemed satisfied and moved on to Revathi, who got up and read her passage flawlessly for Madam Shanthi actually smiled at her. The last girl also got a cuff but got off lightly in comparison to poor Kalpa. My heart was breaking for her, and I longed to turn around and go to her and comfort her and assuage the pain and humiliation in some way.

I think it was on that day, in that hot, sultry, Madras morning, in that strange classroom with the dragon that was Madam Shanthi brandishing that evil little cane, that the seeds of compassion took root in me and I understood, many, many, years later, that no matter how bad my own situation was, I always had space in my heart and mind to feel concern for others, and that quality always lifted me out of my own gloom and despair.

The morning wore on and the stuffy, airless room seemed to close in on us. We were all sweating profusely except for Madam Shanthi who kept fanning herself with a newspaper that afforded a cooling breeze, and that kept the flies and mosquitoes away. I had to keep swatting at my arms and neck and head periodically to keep the insects away, and after a while found it impossible to concentrate as Madam Shanthi made us memorise a maths table, she had printed out on the board for us.

At eleven-thirty, the bell rang and we all stood up, the bench scraping noisily as Madam Shanthi got up and swept magnificently out of the classroom leaving us alone. As soon as the door swung shut behind her, I turned around to speak to Kalpa, who seemed to have recovered from her ordeal, and smiled cheerfully at me. I smiled back and asked her what would happen next.

"Now Madam Judith will come and teach us," she said happily, and as she said it the door opened and in walked a vision of loveliness.

Madam Judith was wearing a dress, and had short black hair, cut like a boy's, and very red lips. I had never seen a woman wear a dress before, and was transfixed by the sight of her bare legs. I knew it was wrong to show your legs in such a fashion, but somehow on this woman it looked just right, and I could not stop staring at her. She was very young and seemed full of life, and beamed at all of us as we got up again to greet her. She handed us pieces of paper, and told us we were going to play a game. I was entranced… a game while at school; this was an entirely new concept for me.

She made us fold the papers, and write our names and then fold the paper again. We then passed the folded papers to our neighbours and Madam Judith made us write what we wanted to become when we grew up. We did so, and passed the papers around again, and wrote what our favourite food was… And this went on six times. We finally opened all the papers and the results were hilarious. The paper, with my name read that I was Madhuri, and that when I grew up I wanted to be very fat, and that my favourite food was dry chappatis and that my favourite activity was beating Madam Shanthi.

We all were giggling helplessly by this time, and once we had sobered up, Madam Judith gave us a history lesson. She told us about how we had been ruled by the British and how the great Mahatma Gandhi had united the whole country into driving them out. She made it sound like it was happening around us that very minute, and she described how Indians had died fighting to regain their land and how the Mahatma himself had almost starved himself to death to try to convince the country to use peace as our battle strategy. I was entranced. Never had history seemed so real or colourful and I felt my eyes fill with tears as I heard about the many who had died to give me this freedom I now had.

Two hours sped by on silken wings and Madam Judith took us through a treasure trove of information and knowledge. We wrote down what we remembered and then gave our books to be corrected. Mine came back, with a big red tick, and the word 'good' scrawled at the bottom. Madam Judith looked at me, and smiling said,

"So you are the new girl. What's your name?"

"Madhuri!" I said, suddenly shy and looked down at my feet.

"Well Madhuri! I think you will be one of my star pupils as I can see you enjoy learning."

I almost swooned from the joy of hearing these words and went back to my place, feeling happier than I had in two days. At one-thirty the bell rang again, and Madam Judith smiled at all of us and left the room, leaving behind an air of good cheer and general well-being. Even Revathi seemed less miserable than usual and sauntered out at the head of the little group with a thin smile playing across her lips.

We headed back into the huge hall, and the sight of the children lying across the mats wiped out my sense of well-being almost immediately. The same table was there laden with bowls of lentils and rice and vegetables and this time I knew the drill. The women from the morning were there already feeding some of them, and I followed suit. I picked up a bowl and started helping. My first spat out every mouthful and I had to place a towel over my clothes to avoid further damage.

My heart sank when I saw the next one was the same boy I had fed the first time. I went to him with my heart in my mouth, and tried to cradle him and surprisingly he nestled against me comfortably and opened his mouth in anticipation. I put the spoon in with a trembling hand, and he swallowed and then opened his mouth again. Kalpa came up with a fresh bowl and sat down next to me to feed the baby next to us.

"Don't be so afraid of him. He only attacks when he does not recognise someone for the first time. Now he knows you, you won't have any problems."

We sat together in companionable silence moving from one child to the next and when all of them had been fed, we spent some time putting the younger ones to sleep, and playing with the older ones. I had loved playing with my younger sister and her sweet, affectionate responses had always gladdened my heart, but playing with these children was so different. Most were unable to focus, and would cry out and make strange noises and drool for no apparent reason. An even though they had the same eyes, ears and nose and hands and legs like me, they seemed to belong to a different world. I have to admit, that the whole process of feeding them and caring for them filled me with a revulsion I never quite got over, despite the pity I eventually came to feel for these hapless beings, who were suffering this lifetime locked into malformed, twisted bodies, imprisoned by their own mental processes. As for the little boy who attacked me – eventually, he would eat no food, unless I was feeding him, and over time, Raghu, for that was his name, became my responsibility, even when he was ill, as he would not allow anyone else to give him his medicines. His strange attachment to me was a tiny balm to my wounded soul, which had never stopped feeling abandoned and betrayed, and I drew comfort from the fact that this misshapen, hapless creature seemed to love me more than my own family did.

Close to five 'o' clock, two old women came into the hall from a door at the side, which Kalpa told me was where the kitchen was and where we would take turns each week to cut and chop vegetables and clean the dirty utensils. They carried in huge teapots and steel glasses, and we were all allowed to take a cup of hot sweet tea. When we finished we washed our glasses at the row of taps that ran down one length of the room, and then we were sent to the dorm again. Kalpa walked with me, and after we had washed our faces taking off the sweat of the day, we went out through a side door that led into the large courtyard I had seen from our dormitory window that morning. There was a slight breeze, and the dusty coconut palms waved their fronds thankfully against the setting sun. It was a relief to be out in the fresh air, and we walked silently to a corner and sat on the cement paving and looked around us.

"We can do what we want now, for two hours" said Kalpa, picking up a stick to trace little patterns in the sandy mud that lay next to the concrete.

I picked up another and added to her little designs and in a few minutes we had etched the most fantastic pattern. It became a routine with us and most evenings, when we did not have kitchen duties, we would sit together and talk about our families, and our hopes and draw comfort from our deepening friendship, as only two young girls can. From this dusty, sandy corner I learned of the circumstances that brought her to this ashram, and she learned of mine. I learned about the ashram itself and its ways, I learned about Madam Nalini and Madam Judith and Madam Shanthi, and I learned that no matter how much your heart aches, there is always room for a little laughter and that after a while anyone can get used to any situation, especially after a hot cup of tea, and a little bit of fresh air.

We were served dinner, some tasteless rice dish that looked and smelled bad. I left most of it and went to bed silently, overwhelmed by the experiences of the day. Revathi closed the door and turned off the light and slowly the breathing around me took on a regular pattern as the girls around me fell into slumber. I lay on my side and stayed awake watching the light stream in through the locked down window. My thoughts drifted randomly coming back to settle on memories of this strange and unwelcome day. I remembered I had forgotten to drag my box of new things from under the bed to have a better look. It was too late now, and if I tried, I would probably wake everyone. And unbidden some of the new learning came back to me. "Damn it" I said to myself under my breath, and then closed my eyes as tightly as I could and let sleep envelop me in her comforting embrace.

Chapter Four
THE ADOLESCENCE

The days that followed flowed from one to the other with little variation. Breakfast, helping with the children, classes, lunch, helping put the children down for their afternoon nap, and then the chores around the ashram, the two free hours in the evening, helping the children again with dinner and then bed. The first few months were especially hard for me and I ached for my family every minute of the day, with every fibre of my being. Falling asleep each night and waking up each morning were the hardest, as I invariably woke and fell asleep to a terrible sense of being alone and a sadness that went beyond words. I think in those months I would have cut my own arm off to see my mother again. But over the months, the sense of being abandoned took over, and a slow bud of resentment began to unfurl in the recesses of my mind. It blossomed into an unyielding anger at having been cast aside without a word of explanation, and with it came a sense of being unloved and worthless that never quite left me.

The daily handling of the children at the ashram made every day more horrific than the last, and the job never got easier. I could not bring myself to understand them or feel any affection for these irregular, twisted beings that were locked into the horrors of their bodies and minds; they frightened me, and having to pick them up and handle them made every day a living hell. The older ones were strong and violent, and the younger ones unpredictable and intractable.

I was scratched, bitten, kicked, shouted at, dribbled and spat on, and worst of all was the smell. They would soil themselves regularly and it was always left to us girls to clean them. We seemed to be the lowest in the pecking order at the ashram, and I soon learned when you are the lowest of the low, you get to do the dirtiest jobs and are expected to do them uncomplainingly.

There were a group of ladies who came in the morning to help with the ashram. A few taught us, others just held the children, cooed to them, walked them around, and helped feed them. These ladies dressed well and came from outside the ashram every day and barely acknowledged us, the six girls locked into this prison-like existence that we were meant to be grateful for. Kalpa told me they all came in big cars with drivers and were very rich, and she whispered to me one day over lunch that these ladies were 'doing charity'. I mulled this over in my head and then decided that 'doing charity' was when rich people pretended to care about us poor people. Kalpa also told me that these rich ladies provided money so that we could be clothed and fed, and that it was because of them we were so well looked after. I could not understand any of this. Why should anyone give money to help these twisted children, or assist us forgotten young girls? I learned much later in life, that this 'doing charity' made rich people feel less guilty about being rich, and I learned to manipulate that emotion to my advantage. But for now, as a young girl, all I wondered was if any of them knew where my mother was, but I did not dare ask the question.

Over time the blur of faces at the ashram became separate entities, each with distinct personalities. The one I grew to love the most was Kalpa, and during our free time in the compound each evening I got to know her and her gentle nature well. Kalpa had the ability to accept and let go of situations with an equanimity that I envied, and she took me under her wing. I learned she was younger than me by a couple of years, and yet she mothered me with a gentle steady hand that was a balm to my wounded soul.

One evening she told me about her life before the ashram. She said she came from a family of six girls, and her mother was a fisherwoman who lived in a shack by the sea. Her father was rarely present and she said she did not remember what he even looked like. She just remembered his voice and the way he would stand and shout outside their shack whenever he was drunk. I nodded in understanding as she said that. I knew, only too well, the oppressiveness of a drunk father. When Kalpa was born, another girl, her father swore never to return to the shack leaving her mother and going off in search of a woman who could provide him with a son and heir. Kalpa grew up playing on the sand, eating copious amounts of fresh fish.

"I miss fish," she confessed to me softly, "and the sound of the sea still plays in my mind. One day I will go back and live by the ocean."

I asked her what the ocean was. She smiled and said,

"It's a great big body of water, bigger than anything you have ever seen. It's blue and black and green and brown and makes a whooshing noise and all sorts of things live inside it … animals that you would not imagine. I've seen fish bigger than you and me, and little crabs and big birds that fly over the sea. Once I saw a massive turtle shell washed up on the sand. There's nothing more beautiful than the ocean," she said, smiling her slow, peaceful smile.

I tried to imagine this magical place but all that came to mind was the green marble from long ago. Kalpa shook her head as she saw me trying to picture what she had described.

"Don't! You cannot understand unless you see it." And I hoped that one day I would.

I told her about Thousand Lights and being up high on the roof and watching the sparkling traffic and listening to the roar of the traffic, but somehow I could not make it sound as exciting as the ocean with its unusual animals and changing colours. Kalpa did not seem to think so.

"How wonderful to be so high up," she said, and then looked at the flat roof of the stained grey Ashram building.

"I wonder what we would be able to see if we climbed up to the roof?" she wondered.

I looked at the flat, grimy walls and then at a set of pipes that ran down one side. Kalpa saw me looking at it, and laid a restraining hand on my knee.

"Don't," she said warningly, "or you will be in so much trouble. One of the boys, a few years ago, tried to climb up those pipes, and fell down and broke his leg. Madam Shanthi had him thrown out of the ashram immediately, even though he was mentally ill and had nowhere to go."

"So where did he go?" I asked stupidly.

Kalpa shrugged. "The watchman took him away one day, and we have no idea what happened. So don't even think of trying to escape, because if you have no one to go to, you will be on your own on the outside."

I did not say anything to Kalpa, who was obviously scared of the outside world, but I wondered mutinously if the world outside the ashram walls would be as awful and soul-destroying as the world inside them.

We sat in companionable silence for a few minutes, and then as if she had read my thoughts, she said, "Madhuri, it is worse outside. When I was five, my mother left us girls in the shack and wandered into the ocean and never came back. We sat around for two days in our shack, waiting for her. Finally one of the neighbours noticed we were on our own. They stood around us talking and wondering what to do with us. The three eldest girls were taken away by some men and a strong-voiced woman. I have no idea what happened to them, but my eldest sister picked me up before she left, and held me close and said, 'I hope this does not happen to you', and then turned to follow those that had come to take her away. The other two girls were taken away by a pair of women in white sarees and then I was the only one left and my neighbours brought me here and left me."

She said all this without a trace of sadness, in a matter-of-fact voice that made me ashamed of my own bouts of anger and resentment against my family. At least my mother had not wandered off without making arrangements for me to be looked after. But Kalpa's story made me fiercely protective about her, and she became a substitute of sorts for my little sister. I knew she loved food, so whenever we got sweets to eat, I saved my share for her, and together we made plans for a wonderful life we would eventually have.

Our favourite one was where we both lived in a shack by the sea, and caught fish and sold it, and made money and never had to worry about getting up late, or cleaning dirty, deformed children again, or being scolded by rich women who swept past us magnificently as soon as they finished their charitable deeds at the ashram. Kalpa promised to buy me a sack of marbles with the first catch we sold. I told her I would buy her all the sweets she ever wanted. And so on those blistering evenings, with the buzz of flies around us, and the sound of coconut trees creaking in response to the odd gusts of wind, we planned a life of peace and plenty, and it sustained us against the harsh realities of our present existence.

Kalpa also became my source of gossip around the ashram. She was the one who told me about Madam Judith. Pretty, lively Madam Judith, who treated us like her friends and taught class for us on Mondays, was an Anglo-Indian, she whispered confidentially, making it sound like a terrible disease.

"What's an Anglo-Indian?" I asked curiously.

Kalpa tried to explain. "They're like us, Indians, but not really Indian. Their ancestors married foreigners," she said, wrinkling her nose.

I immediately thought back to the big red-faced man who had come to my old school all those years ago. Marry one of those? I shuddered and then wondered if Madam Judith would have to marry one of those big-faced, big-boned people, and asked Kalpa.

"Oh no, they can marry whom they please," she answered knowledgeably, "and wear what they like. I've even heard Madam Judith speak about dances, where she goes late in the evenings and dances with men."

I shivered in delicious horror at the thought, and I must confess, despite my genuine affection for the free-spirited Madam Judith, I thoroughly enjoyed my first feelings of moral superiority over another human being.

Kalpa continued, "In fact, she told us that it was not necessary for girls to marry and it was possible to work and be independent."

I shook my head wonderingly at this new bit of information. Even locked away into the ashram, we knew the only course of action for us was to eventually get married and have children. To do otherwise would be to visit utter shame upon ourselves, our families and society, and to deny the very reason for our existence. Of course, girls like Kalpa and myself lived on the fringes of society with no families of our own, but we had no doubt that our lives would pan out in a similar fashion to our mothers'. That Madam Judith could consider a different way was almost blasphemous and I wondered how she could be happy, in her short skirts and short hair and strange way of life. I spent a lot of time wondering about her after that, and tried to imagine her life outside of the building.

She once saw me staring at her curiously in class with a million unasked questions in my eyes. That afternoon, she stayed back after class and asked me to help her clear up the desk. Revathi stared at me jealously when I was given this special privilege and nudged me sharply with her elbow as she went out. I stayed back and began to collect the little pieces of chalk she had distributed earlier to us to write on the board and took them to her desk.

Madam Judith was wearing a pale pink skirt with a white blouse and had sparkly earrings falling down from her ears. Her short hair was brushed back off her face and she looked neat and cool and elegant. She looked up at me and smiled.

"How are you liking it here?" she asked.

"It's nice," I answered cautiously, not wanting to seem ungrateful.

Madam Judith, looked at me searchingly and said,

"I know you don't like it and I don't blame you. It's hot, and uncomfortable, and they treat you all like unpaid ayahs. I wish I could help more, but I can't."

This was said in a matter-of-fact tone of voice, and the honesty of her remark made me open up.

"Are you married, madam?" I asked. She laughed as I said this and shook her head.

"No," she said with a smile, "I am not and I am in no rush to get married. I have a boyfriend I see every week, and that's enough for now."

"A boyfriend?"

Another new word. Madam Judith tried to explain.

"A young man who loves me, and we see each other as often as we can. We go for movies, and write letters and have dinner together …" she trailed off seeing I had absolutely no comprehension of this world she was describing. "Like in the movies." she added.

I shook my head and shrugged.

"I have seen movie posters, but never a movie. I would like to," I said, and quickly added that I wanted to see the ocean too.

Madam Judith, laughed at me and ruffled my hair and said I was clever and she was sure one day I would see all those things, and maybe even have a boyfriend. She left me feeling confused and ignorant, and much as I adored her, I secretly wondered if this young woman was what my mother used to call a 'bad woman'. When I spoke to Kalpa about it, she just shrugged her inevitable shrug, and with her air of all-knowing wisdom said, "She's an Anglo-Indian and they don't live like Indians. They are very lucky." To me, Madam Judith was like a divine being, but nothing like the goddess I knew. For Madam Judith was larger than life and very visible.

Our next favourite topic of discussion was Madam Shanthi. We all received the business end of her cane on more than one occasion, and we all lived in fear of her sharp tongue and all-seeing eyes.

Madam Shanthi was the head of the Ashram and lived in a separate room down the corridor from us. None of us had ever seen it and rumour had it that it was finely furnished with soft chairs and cushions and had beautiful pictures on the wall. Madam Shanthi herself was a large woman who always wore crisply starched cotton sarees that enveloped her in stiff, pleated swathes. She had a heavy hand and it came down on our backs and arms swiftly, for the slightest infraction. She seemed to have taken an utter dislike to poor Kalpa, and Kalpa had no idea why this was the case. When I asked, she gave her usual shrug, and said, "Maybe it is because she is not married."

This confused me. Madam Judith was happy because she was not married, and Madam Shanthi was miserable because of the same thing. How was this possible?

The truth emerged in the most unexpected and entertaining way. Madam Shanthi was nasty not just to us, but to the rich ladies who visited every day to help with the children. She treated them with scant respect, and was most dismissive in her dealings with them. It was obvious they came from a better background than her, and I think it made her feel better to treat them in this fashion. Mostly, they ignored her, and went about their work, chatting with Madam Nalini and sorting out the series of cooks and ayahs that came and went from the Ashram.

Every week we took turns to help in the kitchen. It was only marginally better than helping with the children. The kitchen was a long dark room behind the huge dining hall, with just two ventilators far up on one of the walls. Other than Ramu, the full-time cook who lived with the watchman in the little hut just beyond the kitchen, the rest of the kitchen staff were a rag-tag bunch of people, and not one stayed longer than a few months at the most. Ramu was a wizened old man, with a few strands of grey hair that were oiled in single strands across his shiny head and he wore an unvaried uniform of tattered old khaki shorts with a dirty white vest. He sported a pair of thick, black-framed glasses through which he peered out at the world, and was sullen and terse with anyone who addressed him or questioned him. He had been at the ashram for an impossibly long time, and I think even the formidable Madam Shanthi treated him with a modicum of respect.

A few weeks after I had joined the ashram, a new lady had started visiting us and it seemed to me she was nicer than the others. Her name was Rani, Madam Rani to us, and she smiled often and said please and thank you and appeared to genuinely care for us. She taught us as well, and one day, it suddenly dawned on her that every day one of the girls was missing from class. She looked up suddenly from the book she was reading, and asked,

"Why do you all skip class like this?"

She sounded stern and we all looked at her wonderingly, not knowing what the problem was.

"You," she said, pointing at me, "You were not here yesterday. And today Sindhu is missing, and this happens every day. Why don't you all attend your classes regularly?"

We all sat still for a while and it was Revathi who finally answered.

"Madam, today is Sindhu's turn in the kitchen."

The lady, who we knew as Madam Rani, looked at her surprised.

"What do you mean by that?"

Revathi answered steadily, and I admired her composure, as Madam Rani looked most annoyed.

"Madam, every day we help to make the food and clean the ashram."

It was almost time for the lessons to end, and Madam Rani got up swiftly, and said abruptly, "Class is over," and stormed out of the room.

We stood up, looking at each other uncertainly, wondering what we had done wrong and if she had gone to complain about us to Madam Shanthi. It seemed like the bell took forever to ring, and as soon as it did, we trailed after her to go to the dining room, wondering what punishment awaited us. We arrived to find Madam Rani and Madam Shanthi, facing each other across one of the trestle tables indulging in a screaming match that drowned out the sounds of the children.

"How dare you make them slave in the kitchen? They're not here to be servants. They are here for shelter and food and to get some sort of education."

Madam Rani was bristling with rage.

"Don't you yell at me," screamed back Madam Shanthi. "You have no idea how difficult it is to run this place on such limited resources. It's impossible to find staff to help in the kitchen. Do you expect me to cut the vegetables and do the washing and cleaning?"

"The reason no one stays here is because of how you treat them. You're a disgrace to this institution. Just because your husband left as you were unable to give him a child, does not mean you can take it out on these unfortunates who end up here. Your bitter nature is destroying this ashram which is meant to be a place of peace, not suffering."

The words came out of Madam Rani's mouth like poisonous darts, and Madam Shanthi paled under the vicious onslaught. I was personally glad to see someone take on this woman who ruled us with such brutal discipline.

"Get out!" said Madam Shanthi, "As long as I am in charge we will not need over-privileged women coming in here with their high and mighty ideas trying to tell us how to run the place. Run back to your cosy life and never come back here."

She spun around and left the room, and we all stared at Madam Rani, who let out a sigh and spoke to Madam Nalini.

"The girls cannot be made to serve and help in the kitchen. Someone needs to take action. You're the Assistant Head and you should do something."

And with that she walked out of the dining hall and out of our lives for we never saw her again.

Madam Nalini shook herself, and with a bemused expression went to the trestle tables and began ladling out the food.

We all followed suit and an hour later, all the children were fed and we were allowed to eat after, as usual. We helped lay the children out to sleep on the straw mats and then trooped out to our dorm. Sindhu went back to help clean the pile of vessels and help the ayahs mop the place down. None of us spoke very much, and my mind was buzzing with questions - Was our life meant to be different? Was Madam Shanthi doing something wrong? The questions were never answered, and the only outcome of that battle was that Madam Shanthi was even more brutal in her dealings with us; as if to exert her authority after that public debacle, she was even more generous with her cane than ever before. I felt the sting of it over every mispronounced word, and every spelling mistake, and every sum calculated wrongly. I came to dread lessons and my love of learning disappeared under the cloud of Madam Shanthi's anger and judgment.

Nothing ever came of Madam Rani's screaming match with Madam Shanthi, and our lives went on mostly unchanged. Raghu still, and without warning, attacked anyone new who came near him, Revathi continued to dislike me, the ayahs came and went … a faceless, nameless mass of bent and worn out women … the sun blazed our very souls in the summer months and I grew older and more resigned to this life with each passing day.

The pattern was harsh and unremitting except for our lessons with Madam Judith. I never forgot the sound of her voice and the scraps of information I managed to glean from those smouldering afternoons in the stuffy classroom. Those stayed with me long after my days at Anni Ashram.

Chapter Five
THE PASSAGE OF TIME

They say time passes much slower when you are children. Certainly, the initial years at the ashram seemed to crawl by. There was no fun, no games-- just the daily routine of caring for a group of children that offered little back in return. The rudimentary education we were given taught us all how to read and write very basic Tamil, but my written English was still sketchy at best. Revathi informed us loftily we were lucky we did not have to write exams, and from the faint memory of my earlier school, of those nerve-wracking events, I was pleased that this was the case. I got to know the other girls quite well. No one new came to us during the time I was in Anni Ashram, and so the six of us grew as close as it was possible to in those limiting circumstances.

Revathi, who was the oldest, always maintained her aloof distance from us and only ever smiled when she was praised by a teacher. She was not above prodding and pinching us younger ones slyly, especially when she felt we had outperformed her in the classroom; but we had no one to complain to, so she got away with her bullying and violence. After a while I learned not to pay any attention to it and shrugged it off as just one of those other things I had to cope with. Sindhu was a plump, cheerful little thing. Orphaned at a very young age, she had only ever known life at the ashram, and was the most comfortable in it. She was the same age as me and wanted to be a teacher, she said. She was not very good at her studies, however, and though she struggled diligently through her work, she, along with Kalpa, felt the force of Madam Shanthi's cane the most in class.

Sindhu and I would spend our evenings together when Kalpa was on kitchen duty, and I liked her well enough. She told me she had an uncle somewhere who visited her once a year. She confided to me that her uncle had promised her that if he ever got a well-paying job, he would come and take her away from the ashram and she was waiting for that day. I said nothing, as by now, I knew we girls were unwanted and no one would come to take us away, but I smiled at her encouragingly, not wanting to burst the only bubble she had.

The other two girls were sisters, Latha and Leela. They seemed not to need the rest of us very much and did every-thing together, including sleeping in cots next to each other. They looked remarkably similar. They had come to the ashram a year before I arrived and from similar circumstances as mine. Their father had passed away, and their mother could not afford to look after them, so they were brought here to be raised and educated.

Education is a loose term to use for what was actually im-parted to us. Kalpa told me in hushed tones that the rich la-dies who dropped in to teach provided the ashram with money they donated and expected education to be a part of the pro-ceedings. But there was no formality to the learning process, unlike my old Government school. There was no curriculum, no exams, no real text books. We were taught according to the whims and fancies of the volunteers who came and went with such monotonous regularity, that after a while they all blended into one faceless mass of richly clad women who did not really care about much other than the ability to be part of a charita-ble cause. Often they came in groups, chattering gaily, and it seemed the visits to our ashram served a social purpose more than anything else.

It was clear the real purpose of us young girls was the up-keep and running of the ashram itself. Other than our duties of feeding the children, we took turns to clean our dormitory, the dining room and all the bathrooms. Ramu cleaned the kitchen, or so he said, but the grimy floor and dank smell of rotting vegetables said otherwise. Madam Shanthi or any of the other staff never went in there, and we dared not tell them how unsanitary it was inside the kitchen. Ramu was not above slapping us hard if we displeased him. I hated going there.

My day in the kitchen was on Wednesdays, and as soon as the bell rang in the morning and I had finished my ablutions, I would run to the dark, stuffy kitchen where Ramu would be waiting with a grim expression and a pile of vegetables to be cut and peeled. From morning till evening I would cut onions, my eyes watering furiously, skin potatoes, knead dough and run around doing his bidding till I was ready to weep from exhaustion. It was a hard job for anyone, but much more so when you are twelve or thirteen or fourteen. On those days I did not get to eat lunch, but if I was lucky I would get to wolf down a meal around four in the evening. There would be piles of washing up afterwards, and I would have to take these vessels out, along with whichever ayah had turned up that day, and rinse out the dishes in the three taps behind the kitchen.

I would only finish long after the sun had set, and after a cup of lukewarm leftover tea, I would drag my aching self across to the bathroom, wash and collapse into mindless slumber, until the bell broke the stillness of sleep the next day. On Saturdays we all got together and cleaned the entire building. We took turns to sweep and swab and dust and wash the children's clothes, and if there was any work leftover we did it the next day.

On Sunday evenings Madam Shanthi would lead us all in a puja. There was a small shrine outside the main door, with a stone statue of a goddess. It was a different goddess from the one I remembered, and she wore a bright blue saree and had flowers and ornaments draped across her. We would stand there, while Madam Shanthi sang a hymn, lit a lamp, and told us a story from the Ramayana or Mahabharatha. None of it made much sense to us, but we obediently closed our eyes and prayed for our time at the ashram to end soon, and gratefully took the tiny sliver of prasadam that was offered. Madam Nalini always went out on Saturday afternoons and came back late on Sunday evenings, long after we had turned in for the night. None of us knew where she went, or what she did on these weekends.

Life in the ashram was not without its excitement. One event especially stood out. It was a day's excursion into town one Sunday. Madam Shanthi was away for a few weeks, none of us knew where or why she had gone; but the ashram was considerably more relaxed and happy as a result, and even the children seemed to rest easier without the shadow of her overpowering presence. I keep saying children, but these poor creatures were only a few years younger than us, and many were the same age as us. I guess the six of us stopped being children the moment we walked through the doors of that ashram. But for one glorious day we were allowed to be our age, thanks to Madam Judith, who spoke to Madam Nalini and arranged to take us all out for the day on a Sunday. We were told on Friday, by Madam Nalini herself, and I must confess none of us slept much that night.

On Sunday we were up before the bell rang, and having fed the children at record speed, we were waiting in the reception hall, silent with excitement. Madam Judith arrived at half past nine, in a beat-up old Matador van that, to us, was the last word in luxury. The fat, cheerful looking man driving it was her father, she said, and we all smiled at him shyly, as we piled into the seats at the back, and set off giggling nervously, pointing out everything we saw to each other. Madam Judith's father was a jolly old man, with wispy white hair that kept falling into his eyes as he drove. He insisted we call him Uncle Kevin, and he and Madam Judith sang songs together and tried to teach us some, but we could not get our heads around the tune or the words.

I was sitting right behind him and at one point he grabbed my hand and showed me how to use the horn. I went quite mad and at every opportunity I got, I would lean over and press on it as hard as I could, causing a terrible racket and making the girls scream in delight every single time it happened. Uncle Kevin eventually made me stop as he said this would make us have an accident. But I will never forget the fun of being part of the driving process, and it stands out as one of my happiest memories ever.

We drove along the dusty roads of Chennai, and revelled in the freedom we were sensing. I was reminded of the two auto rides I had had, and despite the happiness I was feeling, that permanent knot of pain in my stomach hardened a little more. We drove down busy roads, past buses belching thick grey smoke, autos that wheeled around like flies in a stagnant pond, and motorcycles with young men on them who whizzed away to freedom somewhere beyond my understanding. There were huge billboards everywhere dominated with giant pictures of beautiful women in wispy clothes, and the occasional cows and dogs stood by the side of the road, looking thoughtfully at the merciless traffic that whirled by them. It was all incredibly colourful and noisy and made me want to jump up and down and clap my hands in excitement. Uncle Kevin turned off the big busy road onto a smaller one and went through a pair of enormous gates to a towering building. He parked the car amongst a thousand others it seemed, and bade us all get out. We trooped out, chattering excitedly, asking Madam Judith where we were going.

"Hush," she said, "You'll see in a minute."

We shuffled indoors into an enormous foyer, and Revathi figured it out first from all the posters on the wall.

"We're going to see a film," she said almost reverently.

And yes, we were. Madam Judith bought us all tickets and twenty minutes later we were transported into a whole other world. We watched with awe as tall men, with big moustaches jumped over buildings, and gorgeous women danced and sang around gardens, and we wondered if life really was like that for the rich and beautiful. We watched transfixed as the hero rescued his girlfriend from the evil villain, and battled with his prospective father-in-law in order to marry his daughter. I finally understood what Madam Judith meant when she said she had a boyfriend, and in the dark, I looked across at her wonderingly, trying to imagine her singing and dancing under trees and around flowers with a man lovingly following her. I couldn't see it somehow. Despite the thrill of the movie, I still saw her as the pretty teacher who taught me English, history and maths and smiled encouragingly at me, and I hoped she would not marry and leave us.

After the movie, we all walked, holding hands so as not to get lost, to a nearby restaurant where Madam Judith ordered the most delicious and crisp dosas for us. We all must have eaten at least a dozen each. After the dosas, the waiter produced bowls of a pink, creamy stuff, with a spoon in each bowl and set one down in front of each of us. None of us had ever seen anything like this before and stared at it curiously, unsure as to what to do.

"Eat it up before it melts," said Madam Judith, laughing, "Like this."

And she scooped the spoon into the pink stuff and put the spoon into her mouth. I happened to look at Uncle Kevin while this was happening; he was looking at us with a strange expression and had tears in eyes, and I had no idea why and was worried we had done something wrong.

We all followed suit tentatively. As soon as the pink substance hit my tongue, I got a shock. Admittedly it was the best shock anyone could ever have, but it was a shock. It was icy cold, creamy, sweet and the most delicious thing I had ever tasted. I took another spoonful and rolled it around my tongue and swallowed it and then started eating faster and faster.

"That's strawberry ice cream," said Uncle Kevin. "It's my favourite sweet."

"Everything is your favourite sweet," said Madam Judith, laughing, and scooped the rest of her ice cream into his bowl. How I wished she had put it into mine instead.

Lunch was a leisurely affair, filled with jokes, and laughter and conversation, and my first taste of a meal that was not soured by a drunken father, screaming children or overbearing teachers and sullen ayahs. I savoured every minute of it, and the experience of it was better than the actual meal itself. I imagined all the children in the world who got to experience this every day and envied them the ease and comfort of their lives. To be able to eat your food in good company, without the threat of imminent punishment … this was a true privilege.

We ate our food and piled back into the van and after driving for about half an hour we stopped and got out outside a row of houses. Madam Judith led us to a blue gate and we followed her up a flight of steps into a room that had big comfortable looking chairs. There was a television in the corner, and curtains on the doors and windows. I stared at the television longingly. It was rumoured that Madam Shanthi had one in her room, but none of us had ever seen one before. The whole room was so pretty and light and airy and all of us fell silent because we had never seen anything like it. Madam Judith made us all sit down on the soft sofas and we collapsed into the piles of cushions unsure of where we were or what to expect. Uncle Kevin went through a door and as we stared after him, he emerged a few minutes later, pushing a wheelchair on which sat an old lady. Madam Judith went up to her and laying her hand on her shoulder she introduced this lady to us.

"Girls, this is my mother," she said with a smile. "You can call her Aunty Charmaine."

That's when it dawned on us that we had been brought to Madam Judith's home. We all stared at Aunty Charmaine unsure of what we were to say. Kalpa took the lead, stood up, and raising her hands, she folded them, and offered a namaste to Aunty Charmaine. We all followed suit, as it seemed the right thing to do.

"Please sit. I want you all to be comfortable," said Aunty Charmaine, and so we all tumbled back into our seats, and stared around wondering what would happen next.

"I'll make us all some tea," said Madam Judith, and beckoning to me, said, "Madhuri, come help me."

I got up and followed her through the door, weak-kneed at this honour. The room beyond was as pretty as the front room, with curtains and flowers on the table and pictures on the wall. I stared around me curiously, taking in the gentle, welcoming air, and then trotted after Madam Judith into the most lavish kitchen I could have ever imagined. There were neat cupboards all around, and something Madam Judith told me was a fridge and that kept things cool. There was a sink, with piles of gleaming vessels next to it and, once again, pictures on the wall. Madam Judith pointed me at a cupboard and told me to take out cups and saucers. I opened the door and stared inside in wonder. There were piles of beautiful glass plates, and cups with matching saucers, and lovely deep dishes, all patterned with pretty blue and pink flowers. The sight was unlike anything I had ever seen, and I took out the cups one by one, gingerly putting them on the shelf next to the gas rink.

Madam Judith, in the meantime, had boiled a kettle, and the smell of fresh leaves and cardamom filled the air. Madam Judith poured the delicious smelling brew into the cups and setting them on two trays, gave me one to carry out, and took the other herself. We went back into the front room, where the girls were giggling at something Uncle Kevin had just said and handed the tea around.

I served Leela and Latha, Sindhu, Kalpa and Revathi, who scowled at me, as she took her cup; clearly she thought this honour should have been hers and I knew she would extract revenge at some point. But later would deal with itself, and I took the last serving and sat down and had my first sip from a proper cup. It was delicious. The glass was hot to the touch and yet felt smooth, and drinking tea from such a beautiful object undoubtedly made it taste better. We slurped down the tea, revelling in the sense of being in this lovely home, with people who seemed to accept and like us.

"Have you always lived here?" asked Revathi, suddenly in the middle of her drink. "This is such a big house! How many people live here?"

We all looked up in horror, as she said this, and waited for the storm to burst over our heads, at this gross expression of curiousity. My temper flared immediately at her ingratitude to these nice people, and I wanted to run to her and hit her as hard as I could. I was afraid her cheeky question would result in our outing coming to an abrupt halt. Uncle Kevin answered gently, however.

"After you finish your tea, we'll show you around the house. We only bought it some years ago, and we still have to do a lot of work on it," he said with an understanding smile.

We all drank our tea as fast as we could after that. All of us were curious about this big, airy house, its fine furnishings and the people who lived in it. We all glared at Kalpa who was lingering over her tea and as soon as she was done, Madam Judith led us through her home. The girls shuffled through silently, and like me, they too were astonished at the size of the house. The dining room, as Madam Judith called it, and the kitchen amazed us; as did the pretty colours on the wall, and the upholstered chairs, and the dining table with carved legs. But it was the bedrooms and bathrooms that made us all sigh. There were so many, one for Madam Judith's parents, one for Madam Judith and two for visitors. There were lovely, tiled bathrooms that smelled of flowers, with mirrors, and every room was filled with paintings and pictures and little knick-knacks, and soft and pretty fabrics and carpets, and we had no idea how to process all of what we were seeing.

The very idea that one person could have a room to herself to sleep in was a concept that was alien to us. Madam Judith's room was the best. It was a soft pink, with peach and green furnishings everywhere. There was a dressing table with a mirror that had lots of bottles on it. Madam Judith picked up a bottle and gave us a shock by spraying some of the liquid on us.

"That's perfume." she said with a smile.

The room was filled with a fragrance that we had come to associate with Madam Judith and now we all smelled like her as well. The thrill of it was indescribable and we all grinned foolishly at each other, savouring our first real brush with luxury. Madam Judith smiled at us, and then shepherded us back to the front room. Uncle Kevin was already outside and we could hear him tooting the horn.

We said our namastes to Aunty Charmaine and Madam Judith gave her a mother a hug, and then led us all back to the van where we piled in, silent and wondering at what we had just experienced. I must admit I was slightly envious, and wished that I had a life that involved a big house and loving parents and a beautiful, big room to sleep in, undisturbed by the presence of others. But it was hard to stay envious of Madam Judith; she was so kind and sweet and full of fun and this most wonderful day had only come about through her good graces.

What came next was the best surprise of all. Certainly it was for Kalpa. We drove along the dusty, crowded roads a lot more silent than ones we had been on earlier. We were still processing all we had seen during the day. Leela and Latha were whispering together and giggling, and none of us paid much attention to them. They did this all the time, and we were used to it. The van turned off the busy main drag, onto a muddy, potholed road, and we were bumped around quite a bit.

"Damn this government," said Uncle Kevin, loudly and angrily, "Why can't they fix the roads?"

This brought back a lesson learned long ago.

"Dammit!" I said loudly and clearly.

Uncle Kevin burst into a laugh and Madam Judith giggled and turned around.

"Where did you learn that Madhuri? Not in English classes surely?"

I sensed I had said something bad, and I looked down at my feet, not wanting to answer.

"It's okay," said Madam Judith gently, and I heard the smile in her voice and so decided to look at her instead of my feet.

"I heard Madam Nalini say it a long time ago," I said weakly.

Madam Judith grinned at me, "Try not to say it out loud. You can say it inside your head if you want to."

I wanted to protest at this injustice. After all, if Madam Nalini and Uncle Kevin could say it, what was wrong if I said it. But years of holding my tongue made me reign in the question and I smiled back and nodded in agreement. Someday I would try to figure out why it was okay for others but not me to do, say and have certain things. For now, this day was enough.

I turned and looked out of the window, trying not to feel like a stone being rattled around in a tin, as the road was getting rougher and rougher with every turn of the wheels. We held on to the seats in front of us in order to stay steady, but we still swayed and rolled and bounced along, until we came to the end of the road and turned right. We looked up and there right in front of our eyes was a sight I had never seen before. It was what Kalpa had tried to describe to me that dusty evening a long time ago. It lay beyond a patch of golden ground and it sparkled in the late afternoon sun. Sunlight bounced off it and reflected a million points of light and I forgot to breathe at the wonder of it. There in front of me lay the sea. A bright stretch of blue grey that seemed to go on forever, with a frothy fringe that lapped at the land in the most fascinatingly graceful way.

I was transfixed. Of all that I had expected, I had not expected this.

Kalpa, who was beside me, let out a little sigh, and it brought me back to my immediate surroundings. Uncle Kevin was opening the door, and we all tumbled out, and stood in a line looking at the incredible wonder that was the Bay of Bengal. We learned this later from Madam Judith, but for now, all we knew was we were lucky enough to be looking at the sea and none of us had ever seen anything quite so beautiful. There was a tangy smell in the air and Kalpa sniffed this eagerly.

"That's the smell of the sea. I have not forgotten." she said softly.

I took her hand and followed her as she led the way to the fine sand that began just beyond where the van was parked.

"Take off your shoes and carry them in your hands," warned Madam Judith.

We obeyed and carrying our rubber slippers in our hands we stepped onto the sand. It squished between my toes, and was hotter than I expected it to be. It felt soft and gritty at the same time and I loved the feeling of it as I gingerly walked towards the huge body of water. The roar of the ocean filled our ears and it was wondrous. I now knew what Kalpa meant when she had tried to explain what it was to be in the presence of this amazing force of nature. Kalpa unclasped her hand from mine, and began to walk faster toward the water's edge. Revathi followed suit, and Madam Judith kept pace with them to make sure nothing went wrong.

The rest of us went at a slower pace, and caught up with them as they stood a short distance away from the waves. I was entranced by the way they raced up and flowed back and it was like watching a dance. Kalpa looked at Madam Judith questioningly, who nodded her approval. And to my horror, she hitched up her dark blue pavadai, exposing her scrawny legs and walked straight into the path of an oncoming wave. Madam Judith joined her, her skirt short enough to escape the water, and after a minute, not to be outdone, Revathi joined in. We watched the three of them, and slowly one by one, we all walked into the edge of the ocean. I was the last one to go, and Uncle Kevin had to hold my hand and lead me in.

None of us were to go in beyond our ankles, warned Madam Judith, and we were happy to obey. It was both exhilarating and slightly scary. I loved the sensation as the water rolled up and around my feet, but as it melted away back into the ocean it seemed to drag my feet with it and that made me very nervous. I clutched Uncle Kevin's hand tightly for the first few minutes, but after that I got used to the feeling and laughed and began to bounce up and down, jumping in the waves, and rejoicing in the feeling of freedom all of this was giving me. We made up a game where we tried to run faster than the waves and then run after them as they went back to the sea, and avoid the new ones coming in. We were for the first time, children, playing by the seashore; duties, responsibilities, scoldings and aching muscles forgotten in these few hours of absolute pleasure.

We were so unused to fresh air and sunshine and playing, that all of us tired easily, and we sat down on the sand after a while, by the water's edge, and watched as the sun turned from a bright yellow orb into a dusty orange ball that dipped into the hazy and blurred edge at the end of the world. I sat and watched the sunset silently, with Kalpa by my side. I could not recall a happier time in my life, and I tried to remember every detail of the sun and sand, and the way the rough cotton of our dark pavadais matched the inky colour of the ocean that lay reflecting thousands of sparkles from the setting sun.

We drove back to the ashram in utter silence, exhausted by our day of luxury and liberty. Sindhu fell asleep and only woke up as we reached the creaky brown gates of the ashram. I did not dare fall asleep, and I guess neither did the others, as none of us wanted to miss out on even a single minute of this incredible and unexpected treat. Uncle Kevin stopped outside the gate and we climbed out of the van slowly, and made our way up the drive and entered the ashram with sinking hearts.

In my years here, I had never grown to like the place, and this evening it seemed even more foreboding and grim than ever before. Madam Judith, who had escorted us back, led us into the main hall, and we stood there for a minute, lost and forlorn, hoping by some miracle we would be ushered back out into that wonderful life again.

Madam Judith looked wistful for a moment, and then she smiled cheerfully, patted Revathi on the head, and asked,

"Was that fun? Shall we try to do it again another time?"

We looked up at her and, as what she said slowly registered. We all smiled and Sindhu clapped her hands delightedly.

"Yes, Madam, please!" we said excitedly and gratefully, buoyed up by the fact that this was not the complete end of good times for us.

There would be another and then who knows, another one, and another … the possibilities made my head swim. Madam

Nalini had come out in the meantime, and stood watching us in the hall. She clapped her hands sharply, and it brought us all back to the present instantly. We huddled together, and watched Madam Judith set off down the drive back to her lovely home and kind parents. We turned around and went into our dormitory, and gathering our towels and soaps we went to wash away the end of this lovely day.

We rinsed off in silence and went around to the dining room, but it was in darkness and the children must have been fed and put to bed by the ayahs that evening. This was usually our job, but it seems today we had been let off. The only downside to this was, our evening meal would have to be foregone, but none of us complained, and we went back to the dormitory to lie down and take in the marvels of the day we had just had. I lay down and closed my eyes, and tried to remember how the sea felt washing over my feet, but somehow it had already become a distant dream. As the memories unfurled in my mind like a flag blown about by an intermittent breeze, I fell into an uneasy sleep where waiters in restaurants served me food that had been cooked by my mother. And so we woke on Monday, to the strident resonance of the bell, and went about our lives as if that one glorious day out had never happened. But it had, and in my mind, I knew there was a different life out there, and I prayed fervently that this wonderful life would be mine someday.

The wonder of the day stayed with us all for many weeks, and we often spoke about it with delight and laughter in the few hours of playtime we got in the evenings in the dusty, ugly compound behind the ashram. We never had a day like that again, and despite her promise Madam Judith did not bring it up again, and we knew better than to ask. After all, even that one time was more than any of us could have expected or imagined. Life continued the way it always had. Our days went by in a haze of half-hearted learning, being bitten and kicked and spat on by the children and looking after the ashram which somehow never quite managed to get quite clean no matter how much soap and water we used. And in this enormous grey dusty building we passed the hot, sweaty summer months that cooled into muggy, sticky winters, and we grew into silent, unquestioning adolescents, knowing exactly what each day brought for us, and knowing nothing of what really lay behind the walls of the ashram other than what we had seen on that one golden day.

Chapter Six
THE CHANGES

I have no clue how long I was at the ashram. The months and years blended into a single, blurred passage of time and I forgot how old I was, or when my birthday was. There was one mirror in the communal bathroom and that's what marked the change in years and in our lives. I grew from a skinny girl, into a skinny teenager with awkward arms and elbows that were constantly bumping into things. I, like the other girls, was given a new pavadai when I grew out of the old one.

Memories of my brothers dimmed into obscurity, and of my sister Radhi, my only recollection was her gurgling laugh. To this day the sound of a baby's laughter takes me back to the little room on the roof in Thousand Lights, and the image of the homespun cradle rocking, set high above the cares of the sad little world I lived in. After a while, the details of that beautiful day out with Madam Judith and her family faded, and our few hours spent out in the dusty compound, surrounded by the towering coconut trees and the incessant buzzing of mosquitoes, were all the play we girls had.

I never did learn very much here. I could say the English alphabet and read and write very basic Tamil, but mostly my skills were honed around looking after the twisted and bent children that lived under the same roof as me. I learned to feed them, to be patient, to wash my bites with soap and water, and I learned their names. I have no idea where they are today, or what happened to them. None of them seemed to have families that visited, and they all slept in the great hall where we all ate every day. There were no toys or games, but the few chairs and table legs and the view from the grim black iron bars on the windows seemed to offer them some entertainment.

On the days when I was on kitchen duty I would often come out from the evil, dank-smelling kitchen in the evenings after dinner, and find one or two or even three of them standing at different windows staring out into the gathering dusk, at the high compound wall, rocking their heads and softly moaning to themselves. I would take them back to their mats, and make them lie down again, and stroke their heads till they fell asleep again.

Of all the children, Thanga stayed my favourite. He was always quiet with me, and never attacked me again, though he did attack a few of the fine ladies who came to play with the children and made the mistake of trying to hold him. Whenever he acted up, I would be called, and I would have to go and untangle his fingers from their sarees or their hair, and they would always be very grateful, and pat me on the head and say what a good girl I was.

Revathi hated that I was singled out for these special attentions and between her pinches and the bruises and hurts sustained from the children, I managed to stay very clean, as I was forever rushing off to wash my face or my hands and legs to avoid an infection. I had seen what happened to Kalpa and Sindhu when they failed to wash their wounds. Sindhu's hand especially got very swollen, when she was bitten by one of the children and was in a lot of pain, but lucky thing, she was taken out of the ashram to go to the doctors. She came back looking rather unhappy, and said that Madam Nalini had been very cross with her for being so careless, and she had been given an injection which had been terribly painful. I was immediately reminded of that terrible night in the hospital when my father had injured my mother, and I was extra nice to her, even washing her clothes that weekend. Kalpa was not so happy that I was showing Sindhu special attention, and ignored me for a few days, much to my surprise, as I had no idea what I had done to offend her. I moped around for a few days, and then bit-by-bit, perhaps seeing that Sindhu was no real threat to our special relationship, she reverted to her normal cheerful, gentle self and the whole thing was put behind us.

We were lucky that no one really fell seriously ill during my time at the ashram. Rumours stated that many years previously a young girl, like ourselves, had died of neglect during an illness, and we were locked in at night, to keep her spirit out. We heard this from one of the many ayahs who came and went, and we all thrilled to this delicious tale which added a sense of excitement to our mundane, tiring lives. We were of course told to bang on the door if there was a problem at night, and one of the ayahs would come to check on us. We never had cause to and most of us were so tired at the end of all our labours each day that we fell asleep quickly, welcoming the gentle comfort slumber brought, sometimes bringing with it dreams of sparkling oceans, hazy recollections of better times, and the forgotten voices of loved ones calling us back to a time beyond and away from the Anni Ashram.

These years brought big changes other than most of us hitting puberty. That in itself was a tortuous process, and it was Madam Shanthi, at her authoritarian best, who dealt with this delicate aspect of our lives. We already knew the basics from Revathi who was the first of us to 'grow up' as she put it. But we had to deal with Madam Shanthi handing us strips of cloth and instructing us in their use. We did not dare ask her any questions, and of course it was the gentle, laughing Madam Judith who explained to us the finer details of the process. There was no celebration, and no rejoicing in our new-found grace as females, and the only hint we got that there should have been festivities was when the ayahs found out and tutted over us, and told us how their daughters had been given gold, and the entire neighbourhood had been fed to celebrate this most magnificent entry into womanhood. For me, it was about coping with three days of pain, but for Leela and Latha the monthly battle was fierce. They would walk around heavy-eyed, and drooping, almost wilting from the agony.

There was no respite from duties for us on those days, and we plodded on, gritting our teeth, learning that for girls like us, sympathy was a rare commodity. Madam Nalini would often give us some medicine, when the symptoms were very severe, but if we complained too much she too would get quite cross, so we only went to her when it all became utterly unbearable. We tried to help each other on the rough days, and even Revathi would sink to help out the rest of us; I suppose she realised she herself needed our help once in a way.

Of all the days that I hated the most at the ashram, the day of kitchen duty was the worst. On those days roused by the clanging bell, I would rush through my ablutions and scurry down the corridor, to the big hall and run past the screaming, wailing, groaning children, through the door at the end into the dark, musty, smoky room, where Ramu would be waiting, ready to whack me across the back of my head if I was late by even a minute, in his opinion. My first job was to peel the onions which would be lying in a dirty green plastic bucket. At first it took me forever, and my eyes burned terribly and I kept cutting myself. But after a few weeks, I became more dexterous and managed to peel the massive bucket of onions fairly quickly, to a point where Ramu's head did not wobble dangerously at me, threatening me with dire consequences for my ineptitude. After the onions, there was the bucket of tomatoes, followed by vast quantities of chillies and coriander and then there were the kilos of rice to sift through. There were always a couple of ayahs who would help out a little with the cleaning and chopping and peeling, but mostly they cleaned the floors, and bathed the children and washed the piles of dirty clothes that the children went through.

We cooked food for everyone in the ashram - the children, us girls, the gardener, Ramu and the ayahs. We had an unvaried staple of idlis and upma for breakfast, rice, a curry and vegetables for lunch. For tea we would sometimes make samosas or sundal, and dinner would offer the leftovers of the previous day's vegetables. The food was good, and Ramu despite being a foul-tempered old man, was an excellent cook. I adored potatoes and this was the only vegetable I would peel cheerfully. Cleaning the rice was another chore I detested. I would first sift the rice and clean out all the stones, and then soak it in water and lift all the little bugs that floated to the top. No matter how hard we tried, none of us ever managed to get the job done perfectly, and every day we would find the odd worm or insect in our food. Some fell in from the greasy ceiling, and the incessant flies always managed to find their way in. But we all got used to it after a time, and the children rarely noticed.

Food for Madam Shanthi was prepared separately in her own separate kitchen and none of us ever got to see the inside of those living quarters. She had her own maid that she hired privately, or so rumour had it, who did her washing and cleaning and cooking. Madam Nalini ate with us, but always in tiny portions, wrinkling her nose in distaste. She too had her own private quarters and she once confessed she made her own meals on a small stove in there. She seemed slightly embarrassed after this confession, I remember, and the next day she brought around kala jamuns for all us girls that we fell upon like hungry wolves.

Once the vegetables were chopped and peeled, I had to unfold the trestle tables and set them up, carry the plates into the hall, and help one of the ayahs carry the huge water dispenser into the dining hall. Then of course began the arduous process of feeding the children, who no matter how old they got, always needed help with this, the simplest of tasks.

Raghu grew a little, but remained a child, with the occasional wild look in his eyes that spoke of goodness-knows-what terrors that lay hidden inside him. I must admit some of the children were so very quiet and docile that they would have gone on eating as much as we kept spooning in, till they were sick. Others loved meal times and would rock back and forth eagerly in anticipation as soon as I started setting up the trestle tables. After the feeding they were put down for a nap, and we would play with them and try to get them to rest, though they rarely obliged and our reward for these efforts was normally a bruise or a bite. I would then scurry back to the kitchen to wash the piles of dirty vessels with the ayahs, and then I would take a broom, and sweep and swab the kitchen. Then began the job of peeling the vegetables for the evening meal…

And so it went till the children were lying in rows on their mats, asleep, with an ayah watching over them. It was back-breaking labour, my muscles never got used to the work, and I was exhausted at the end of the day. I would walk back wearily to our dormitory, and I often cheated on my evening ablutions because I was too tired to even wash my face.

Two big incidents marked the rest of my years in this place and they both happened towards the end of my stay at the ashram.

No one ever told us how long we would be there. After the first year all of us gave up any hope of seeing our families. We had no idea how long we would stay on in the ashram but we all hoped someday we would get out. We were too timid, too cowed down by life, and too scared of punishment to ask questions, and we were, I suppose, grateful that we had a roof over our heads and food to eat. Sindhu was the beauty in our group with long dark hair and almond- shaped eyes. Kalpa was the peacekeeper and the one we all turned to for comfort. She had amazing reserves of kindness and compassion and whenever I looked back on my life, the memory of her gentle smile always calmed me in a way I cannot explain. Latha and Leela only ever needed each other, and seemed to have a secret life, a bond that none of us could participate in.

Revathi was the eldest, the most powerful and the one who possibly made our life most hellish, for her authoritarian disposition and need to subjugate us was all-pervading and we were never free from her dominating personality. The worst thing about her was that she was always good at everything she did. She picked up lessons with remarkable ease, did her chores with a thoroughness that none of us could achieve, and managed the children with keen efficiency. Yet despite her clever, competent ways, she lacked a sense of humanity, any sort of kindness, and she somehow managed to make us all feel inferior and just a little afraid of her. In the evenings she sat by herself in the big compound, under a tree that only she sat under. She would choose who to call to her, and when she did we would leave whatever we were doing, and go and sit with her and listen to her and do her bidding. She rarely called me, as for some reason she disliked me more than all the others, and often called Kalpa, just to make sure I was deprived of her company. The few times she ordered me to go sit with her were strained and uncomfortable.

She once asked me, "Do you know where your parents are?"

"My father died," I replied, "and I do not know where my mother is."

She leaned across to me and with a glitter in her eyes, she smiled cruelly, and said, "I know how to get in touch with your mother."

I stared at her in shocked silence.

"Yes!" she continued, "I know where all the details of all your parents are. They are in Madam Shanthi's office, in a file on her desk."

I did not doubt this. As she was the eldest and smartest and had been at the ashram the longest, she was often asked to go and help with filing and managing, and for some reason, Madam Shanthi liked her. I realised much later that this was because they were remarkably similar in nature. But at that moment, I stared at her, hope jangling in my heart, that here at last was a real connection to my family. I looked at her hopefully, and the question in my eyes must have been obvious, for she laughed at me mockingly, and said,

"Why do you want to see your mother. She left you here because she did not want you, remember?"

And with that well-delivered blow, she got up and sauntered away indoors, leaving me in the gathering dusk, to collect myself and cope with this awful truth that I had never dared acknowledge before that day.

There is little worse that can happen to a child than to realise fully that his/her parents do not want him or her. Revathi had delivered her poison with startling accuracy and it spread through me, killing off every last vestige of hope I had ever had, that one day my mother would return to take me away from this unfeeling place and its unfeeling people. I cried myself to sleep again that night, and in the morning I awoke and decided that no matter what, I would never allow myself to think of my family again.

A few weeks after this, as the blaze of summer was disintegrating slowly into a sticky monsoon, as we struggled over our English spelling one morning, Madam Shanthi walked into our class to make an announcement. We were being taught by one of the long line of fine ladies who came and went with monotonous regularity to 'teach' us. This one wore spectacles, and like all the others adopted an air of false cheer and kindness in her dealings with us. We had learned long ago that these ladies only came for very short periods, to be replaced swiftly by others like them when they left.

I remember on this particular morning, I had a heat rash down my back and was itching most terribly, but I did not dare complain or move. I had sprinkled powder liberally down my back, but that had offered little relief. As Madam Shanthi walked in I froze, the itching forgotten. We all sat up straighter, and the lady teaching us seemed a little put out by this interruption to her class. Madam Shanthi glanced at her dismissively, and then in her strident tone started to speak to us.

"I have come to tell you that Madam Nalini will be leaving us to get married," she said, the words coming out of her mouth like little daggers. "You will all attend her wedding which is in a month. Her replacement will be Revathi, who will start training to take over her duties, immediately."

She looked at Revathi and smiled, a sly predatory smile that sent a shiver of unease running down my spine. I glanced at

Revathi, who was sitting up very straight. She was looking back at Madam Shanthi, with a knowing expression in her eyes and just a hint of a smile played around her lips. She obviously had known about this for a while and was delighting in the shock that the announcement had created. There was utter silence as we took in the news. The hum of traffic and the buzz of flies reverberated loudly in our heads and it seemed that time had stopped still. It was our first inkling that life inside the ashram could change and change dramatically for us. Madam Shanthi stayed for a minute looking at all of us, and then turned on her heel and swept out of the classroom, leaving behind an air of impending doom.

The spectacled teacher looked after her, shook her head as if annoyed, and then continued to try and make us read some simple English texts. We stumbled through the lesson unable to concentrate, caught up in a maelstrom of emotions and thoughts not the least of which was how our lives would pan out with Revathi taking over the reins from Madam Nalini. Madam Nalini was not the kindest person to us, but she was always fair, and for girls like me that was a real blessing. Now Revathi would have even more power over us, and me, and the thought terrified me as I knew how much she disliked me. When it was time for lunch, we all walked to the hall slowly with Revathi leading the way, and went about feeding the children with even less enthusiasm than before. Somehow life had never seemed more unfair.

I sat with Sindhu during our time out that evening as it was Kalpa's turn in the kitchen that day. We were both silent, and then Sindhu said in a whisper,

"She will make our lives miserable now."

I nodded and we both sat wondering what horrors would be visited on us, with the supercilious Revathi now second in command. None of us could understand how she had come to receive this privilege. I learned why a few months later, but it was not something I could not share with anyone, not even Kalpa.

It happened a couple of weeks later. One evening after kitchen duty, which had taken even longer than before, I was told by Ramu to go to the office and inform Revathi that we were getting low on kitchen supplies. I knew that Revathi worked most evenings in the little office with the big steel cupboards, as she was still learning the ropes. The girls were back in the dorm, and there was a hush over the entire building. The roar of traffic outside was its usual muted thrum and the chirping of crickets was starting to define the sounds of the night. I walked into the hall, and as I came up to the door to the office I saw it was slightly ajar … and even though they did not see me, I saw them. Revathi was sitting on the chair behind the desk and Madam Shanthi was standing beside her, her arms wrapped around the younger girl's neck, her face pressed close to her face, and she was whispering into her ear. I could not hear what she was saying, but even from here, with my limited experience of the world, I could instinctively tell it was an intimacy that defied the bounds of propriety. I stood stock still, not understanding what I was seeing, but some instinct told me what I was witnessing was not right. Then it happened. Revathi turned and saw me through the crack in the door and even from this distance I could see her gaze darken as she saw me watching; she smiled slowly, and took Madam Shanthi's hand and kissed it, slowly and tenderly, all the while holding my gaze with hers. She knew then that I would never tell a soul, and I knew then why she had been selected for special privileges by Madam Shanthi.

I turned and fled, and went scurrying back to the dark kitchen to tell Ramu that there was no one around - to which he promptly responded by hitting me across the back of my head with a wooden ladle. I said nothing and continued my chores, and when I had finished I went back and lay on the cot, my eyes staring up at the dark ceiling trying to make sense of what I had seen. I fell asleep to tangled dreams of Revathi standing by my bed and staring at me, while Madam Shanthi lurked in the background like a malevolent monster intent on destroying me.

While I struggled with the weight of my newfound knowledge, everyone else was all excited at the thought of Madam Nalini getting married. Or to state it more accurately, they were excited about attending her wedding and even more excited about the rumour of the new clothes we were to be given to wear to it. We all watched her closely, and wondered about her marriage in our spare time. Leela and Latha were convinced that she had a boyfriend that she saw when she went away on the weekends. The rest of us were of the opinion that she had a family, and they had arranged this wondrous union for her. Revathi declined to participate in the general wondering. She was more aloof than ever before and had stopped attending classes, as she was now in training with Madam Nalini. She was there, unsmiling and grim as we went to collect our monthly toiletries. When it was my turn she slammed the soap into my hand as hard as she could, and I let out a little gasp of pain. Madam Nalini saw this, and she bluntly told Revathi to be gentler. I knew this would not earn me any favours with Revathi, and I wished that Madam Nalini had said nothing instead. We saw her every now and then trotting behind Madam Nalini or Madam Shanthi, carrying papers around and looking self-important. She stopped helping with the children, and it seemed that her life was suddenly free of the impositions that weighed the rest of us down. And only I knew why.

Then one Saturday, as we were having lunch, Madam Nalini got up and clapped her hands for silence. We fell quiet, though the din from the children did not abate, and she spoke above the general clamour.

"I will be leaving after this lunch. Today was my last day, and I wanted to say goodbye to all of you. I hope I'll see you at my wedding."

We stared at her, unprepared for the immediacy of her departure, and I must confess my heart plummeted from my chest deep into my stomach, as I absorbed the news. I realised only then how safe she made us feel with her no-nonsense ways and her bluff kindness. She nodded at Revathi who came forward with a pile of boxes. Madam Nalini took the boxes from her and came over to each of us, giving a box to each. We opened them curiously and our expressions of curiosity changed to expressions of joy and wonder rapidly. Inside each of the boxes were pattu pavadas in gorgeous jewel colours. Mine was a bright blue with a peacock green border and a gold edging, with a pink and green scarf to wrap around it. I stared at it in utter delight, and then looked up at Madam Nalini, who smiled at me, and then addressed all of us again.

"Please wear these clothes to my wedding." And with that she was gone and we never saw her at the ashram again.

We attended her wedding on a cool evening. Madam Shanthi had organised a small bus to take us to the reception and we piled into it, resplendent in our new finery. We looked like a group of wealthy young girls, and the thought filled me with delight. We had no idea what to expect, and we kept our excitement to ourselves as Madam Shanthi was sitting in the front row, with Revathi next to her. My heart was beating so loudly that I thought everyone would hear it, and Kalpa and I clutched each other's hands in excitement till we left nail marks in each other's palms.

The bus trundled across busy, loud roads and bright traffic lights, passing by giant posters advertising beautiful women and moustached men, meandering through lorries, cars, scooters and the odd cyclist, till we reached a large building that was lit up with thousands of sparkling lights. It glittered like a sky of stars had fallen down on this building, and we all stared at it in wondrous delight as the bus pulled up under a porch that was filled with flowers. We climbed out single file and stood waiting for instructions as we were unsure of what to do next. Madam Shanthi counted us off, and then she and Revathi shepherded us up a flight of stairs at the top of which was a table. Two women stood behind this table, handing out little garlands of marigolds which we accepted in utter delight and tied them around our hands and hair. Thus, even more resplendent, we entered the biggest, grandest hall I had ever seen. It was massive, with huge ornate pillars and was painted in yellow and blue. There were flowers on the pillars and paper decorations swung giddily from the ceiling, swaying and twirling in the cooling breeze created by the massive fans that spun overhead, wafting air over our hot, excited heads. There was the most glorious smell of incense and it reminded me of our little Sunday pujas at the ashram, and music from huge speakers competed with the roar of conversation.

The hall was packed with people. Many, many people. The women all bedecked in sarees and pavadais of the most astonishing colours, laden with gold ornaments, and laughing and chattering to each other gaily. The men wore crisp shirts or jubbas, and everyone looked most resplendent, and we all suddenly realised despite our finery, how shabby we were in comparison. I realised then that nothing quite separates the rich from the poor than the clothes we wear. I felt dowdy and ashamed and suddenly wished I was back at the ashram, where things felt a little more equal.

But that thought soon fled as we were pushed into an adjoining hall filled with benches and long tables. The smell of food was mouth-watering and we sat down at a single table that was set with crisp fresh plantain leaves. Even we young unwanted girls knew what an honour this was, and our deprived souls thrilled to the idea of it. Men carrying buckets of delicious smelling foods came up to us ladling things onto our leaves and we fell upon it like ravenous little curs. We asked for seconds and thirds - and ate till we could hardly lift ourselves off the benches, so heavy and replete we were. We went in pairs to wash our hands at the long row of taps outside and came back in and waited by the door to form our little group again. We were all grinning vacuously by now, and I saw that Sindu had sneaked some sweets into her scarf for later, and I wished I had had the presence of mind to do that as well, to give to Kalpa later.

The crowds had thinned out a little back in the main hall, and we made our way down the side of the hall to the front of this vast room, to a podium that was richly decorated and on which sat the bride and groom on big fat golden chairs. At first we did not realise it was Madam Nalini, as she looked utterly different. She was wearing a maroon saree that seemed to have been spun out of gold, for it shimmered with every move she made. She was wearing an enormous maroon bindi and her hair was piled up to the top of her head and cascaded down her back in a profusion of roses and marigolds. She was wearing so much gold, I wondered how she stayed upright and did not fall down from the weight of it all. But she looked like a goddess and we were entranced by the transformation from ashram deputy to bridal beauty. She saw us all approach and smiled her collected smile, and then we knew it was really her. The big disappointment was her husband. He was short, squat and balding and next to Madam Nalini, especially in her current finery, he looked even plainer than he actually was. I think we were all offended on her behalf. For some reason, as Kalpa and I later discussed, we had expected him to be a tall, handsome man, with a big, fine moustache and a hearty laugh. Still, it was all most exciting and we went up to Madam Nalini and smiled shyly at her, not sure of what to say, and even the cocksure Revathi seemed to be at a loss.

Madam Shanthi congratulated her stiffly, and her smile was insincere at best. We then stood around the couple and blinked as a flashbulb went off and we were photographed together -- a little group of lost girls with the two women who were the closest thing we had had to parents for many years now. I never saw the photograph and I wish I could have had a copy. I can see us clearly in my mind's eye still, standing on that stage, looking slightly bewildered and intimidated by it all, yet hopeful that someday this would be our fate as well. That one day we might be the brides, all dressed up in gold and silk, with a life that was a far cry from the ones we had at the ashram.

Chapter Seven
THE LOSS

Life resumed its normal course after the excitement of the wedding had died down. We spoke about it for days afterwards and sighed over how wonderful Madam Nalini had looked. All of us hoped we would look as resplendent as her when we got married. Each of us had dreams of the man we would marry. Leela and Latha wanted to marry brothers, Sindhu hoped her husband would be kind, and I just hoped he would not be like my father. But we all could not wait to dress up in beautiful clothes and have a big ceremony that honoured us. I do not know if these dreams came true for any of them, but I have always hoped that they found happiness and contentment. These were good girls with kind hearts, and the awkward and hesitant friendships that we built within the walls of the ashram offered us some comfort in the face of the abandonment and uncertainty we all faced. We never saw Madam Nalini again, but after a few months we grew bored wondering where she was and what she was doing and stopped discussing her. I still remembered her though, every time I said, 'dammit' under my breath when things got even bleaker than usual.

Even Madam Judith had no idea when we asked her in class one day. She merely shrugged her shoulders, and in her usual merry way said we should stop wondering about it so much. We then asked her if she would be getting married soon, and to our surprise her face darkened, and her eyes filled with tears and she shook her head and looked away. We stared at her in dismay not knowing what to do.

Then Kalpa in her usual gentle way asked, "Madam Judith are you okay? Are you not well? Shall I go and get you a glass of water?

Madam Judith looked up at all of us red-eyed. She gave us a watery smile and then spoke in a voice that did not carry its usual happy note.

"My boyfriend married someone else," she said shakily.

We stared at her not knowing what to do with this bit of news. I could not understand why this had affected her so much. But it was obviously a loss to her and she was suffering, and that we understood only too well. We had all lost people we loved security and a sense of belonging, and our hearts went out to the pretty, elegant little woman before us who had done so much to bring us comfort and joy.

"Maybe you'll get another boyfriend, Madam. You are so beautiful," said Sindhu tentatively.

We all nodded vigorously at the proposal.

Madam Judith smiled weakly and said she did not want another one, only the one she had lost. It was Kalpa with her inborn wisdom who asked the more pertinent question.

"What happened, Madam? Why did he marry someone else?"

She answered slowly, her face reddening as she told us. "His parents objected to him marrying an Anglo-Indian girl. They wanted someone from their own caste for their son."

This we understood. From our interactions with the ayahs at the ashram, our memories of life outside it, and the conversations we overheard between the rich ladies, we all understood caste and how it worked. Most of us were unsure of our own caste, but I knew from my mother I was a Vanniyar. What that meant in actual terms was a mystery, but I had jealously clung to the fact, imagining it bestowed on me a sense of being part of a community, even though the only one I really belonged to was composed of a group of unwanted girls and malformed children. Certainly we knew how important issues like caste were and how important it was to maintain the purity of these castes. What we did not understand was why Madam Judith had settled on someone outside of her own tribe to marry. Surely she must have known this would end in disaster. She must have sensed our thoughts, for she looked up, and shook her head as if to clear it of its cobwebs.

"I guess it's my own fault for choosing unwisely, but sometimes our hearts speak louder than our heads," she said. "But it is not for you all to worry about my problems. So let's continue with the class."

And so we bent our heads and studied even harder, hoping it would cheer up our favourite teacher. And none of us spoke about it ever again. I did not understand what it was to be in love and have a boyfriend and I was quite sure I never wanted to find out. It somehow seemed like immoral and inappropriate behaviour and I wished to remain as pure as Savitri. We had all heard her story at one of our Sunday pujas recently, and as a consequence we were all trying to be as virtuous and pure as possible, given that the place we lived was one where forgetting to wash your night clothes was considered a major sin against Madam Shanthi and the entire pantheon of gods and goddesses.

Madam Judith was never her merry old self again, and even though she smiled and laughed with us as she always did, it seemed forced, as if her heart was not in it anymore. Her eyes always looked sad, and when she thought no one was looking, she would gaze into the distance with a faraway look in her eyes. I always wondered if these were the moments she was remembering her boyfriend, and I wondered how she could be so sad. After all, I had seen her life, we all had, and she had a beautiful home and clothes, and parents who loved her … surely they would arrange a husband for her and she would have nothing to worry about. In fact there were times when I thought she was quite stupid for pining after a man when she already had all she needed within the four walls of her own home. But I kept these thoughts to myself and did not share them, not even with Kalpa, and after a while stopped thinking about that as well.

Boys, boyfriends, men or relationships were not things any of us had the time for. The only men we saw were Ramu, the cook, and the even more ancient gardener and gatekeeper we all called Anna on the rare occasions that we saw him. I spoke to him once. He had come around the back to the smelly, greasy kitchen on one of my duty days. He had purloined a glass of tea from Ramu and was drinking it noisily as he stared emptily at the wall. I walked past him to go out the door with an armful of vessels, and as I started rinsing them out in the long cement sink, he came out and used one of the taps to splash cool water on his face. He then looked at me and grinned, the water droplets glistening on his face in the dusty sunshine.

"How old are you?" he asked me.

"I think I'm fifteen," I said, wondering why he wanted to know.

I did not like him and for some reason, rather unfairly, blamed him for the separation from my family all those years ago. After all, if he had not opened that gate that day and let us in, I would still be with my mother.

"Your mother has not come to see you in all this time," he said matter-of-factly.

I nodded. Somehow the pain of that fact had never left me. I had no idea where she was, where my brothers were, what had become of Radhi … indeed if any of them were even alive anymore.

I tried my luck.

"Do you know where my mother is?" There! I had finally asked someone the question.

He shook his head ruefully.

"No, I do not know these details. I knew the vegetable seller from your building, and that's how you came here when your father died," he said, nodding his head and screwing up his eyes. A humid breeze wafted across the walls and over us as he said this, and he looked down at me and said the words that crushed every last vestige of hope in my poor, miserable heart.

"You may not see her again. But they will not keep you here forever. Sooner or later all of you will have to leave from here. Be prepared."

And with that unsettling remark he turned around and shuffled off around the corner, back to his post by the gate, leaving me wondering what he meant by that.

I told Kalpa about it the next day as we sat outside in the muggy evening, scratching out one of our fantastic patterns in the mud. She stopped, with her twig mid-air, and stared at the ground. She was silent for a few minutes and then, without looking at me, she spoke in a monotone which was utterly unlike her usual soft and measured tones.

"Usually the rich ladies who come to play with children take them into their homes." One of the girls who was here some years ago, before you came, got a job as a cook with one of the ladies, and she used to come back, once in a while with the lady on her visits to the ashram. She told us she had her own room, was well-looked after and said it was a better life, and the lady was kind. But then the lady stopped coming so we don't know what happened after that."

I digested this information slowly. So the ashram was not all there was for us, till we got married. Logically, I then realised, there would be slim chances of any of us getting married if we were confined to the ashram, and in that moment I grew up. It coalesced in my head all of a sudden, this realization that we were unwanted. By our families and societies, and even the ashram seemed to keep us on only by tolerance. There was to be no marriage for us, no future, just a lifetime of drudgery with little or no chance at anything better. I bent my head down and continued to add to our artistic work on the ground, and a tear slid down my face and fell. If Kalpa noticed she said nothing, and I continued to cry silently, railing inwardly against this cruel hand that fate had dealt me. Unaccountably, I was furious with Madam Judith in that moment, who had everything I could have ever hoped for, and yet was sad and disappointed with her lot in life. Even in later years I always wondered how the people I sometimes encountered, those with cars, jewellery, families and houses, managed to be so unhappy in the face of the many riches they had been so freely given. Maybe if one day, just for one day, they could live my life and see the world I inhabited, they would realize how lucky they were to have been so blessed by the Goddess I was yet to see.

I remember that night well. I had stopped crying and got into my coarse night clothes, and lay awake the better part of the night, staring up into the darkness wondering what the future would bring for me. The thought of being trapped in the ashram forever was unbearable. I still had clear memories of being part of a family, and somehow I knew now that I had to find my family again. And that's the first time I decided to run away. I had no idea how I was going to do it, and I had no idea where to even begin planning this miraculous escape, but as the dawn broke into our dingy dormitory, I fell asleep feeling comforted by the thought that I had decided to leave the ashram. There would be a time in the not-so-distant future that I would look back on this sleepless night and wonder at how little I knew and how easy my life at the ashram actually was, and I would pray every single day that somehow this bleak and meaningless life would be given back to me. But before all of that something terrible happened at the ashram and I remember it vividly.

It started with Kalpa complaining about a pain in her stomach which got progressively worse over a couple of days. She was unable to sleep most nights, and one night she vomited a few times. The morning after, she and I had walked slowly to the great hall to feed the children their morning meal. Madam Shanthi was there, standing and watching the proceedings, looking grim-faced and unbending in one of her starched cotton sarees. I was next to Kalpa as she reached to pick up one of the children, a new little baby that had come to us some months earlier, a tiny little girl with one side of her face twisted outwards, and a right arm that hung off her, limp and wrinkled like a piece of fruit that had never had the chance to grow. As she bent down, I heard her whimper and wince.

"Are you okay?" I whispered to her.

"My stomach hurts more than ever," she whispered back, gritting her teeth.

I stared at her. I had never known her to complain and had no idea how to deal with this information she had given me.

"Do you want to tell Madam Shanthi?" I asked worriedly.

"No!" she hissed at me and began feeding the little girl. "I told her yesterday morning, and she got very angry with me, but she gave me some medicine."

I nodded. I knew how scary it was to tell Madam Shanthi anything, and she did not care for it when we complained about physical ailments. Most of us had nursed our colds and fevers with cool cloths and hot tea whenever we could get it, and if it got too bad we would tell Madam Judith, who inevitably comforted us, and offered pills and sweets to soothe us. I continued down the line to another child that needed taking care of, and kept glancing at Kalpa the entire time. It was still cool at this time in the morning, but she had beads of sweat dotting her forehead and her face was screwed up in pain. We trooped into our tiny box-like classroom after helping clean and put the children down and took our usual places. Kalpa sat behind me and I could not see her anymore. But every now and then I would hear an intake of sharply drawn breath and I knew it was her, and I grew more and more worried. It was not Madam Judith's day to teach us unfortunately, and I wished it was. I was sure she would have noticed my friend's discomfort and done something about it. The morning seemed to last forever, and we trooped out single file to go to the dining room. I was at the front and walked as sedately as I could with one of the rich ladies, by my side. We entered the big hall, and I went straight up to get food for the children. Halfway down I turned around to look for Kalpa but there was no sign of her in the dining room as I cast my eye across the room. And I knew then something was terribly wrong. I stared around, and then a few seconds later I ran towards the door, the blood pounding in my head. I could hear Madam Shanthi calling to me somewhere in the background of my mind, but all I cared about was finding Kalpa. I got the door and stopped in my tracks and screamed. There lying on the floor, senseless, was Kalpa, her skirt spread out around her like a shroud.

My scream brought Madam Shanthi to the door, and then the rich ladies and ayahs followed suit, and then the girls. Madam Shanthi was the first to get to her, and kneeling down, picked her up and cradled her in her arms.

"Water!" she barked to one of the ayahs.

One of the rich ladies pushed passed her and checked Kalpa's wrist and felt her forehead and told Revathi who had magically appeared from Madam Nalini's old office, to call the doctor. Madam Shanthi looked up and saw the rest of us huddled around the room and she shouted at us to go back into the room and finish feeding the children. I walked back slowly, and the image of Kalpa lying on the floor stayed with me. I was horribly worried for her and as if the children sensed our solemn and sombre mood, they decided to be even more difficult and aggressive than usual. They screamed louder, and drooled more, and kicked and bit harder than normal, or so it seemed to me. I could not wait to get to the dormitory and see if Kalpa was okay and resting. It took forever to clean the hall and put away everything and put the children down for their afternoon nap. As soon as I was done, I rushed back and pushed open the heavy metal door and found that the room was empty. I then ran to the little dark bathroom, and pushed open the door, but that was empty too. I looked around me wildly wondering where she could be and then ran out back into the hall, and into the dusty courtyard at the back where we sat in the evenings making our patterns in the sand. The rest of the girls were all out there and looked at me sadly. Revathi was there too, sitting at the spot Kalpa and I normally sat and I noticed she was scratching away with a stick at the sand patterns we had made the previous days. She was rubbing it out systematically and said nothing as I came to stand in front of her; she did not even look up.

"They've taken her to a hospital. The doctor came and said she was seriously ill and would need an operation," she said in a monotone.

The usual biting edge to her voice was missing, and I realised that she was worried too, but I did not care.

"When will she be back," I asked shakily.

Revathi shook her head and looked up and away at the compound wall. I followed her gaze and saw a flock of sparrows sitting on a branch of a tree that lay beyond the compound wall.

"If you are her friend you should hope she never comes back to this place," she said morosely.

That night we were all silent, and none of us ate much. We went to bed, and I do not know about the others, but I stayed awake praying to the goddess of my childhood, beseeching her to help my friend. I slept badly, and kept waking up and rolling over to see Kalpa's empty bed, and the sight of it made me want to cry as I missed her so much. Worry about her was eating a hole into my heart and mind. But I bit my lip and stayed strong, hoping the next day would bring her back to me.

We woke up, and all of us were still very quiet, and did not talk to each other much; even Leela and Latha who constantly whispered to each other stayed silent on this awful morning as we wondered how our friend was. We shuffled together to the dining hall after our morning ablutions, breakfast and classes, made our way back to the dining hall for lunch. As we began feeding the children, Madam Shanthi came into the dining hall, followed by Revathi who was visibly red-eyed and looking disheveled for the first time ever. Madam Shanthi clapped her hands and as the room felt silent, except for the moans and grumbles and occasional cries of the children, she spoke to us, her words dropping like knives into all our hearts.

"Kalpa died last night in the hospital. She had a ruptured appendix and she did not survive."

I stared at her as she said this, a red mist forming in front of my eyes. In a flash of a blinding clarity the thought came to my mind and it came hurtling out of mouth like a gale force monsoon wind.

"She told you three days ago she was not well. Why did you not take her to the doctor then?" I screamed, my voice falling around the room like a blanket of blame.

The rich ladies looked up, shocked, and the girls and ayahs froze into a tableau of fear and dismay.

Madam Shanthi stared at me, and then without saying a word, walked up to me, and slapped me hard across my face. I fell backwards on the floor, but the rage had taken over me, well and truly. I knew beyond a shadow of doubt that my only friend had died thanks to this cruel woman's heartless response to her ill health. My fear for Madam Shanthi had died along with Kalpa and I did not care anymore; in fact, I hoped she would kill me then and there and spare me facing another day without the quiet, gentle girl who had made my life bearable these past few years. I glared at her from the floor and hissed at her with all the loathing and anger I was feeling.

"You know you are responsible, and I will never forgive you,"

Her response was to reach down and slap me again. She then caught hold of my arm and tried to drag me up, scratching my arms in the process. She was about to hit me again, and as I cowered away from the blow, one of the rich ladies who was closer to us than the others, reached out and grabbed Madam Shanthi's hand.

"That's enough," she said crisply.

And that short, clearly worded order seemed to bring us all back to our senses; Madam Shanthi looked at me and then put down her raised arm and turned on her heel walking away and out the door. Revathi followed her and suddenly the room sprang back into life. The sounds began to register around me, and I could not believe how normal it all sounded. No one came near me, and I got to my feet and walked out the door to the bathroom cubicles to wash the scratches that Madam Shanthi had inflicted on me. I was reminded painfully of my first day at the ashram and having to wash off Thanga's scratches. Only this time there was no Kalpa to nurture and comfort me.

I went back to the dormitory and lay on Kalpa's cot. The smell of her clung to it and I turned over and buried my head in her knobby pillow, willing the world to turn back time and bring my gentle friend back to me. The hurt went too deep for tears and the pain was so intense that no words could ever describe it. I would have exchanged all the weddings, and all the sweets, and even my one beautiful pavadai that had been given me by Madam Nalini to bring back sweet Kalpa. Why is it that only when we lose someone we realise how valuable they were to us. In my head I went over the years we had had together. I remembered our dreams of living in a shack by the sea, her delight on that one trip back to the ocean, the sound of her voice, her kind eyes that were far older than she, the tunes she hummed as she fed the children every day, her unruly hair that escaped the confines of the firmest plaits… all these I remembered and went over in the tiniest detail. If I could not keep her alive in the real world, I would keep her alive in my mind and heart, where no one could take her away from me.

I rarely went out into the compound again. The memories of Kalpa were too strong and it hurt to be in the place where we played. So every evening, after the day she died, I went to help Ramu in the kitchen instead, and scrubbed, cleaned, chopped, cut and stirred as if my life depended on it. He was happy for the extra help, and I think he even felt a little sorry for me, for everyone knew of the friendship Kalpa and I had shared. He never hit me again, and even though his tone to me always stayed gruff, every now and then I would get a grunt of approval, which for some reason always calmed my angry and battered soul.

On Madam Judith's first teaching day the week following Kalpa's death, she asked us to stand up and observe a moment's silence for our friend. We stood up, all of us closing our eyes, and prayed that Kalpa would find a better world to greet her in her next life. Then when we sat down Madam Judith asked us if there were anything we remembered about Kalpa and if we would like to share the stories. Leela spoke first.

"When we first came to the ashram, Kalpa shared her soap with us."

Latha chimed in with, "Also her powder."

Sindhu smiled and said, "Kalpa helped me wash my clothes as I was very small and did not know how to."

Madam Judith looked at me, but I shook my head and refused to answer. She nodded sympathetically and then continued her lesson. I do not remember what it was about, for I paid little attention to anything that happened around me these days. After class she asked me to stay back, and after the other three had left, she came to my little bench and sat down next to me. She put her arm around me and pulled me close to her and I rested against her … it was the first time another human had held me and it felt strange, but I did not want to offend Madam Judith who was trying to be kind, by pulling away. She then spoke to me in quiet tones and in a way that almost felt as if it were Kalpa speaking to me through her.

"Everything keeps changing. Accepting that change is the only way to get through life, Madhuri."

I said nothing and she continued.

"Kalpa's greatest gift was her ability to accept her circumstances. You were her best friend and you must honour her by following her example."

That made a lot of sense, and I suddenly felt lighter than I had since I had lost my friend.

"Madam Shanthi knew she was sick and did nothing," I said bitterly, that knowledge still biting at me every chance it got.

"Yes, I know," she answered, "but there is nothing you can do about that now. And Madam Shanthi is still very angry about what you said to her in front of everyone."

I nodded mutely. I knew I was in trouble and it was just a matter of time before Madam Shanthi extracted her revenge.

"I think you should go and say sorry to her, before she does something really bad to you," suggested Madam Judith.

I nodded slowly and then moving away from her so I could turn sideways and look at her, I asked, "Why should I say sorry when she is the one who killed my friend?"

Madam Judith shook her head wearily and said, "There are worse things than the ashram. Did Kalpa ever tell you what happened to her older sisters?

I shook my head.

"Sometimes girls who have no place to go end up begging on the streets, or worse, get sold into places where you have to do terrible things." she said tautly. "Now stop asking questions, and go and apologise. You have levelled an accusation against Madam Shanthi and some of the ladies are starting to ask questions; she will do everything in her power to make sure her position is left unharmed. Go today, after tea, and tell her you are sorry.

With that she gave me a little push and sent me on the thankless task of feeding the children. That evening I padded softly to Madam Shanthi's office, fear filling my heart and turning my stomach to water. I knocked on the door and Madam Shanthi's harsh tones called out to me to enter. I pushed open the door and went into her office. She seemed genuinely surprised to see me and also most annoyed.

"What is it?" she asked unsmilingly, her heavy features settling into an uncompromising mask of dislike.

"I came to say sorry for what I said in the dining hall the other day," I said nervously.

She stared at me, holding me with a long, hard, angry, gaze, and finally asked me, "What did Kalpa tell you?"

"She said she had come to you saying she was in pain and you gave her medicine and sent her away," I replied, anger beginning to form a knot inside me again as I said this.

Madam Shanthi looked at me, her eyes narrowing into thin slits, and she said threateningly, "If you ever repeat that to anyone else, even to the girls, you'll be really sorry. If anyone, ANYONE, asks you again about this, you will say you were lying that day because you were upset and did not know what you were saying. Do you understand?"

I nodded silently and looked at her carefully. And in that moment I knew she was afraid. The big, powerful, angry and mean Madam Shanthi was afraid. Of me. Of the knowledge I had. She had allowed a girl to die and only she and I knew this. And I knew then she would find a way to get me out of the ashram. My days here were numbered as I was now a threat to her position and power. And perhaps it was Kalpa's gentle nature that came to my rescue at the moment, for in that brief look we exchanged, I felt sorry for her. I understood her in a moment of blinding clarity. Here she was an unmarried, childless woman and all she had was this ashram and her position in it, and her need to cling to this security was her only defence against the world. There I was, a young teenage girl, abandoned and unloved, and yet I felt sorry for her.

She must have seen the pity in my eyes, for she turned on me with all the rage of a spitting cobra, and said, "Remember, you'll be sorry."

And then she swept out of the office.

I knew there was more to come, but I did not care anymore. I tried to be a Kalpa to the other girls. I started going back to the compound in the evenings, helped the girls make their beds and braid their hair, and I realised it felt good to do good. Of all the lessons that Kalpa taught me, I learned the greatest one from her while imitating her after her unfortunate and sudden death. And so the weeks and months passed on, and we all slowly grew used to not having Kalpa's benign presence in our midst. None of us spoke of her often, but I know we all thought of her all the time, me more than all the others. I continued to sleep in her bed and I took her box of things and put the contents in at the bottom of mine. No one ever asked for them and I was glad as knowing her possessions were under my bed with all my earthly belongings somehow made me feel closer to her, despite the vastness of life and death that separated us now. In my mind she was a goddess, living in a heavenly realm, not to be seen, but a presence that would remain forever in my heart and mind. I hoped that this realm had many sweets.

I was now the oldest in the dormitory. The other girls were younger than me, though they had been at the ashram longer. And as the sweltering summer faded into the thundering rains of the monsoon my life changed again. Dramatically. It happened one humid, rainy evening. There was a heavy dampness in the air, a humidity that caused our thick pavadais to stick to our skin like they had been glued there. All our faces wore a sheen of moisture from all the water that seemed to hang in a hot film around us and the air was so thick it seemed hard to breathe. We were waiting for the heavy, swollen clouds to release the rain in a deluge, wetting everything, and soak through the walls and leaky roof, and turn the compound outside into a soggy, gurgling mass of mud. We were sitting in the dormitory, and just as the storm broke sending fat raindrops clattering around the building, Revathi appeared at the door and gestured to me.

"Madam Shanthi wants you in her office now," she said snappily, and then was gone as quickly as she had come.

I scurried to the office and the door was wide open, and Madam Shanthi was at the desk with someone else standing before her. She saw me and beckoned me in, and as I walked in, the other lady turned around and smiled - a small, imitation of a smile. She was old and bent, and had a faded cotton saree covering her head, from which wisps of grey hair escaped and settled around her cheeks. She looked familiar and I wondered who it was.

"Well Madhuri, today is your lucky day," said Madam Shanthi bitingly. "You get to leave us today."

And that's when I recognised the lady. It had been so many years and time had not been kind. This was the woman who had left me here all those years ago, and who had now come to take me back. Someone I had given up hope of ever seeing again. But yet here she was... And as much as I had secretly wanted it for so long, actually seeing my mother face to face again after all this time was a shock. I stared at her not knowing what to say.

"Go get your things; you're leaving immediately," said Madam Shanthi victoriously, and looking up at her, I knew she had been planning this for a while. In that moment I knew I did not want to leave. I knew the system, the routine, the people, in this place. My mother was an unknown stranger and I did not wish to go with her. But I also knew I had no choice, and I walked back to the dormitory, got my box and announced to the girls what had happened. Amidst cries of dismay and surprise, I spun around and went back – it was too soon for more goodbyes, so I hardened my heart and left them without a word. My mother and Madam Shanthi were waiting in the front hall, and as I went and stood by my mother, I looked at the woman who had struck me the day my friend died.

"No one else will ever know, but I will always know," I said bleakly.

Madam Shanthi's face darkened in rage, but my mother pushed me out onto the steps, folded her hands in a namaste to this woman, and then shepherded me down the steps, past the little temple, down the drive lined with swaying, pointed Ashoka trees and out the rusty gate, into another new chapter in my life.

Chapter Eight
THE NEXT LIFE

I will never forget that night I left the ashram. I turned to look back at the drive as the gate clanged shut behind me. The gatekeeper nodded at me, a sullen half-farewell of a nod that I did not have the presence of mind to respond to. I stared at him blankly, and I remember wondering where he was from and how long he sat by the gate each day. He was the first person I had seen when I came to the Ashram, and he was the last person I saw as I left. I wondered if I would see him again, and how old he was, and how long he had been at the ashram. I was barely aware of my mother hailing down an auto and as one stopped for her, she briefly haggled over the fare and got in. It was a sticky evening, and as I climbed in after her, I forgot about the gatekeeper and turned my attention to her. I looked at her and as the passing traffic threw in beams of light into the back of the auto, I saw that she had aged terribly. She did not look at me, and all I could see was her profile, which was still strangely familiar. I had so longed to see her all these years, and now suddenly here she was and I realised I felt nothing at all for her in this moment. I felt a sense of complete detachment at this unexpected turn of events, and I had no idea who this woman was, even though a part of me recognised her as my mother. Mostly I felt a conflicting mix of curiosity and animosity as the auto wriggled in and out of the streaming, unending flow of traffic through this enormous city. I had no idea of where we were going, and I wondered if I would be left alone in another place like the ashram. As I opened my mouth to speak, my mother spoke to me, almost as if she knew what I was going to ask.

"You will stay at your Ramesh Mama's house for a few days," she said decisively, looking straight ahead of her.

I nodded. I had no idea who Ramesh Mama was, but it sounded like a relative. I had no idea that I had relatives and wondered why I had never heard of them before when I had lived in Thousand Lights.

I looked mindlessly at the traffic outside and remembered the hum of the traffic from inside the ashram and wondered if I would ever have to go back again. Inside me, a strange new exhilaration was now starting to build up as I realised that my days at the ashram were, perhaps, finally over. No more kitchen duties, being spat on, kicked or bitten, or beaten. No more hostile Revathi, and no more places that held such powerful and painful memories of my beloved Kalpa. Even now, thinking of her made the back of my eyelids burn with the weight of unshed tears for that dear gentle soul who had guided me through these last few years of my life. I shook my head and returned my attention to the woman by my side. The auto jerked to an abrupt halt as a motorcyclist crossed over suddenly in front of us, and my mother was thrown against me. The weight of her against my side was surprisingly familiar, and it reminded me powerfully of the little house we had once shared, high up, in that dingy building at Thousand Lights.

After what seemed like an age in the auto, we stopped on a narrow road lined on both sides with houses that were so close together some shared a wall, and others seemed to crouch down on each other, as if they were preparing to leap down and swallow the next one up. It was dark, and a single street light at the end of the road bathed the entire place in a sickly, grey glow. We got out in front of what looked like a compound with a narrow door in the wall, and my mother pushed open this door and led me into a long corridor. I stared around me curiously. An open drain ran down one length of the corridor, and doors opened off the other side. My mother walked to one of these doors which was wide open, and had a curtain strung up in a lop-sided fashion, and I followed her.

We walked into a room that was painted a bright green and had four plastic chairs, a table in a corner and a row of shelves in which pride of place was given to a picture of a man who seemed to be tied to two planks of wood, and I wondered who this was. But it was the people in the room who really caught my attention. A very fat man sat on one of the chairs looking up at me, smiling, and an even fatter woman sat on another glaring at me and my mother. There was a young girl about my age who emerged from the room beyond this one, and she came to stand by the woman and looked at me suspiciously. But the person who really caught my attention was a young girl sitting on the floor at the corner of the room, playing with a cloth doll. She looked up as I came in and then went back to playing with her doll, but I knew who this was, and I flew across to her and tried to pick Radhi up and cuddle her. She had become even more beautiful in the intervening years, but she did not remember me at all it seemed, and struggled to get away, and wriggling out of my arms she went back to her doll and did not even look up at me. I turned back slowly and realised my mother was no longer in the room.

The man answered the question in my eyes, "Your amma has gone to make tea for all of us."

As he said it I heard a clattering from the room beyond and realised that was my mother in the back of the house. I tried to smile tentatively at the man and woman, but the woman continued to glare at me, while my uncle wobbled his head at me uncertainly. The girl stared at me unsmilingly, and I felt trapped and unsure, diffident of what to say to these people. I stared at them curiously, and then not knowing what to do I turned my attention back to the girl on the floor. Seeing Radhi after so many years brought back all the pent-up love I had for her, and yet it seemed she did not even know who I was and the knowledge hurt. As I was thinking this my mother came back into the room, with little glasses of tea on a plate. She went over to the man first and served him humbly. He took the glass of tea with an air of condescension, and my mother moved on to serve the fat lady, who I realised was his wife, even though I did not know her name. The young girl was served next, and then my mother brought me a cup of tea, took one herself, and we all drank it in silence, the sound of slurping filling the uncomfortable stillness in the room.

"She's much older than you said she was," said the fat lady suddenly, stabbing a fat forefinger in my direction.

"I have not seen her in so many years, akka," said my mother almost in a whisper, and looked down at the floor apologetically.

"We'll have to find her somewhere fast," said the lady gulping down the rest of her tea, and then took off into what I assumed was the bedroom, and I did not see her again until the evening meal later that night. Uncle Ramesh went to a big black box on the table and pushed a button on it, and wonder of wonders, I realized they had a television. I had not seen one in years, but our old neighbours in Thousand Lights had one, and of course, I had seen one in Madam Judith's house. I had watched television at the old neighbour's house one sultry evening, but as soon as we had started watching the first song that rang out, the skies opened up a deluge and with it the power went off almost immediately, plunging us into a sticky blackness, and we were all left sighing and complaining. To now be in a house with a television was quite exciting and I hoped I would be able to watch something on it at some point. Luckily for me it seemed that Uncle Ramesh had the same idea for he turned on a switch which brought the television to sudden life. He waddled back to the chair and sat down heavily and began to watch a man talking on the screen, and the girl sat down by his feet to watch with him. My mother picked up the plate with empty tea glasses, and tugging at my arm she pulled me back through a side door and led me into a kitchen. It was a dark poorly ventilated room that had a row of shelves on one side, and a table with a stove and condiments on another. Reaching into a plastic bag under the table she pulled out some onions and started cutting them. I looked at her for a minute, then gently took the knife from her and began cutting them myself. She stared at me, surprised for a few seconds, and then got on with the rest of the meal. Together we made a meal of lentils, cabbage, potatoes and rice, and then we carried out plates to the outer room. The fat woman was back, and she served her husband and daughter and proceeded to watch television and ignore us the rest of the evening. My mother served Radhi and me, and then we sat on the floor together, separate to Uncle Ramesh and his family and ate our meal quietly. After we had finished, we cleared the dishes and washed the vessels in the little sink at the back of the kitchen. We came back out to find the room silent. Uncle Ramesh and his family had gone into the other room to bed, it appeared, for I heard the sounds of rumbling snores emerging from that room. My mother went to the corner of the room and unrolling a pile of mats, she beckoned me and Radhi to sleep. Radhi quietly went to a mat and curled up and went to sleep with her arm tucked under her. I pulled a mat close to where my mother was and lay down on it. I could feel the hard stone floor underneath, and realised how used I had become to sleeping on a cot with a mattress under me. The ashram seemed so far away now, and as I thought about it, the memory of Kalpa came flooding back, and I forcibly pushed the painful thought away, trying to concentrate on my present situation instead. I shifted position trying to get comfortable, and eventually managed to settle myself, facing my mother.

"Amma!" I said softly, "Are we going to be staying here from now onwards," I asked.

"No!" she whispered back, "Only until we can find you a job."

"A job!" I asked, raising my voice in surprise.

"Shhhhh!" she said, "Don't wake them up."

"Who are they?" I asked curiously.

"Uncle Ramesh is your father's cousin. His wife is Kalyani and their daughter is Selvi. Radhi has been staying with them since your father died. They said they would send her to school but they have not, but at least she gets food and a roof over her head.

"Where are Mani and Senthil?" I had so many questions now.

"Mani and Senthil are big men now," she said, and I could hear the pride in her voice. They now work in a car garage and Mani is learning to drive and will soon look for a job as a driver." I took in this information and put it away at the back of my head. I knew it was a fine thing for my brother to be a driver and I hoped things would work out well for him.

"What about Senthil?"

"Senthil only wants to be a mechanic. He's very good and now earns good money," she answered.

"So can we not go and stay with them, instead of these people?" I wanted to know.

"No, they stay in a small room with one more boy, and there is no place for us."

"What about you and me?" I enquired softly.

"I work for a private hospital as an ayah. The pay is not good, but they give me a room and food as well, so it is better than nothing. Uncle Ramesh found this job for me, and he will try to find you a job as soon as possible as well, perhaps working in a house somewhere. I have to go back to work in one week, so hopefully before that. Now go to sleep. I am very tired and cannot talk anymore."

With that she rolled over facing away from me and soon her heavy breathing told me she was fast asleep. I stayed awake a while, remembering the ashram, the dorm, and suddenly remembered Raghu and wondered who would feed him every day now in my stead. I hoped it would be Sindhu. And with that thought I fell asleep.

The following morning, I woke early to find my mother and Radhi were already up and at work. My mother was swabbing the small room and Radhi was wiping a cloth over the chairs, and I went up to her to help her, but she turned away from me, and moved to the next chair and continued her task. I shrugged and asked my mother where the bathroom was. She pointed me out the door and to the right, and I got up, taking my toothbrush, toothpowder, soap and towel that I had carried from the Ashram, and headed out the front door. The bathroom was at the end of the long alley which was protected from the outside world by a long whitewashed wall. There were already a small group of people lining up to use this communal toilet and washroom, and I took my place in the line. The toilet was a dank, smelly affair, and the washroom was wet, mouldy and slippery. I finished as quickly as I could and returned back. It was still early in the morning, and the sun was barely up in the sky. Outside the wall, I could hear sounds of people talking, traffic, dogs barking and vendors calling out wares and it made me curious. I went through the outer door in the wall and peeked through it.

The narrow road I had seen last night was buzzing with activity. A tea-seller and vegetable seller were pushing carts and screaming out their excellent prices. A few dogs were sniffing around the street looking for food and barking at the scooters and cyclists going past. Some of the houses lining the street had tiny courtyards out front, and I could see women hanging out washing to dry, and sending their children and husbands off to schools and offices. It all seemed so normal, this bustle of early morning life, and I looked at the dirty, dusty street with its swell of life and revelled in the normalcy of what I was seeing. I saw a group of children in neat navy and white uniforms, carrying enormous school bags on their little backs, pile into an auto that then sped away, winding giddily across the potholes and scooters and cyclists that were going about their daily life. I looked at the small, gaily coloured temple at the end of the road that was ringing out its morning prayers, and smiling I turned back to go indoors, back into my life to see what this day would bring me, just so glad that I would not be going back to the Anni Ashram.

I went back into the dark house to find Uncle Ramesh and his wife were already up. There was no sign of their daughter and I assumed she was still sleeping. My mother came out from the kitchen with a rolled-up cloth towel, and she went out the door, to finish her morning ablutions, I guessed. Radhi was curled up in a ball, on the floor, sound asleep again, snoring gently. The woman came up to her, and bending over prodded her in the legs sharply. Radhi woke up instantly, and sat up, looking around wide awake and I saw the fear in her eyes when she looked at this woman and I bristled inside at the unfairness of it; but I had learned a long time ago not to answer back or speak out against those more powerful than me.

"Get up and get dressed, you lazy child," she said curtly, and turning on her heel, spun away and went back into the kitchen. She came out seconds later, bristling, and glared at me.

"That mother of yours has not made the morning tea. This is what we get for helping your lot," she said, and stormed away into her bedroom.

I went into the kitchen and looked around to find some tea leaves, milk and sugar. Taking water from a large plastic pot, I lit the stove and started boiling water for tea. My mother came back just as I was pouring out the tea into the glasses, and she nodded her approval at me. But instead of making me happy, the little nod angered me, but I did not acknowledge it, and pushing past her rudely I went out into the front room with the tea. Uncle Ramesh was not there anymore, but his wife was, and she seemed slightly mollified by the sight of me bearing tea. The young girl emerged from the bedroom, and I almost dropped the plate of tea glasses I was holding. She was beautifully attired in a white and green salwar, with her hair neatly plaited with matching ribbons, and wonder of wonders, she was wearing a watch on her hand. She had a school bag on her back and I realised at that instant she was setting off to school. Not an Anni Ashram kind of school, but a proper one with teachers and regular lessons and proper textbooks. Her mother was patting down her uniform, her pride and love evident, and at that moment I felt a wave of envy wash over me, so strong, so powerful that it made everything go hazy for a second. I was so envious of her. This girl, with her loving mother, her school bag, and a house with three rooms, had everything I had ever desired in life and try as I did, I could not understand why I did not have these things. I did not understand why my father or Kalpa had died, or why I had had to spend so many years locked up in the Anni Ashram, or why children were born twisted or malformed. These questions raced through my head, as I looked at my cousin heading off to school, living the life that had been taken away from me so suddenly all those years ago. The girl turned around, looked at me, and without a smile went and sat in one of the chairs. I looked up to find Uncle Ramesh's wife staring at me, almost looking pleased. I wondered if she had read my thoughts and gathering myself, I went inside the kitchen. My mother was in there, sweat beading her forehead. It was dark and unbearably hot in the small kitchen, and she was stirring some sambhar in a pot on the stove. A stack of fluffy white idlis sat stacked up in a bowl. Once again, I helped her serve it all into bowls and plates and take them out. Uncle Ramesh was back looking fresh and neatly dressed. The three of them ate with gusto, and then Uncle Ramesh took his daughter and went out the door with her. My mother, Radhi and I ate after my aunt had gone back into the bedroom. We washed up the vessels, and then my mother began sweeping the room. I stared at her not knowing what to do next, and my mother told me to take Radhi and get her dressed. I walked with her to the bathrooms and waited until she had freshened up, and then taking her hand I walked back with her to the house. My aunt was back in the front room, and as soon as we entered, she left with a towel tucked under her arm, her printed nightie trailing behind her like some sort of reluctant animal.

I looked at my mother questioningly, but she said nothing, continuing to sweep the stone floor, hunched over the broom which was making gentle swishing noises. I was still angry with her and I did not know why, but I pushed past her and Radhi, who had sat down quietly in a corner to play with her cloth doll, and I went out to the outer wall and stood in the doorway staring at the narrow road in front of me. I don't know how long I stood there and people came and left through the door next to me, but it barely registered on me. A million thoughts were flying through my mind as I tried to deal with this rush of anger inside me that was coupled with a growing anxiety about my future. My mother was telling me nothing, and I was petrified I might have to return to the bleakness of the ashram if nothing else could be arranged. The sun was already fierce in the sky, and I realised I had rarely seen the sun at this time of day. At the ashram we were mostly indoors, except in the evening when the sun set, and I realized I did not like this fiery ball that was burning through the dark blue pavadai I was wearing. And with that I suddenly knew what my next quest was.

I marched back indoors to the little house, my lips pursed up in a determined pucker. My mother was sitting on the mat while my large aunt sat on the chair, my mother pressing her feet. The sight surprised me and I wondered briefly why my mother was serving this woman in this fashion, but the thought passed as quickly as it had come. The TV was blaring some music, and despite that attraction, I now had another more pressing mission. Radhi was still focussed on her doll and it dawned on me she had not spoken a word since I had seen her and I wondered about it, but then returned my attention to the task at hand. Ignoring all of them, I went to my cardboard box, the one I had taken with me from the ashram, and fished into it. I rummaged around, pulled out the pavadai I had received for Madam Nalini's wedding, and marched out of the house.

"Where are you going," asked my aunt shrilly, sounding most annoyed that I had dared to move without her permission.

I did not answer, rejoicing in the spirit of rebellion that was now bubbling around inside my head, making me feel powerful and independent for the first time in my life.

I grabbed the bottle of powder and almost ran to the dark bathroom that I had used earlier; I went in and swiftly removing my ashram uniform, I changed into the beautiful shimmering pavadai I had only worn once before. Even in the dark bathroom the jewel-like colours of the cloth shone, and I put them on liberally sprinkling powder down myself to make sure I did not sweat into my beautiful clothing. I went back out and right outside the bathroom was a little washbasin with a mirror and I stopped to turn and look at myself. I stared at myself curiously and saw a young girl staring back at me. She had long black hair, tied up in two plaits, and her dark eyes were wide and bright. I unplaited my hair and let it fall around my back and shoulders and was very pleased with the effect, so I continued to admire myself for a few more minutes until a noise made me look up. I looked up to find, a short distance away, a young man leaning nonchalantly against one of the doors that lined that row of houses in this compound. He was smoking a cigarette and staring at me, and continued to do so, even when I glanced at him. It made me feel inexplicably pleased and threatened at the same time. I decided to trot back to my uncle's house, and gathering my things, which had fallen about my feet, I scurried down the alley with this boy's eyes still on me. I had to walk past him to get back, and as I approached him I got increasingly nervous. My heart was thudding so loudly, that I was certain he would hear it, and as I went past, I lowered my head and moved as quickly as I could without actually running. I could feel his eyes on my back as I walked away, and while it was just a short stretch, it felt like forever before I reached the door going in and sighing in relief as I made it beyond his prying eyes. As I entered my mother and aunt looked up and the shock on their faces was most satisfying. My mother stared at me, without saying a word, her eyes almost admiring, and it made me feel glad to know she was looking at me this way. But my aunt's eyes went cold with shock as she took in my attire and loosened hair, and after a few moments she narrowed her eyes and delivered a cutting remark.

"What sort of place did you keep her in? I will not keep women of loose character in my house," she said sharply, and getting up, she grabbed a small cloth bag and flounced out of the house.

I stared after her, and then turned around to look at my mother.

"Go tie your hair up," she said in as sharp a tone as my aunt had used. "Girls of good character don't wander about with their hair loose," and with that she returned to her sweeping. Feeling strangely deflated, I sat down on the floor next to Radhi and plaited up my hair into two tight plaits, and then stayed there watching Radhi, who after a few minutes actually looked up at me, smiled and handed me her doll. I forgot all my anger and confusion at this gesture from my beloved sister, and spent the rest of the morning entertaining her and watching her play with her doll, which I discovered had been named after me. My joy at this discovery was untold; my little sister had not forgotten me after all, and the knowledge was a balm to my wounded spirit which had suffered those years of unexpressed anguish of separation from family in a way that only a young child can.

It was incredibly hot in the stuffy room, and I went out to get some fresh air, but it was burningly hot outside so I came back in. My mother had finished her chores and had gone into the kitchen. I left Radhi playing with her doll, and went into the even hotter kitchen, to help my mother. I cut some carrots, and onions which she turned into a simple curry, and we ate it with the remains of the rice from the previous evening. I washed the vessels in the tiny stone sink, while my mother lay down and closed her eyes. I came out to find her sleeping again, as was Radhi, so I went and sat by the door hoping for a cooling breeze to wash over me, but it was as sultry outside as it was inside, and I found little relief. I glanced down the alley, but the boy from the morning was not there, and I felt slightly disappointed, but shrugged it off, and sat there in the doorway in all my finery, staring into space, not knowing how to fill my time. At the ashram every minute was regimented and there was always the company of the other girls, but now I was being left to my own devices and I found it most confusing. Memories of the ashram swam about in my head, and I found myself remembering Kalpa. I recalled that first day, when she had spoken to me in soothing tones, and the times we had sat out in the dusty courtyard and made plans for when we would grow up and live together, and a terrible sadness washed over me at this remembrance of all that would never be. So I sat staring into space, lost in the memories of my one true friend, with my head resting against the wooden door frame, and my beautiful blue pavadai spread out around me like a brilliant shroud. The heat was soporific and I slowly nodded off into a state of half sleep, dimly aware that people were coming and going past me in the narrow alley. It felt like minutes, but it must have been a good few hours that had passed, because I was shaken awake by my mother, and as I shook my head to clear the somnolence, I realized the sun had fallen, I could hear the cacophony of crows somewhere beyond the compound wall and the temple bell was ringing out loudly to announce evening had arrived and it was time to pay respect to whichever god or goddess was presiding over that neighbourhood.

I got up and went inside. Radhi was sitting on a mat, still obsessed with her doll. I patted her head and went into the kitchen and taking a steel glass, I filled it with water and drank thirstily. There was a delicious smell floating about the house. A pot was simmering on the stove, and I lifted the lid gingerly to see what was inside. Fluffy golden rice with vegetables were bubbling, and I was delighted for even after all these years I remembered my mother's pulao well. I stuck a finger in for a taste and almost shivered in pleasure as the heady mix of spices and flavours hit my tongue. I turned around quickly and went back out. My mother was nowhere to be seen, and once again I looked around uncertainly. Had I been abandoned again? But even as I thought it, she re-entered, and following her was my large, hostile aunt.

She came in and sat heavily on a chair and glared at me and my mother, who went back into the kitchen silently and returned with a glass of tea some minutes later and served her.

My aunt drank it down in huge, noisy slurps and then handing back the glass settled back into the plastic chair and turned on the TV. My mother and I sat down on the floor and for the next half an hour we watched the antics of two men who were trying to rob a house and getting it badly wrong. My aunt guffawed loudly and slapped her knees whenever one of them fell, and Radhi and I giggled uncontrollably; even my mother smiled a few times, but covered her face with her pallu every time she did, as if she did not want anyone to see her enjoying herself. The show put us all in a good mood, and we sat in companionable gaiety, until the curtains parted and my uncle and his daughter returned.

My uncle smiled at us affably, but his daughter seemed displeased to see such merriment in her home. She looked at all of us disdainfully, and then her glance settled on me. I knew she was taking in my finery and was unhappy about it, for without a word she turned on her heel and marched off into the bedroom. My uncle settled into one of the chairs and began watching the television with us, but somehow the earlier feeling of good cheer was no longer present. My mother scurried off to bring my uncle Ramesh some tea, and Radhi and I sat silently watching the antics on the screen that somehow were not so funny anymore. After a few minutes of this, my aunt called out for her daughter.

"Selvi, where are you? Come out here," she said, sounding almost affectionate.

She emerged from the bedroom, a few minutes later, resplendent in a red and pink salwar with a shimmering dupatta thrown over her shoulders. I stared at her, first in surprise, and then in envy. Her clothes made mine look shabby and old, and when she looked at me triumphantly, I knew she had done it deliberately in order to belittle me. Her triumph was short-lived. Her mother's eyes narrowed at this show of splendour, and heaving herself out of her chair with surprising swiftness, she reached out and delivered a sharp, loud slap across her daughter's face. We all stared at her in shocked silence, and her mother snarled at her, shaking her fist in Selvi's face.

"What's the matter with you? Don't you know we keep that only for special occasions? How dare you wear that now? Don't you know how much it cost?"

Each short sentence was delivered with biting venom, and I flinched back from this fierce woman. Radhi shrank into the corner as if she were trying to disappear into the wall, and my mother took off into the kitchen as unobtrusively as she could. My uncle stared at his wife, and then his daughter, and then turning the television up, he continued to watch his programme. While I and Radhi stood terrified, Selvi stared back at her mother insolently, and then stabbed her finger in my direction.

"How is it that she can wear such good clothes? If girls like her can dress up, why can't I?" she asked loudly. "Why don't you slap her as well?"

Her mother looked at me, and taking in my outfit once again turned around to face her daughter.

"That is her mother's problem. Let her deal with it. I won't have you wasting your good clothes for nothing at all," she snapped. "Go change. Now!" she added menacingly.

Selvi glared back at her mother for a few minutes and then sauntered back into the bedroom.

Her mother looked at me icily.

"I don't know who you think you are, but in this house there is no need to show off to us. We are feeding you and looking after your sister, and now, you. Go change now, and don't try to be better than us. Know your place," she said bitingly as she sat down on the chair once again, fanning herself with her pallu after her exhaustions.

I went to my cardboard box, took out the dark blue pavadai and made my way to the bathroom at the end of the alley. There were a crowd of people waiting to use it, and in the gathering darkness a naked bulb hung off the wall giving off a feeble light. I waited until it was my turn, and went in and changed and carefully folded the blue and green silky folds and emerged feeling more than just a little beaten.

The boy was back at his place by the wall, but I was feeling too defeated to care. A strange listlessness had come over me, and I dragged my feet back to Uncle Ramesh's house, put my things away and sat down quietly next to Radhi.

My mother served dinner and we all ate silently. Selvi took her food into the bedroom as if she could not bear to be in the same room as us, and after dinner I helped my mother clear up and clean the front room and the kitchen. We all sat in silence. The television had been switched off, and my uncle read a newspaper, while my aunt went out to chat with one of the neighbours. We could hear her just outside the front door, and after she came back, she went straight to bed. My uncle followed soon after, and as soon as he had gone into the bedroom and closed the door, my mother unrolled the mats and we all settled down to sleep. There was a sliver of light coming in from under the front door, and the sounds of activity outside continued. I heard babies crying, motorcycles zooming to and fro on the road, the neighbours talking outside, and it was all strange and familiar at the same time. Through the noise I heard a night bird crying out plaintively; it was a piercing, melancholy sound and it was the last one I heard that night, as my eyes finally closed into a disturbed slumber on my very first day of freedom from the Anni Ashram.

Chapter Nine
THE JOB

The days at Uncle Ramesh's blended into a seamless sequence of boredom, anticipation and fear. I helped my mother clean and sweep and cook, wash the clothes for the whole family, and in the evenings I sat and entertained Radhi as unobtrusively as I could, while the family watched television. Selvi continued to ignore me, and my mother barely said two words to me other than to inform me that Uncle Ramesh was looking for a job for me. I asked her what sort of job I would get, and my answer was a shrug of the shoulders as I was handed the broom to sweep the floor. A week later, one evening, my aunt came heaving into the house, sweating profusely, and it looked as if she had been running. She sat down heavily in her usual place, fanning herself with her saree pallu, and beckoned me to her. My mother was using the communal bathroom and without her presence I was always extra nervous around this fat and formidable woman. I went across and looked down at my feet, as I stood before her.

"Sit down," she barked at me, and I sat at her feet with a thump.

"I had to walk home today; there was no auto coming back from my sister's," she said as if this were my fault somehow.

"Make yourself useful and press my feet," she said, sliding a big and plump foot into my lap.

I stared at this large appendage unknowingly, wondering what to do. My hesitance must have annoyed my aunt, for she prodded my legs with her foot and nodded her head at me irritably. I took her foot in my hand and tentatively squeezed it. It felt like a large and coarse lump of fabric all balled up together. Her toenails were covered in a bright red paint that was chipped, her soles were rough and cracked and her skin felt dry and hard. I kept squeezing, trying to block out the sensation of her foot under my hands, and thought back to my times with Kalpa under the coconut trees in the ashram compound. I must have been doing something right, for after a few minutes my aunt gave a little sigh of pleasure and I looked up to see her close her eyes and start to nod off. My mother came back into the house silently as I was performing this task, and looked at me as I sat at my aunt's feet. She said nothing, but a strange expression passed over her face, almost like pity, which went as quickly as it came, and she silently padded into the kitchen while I stayed pressing my aunt's feet. Selvi bounced back a few minutes later, with her father, filled with chatter about her school and friends. She ignored me completely, and sat around with her school books scattered around her watching the television. Dinner was served as usual, but with one difference. We had a visitor in the middle of it. He was a man wearing a very smart cap, and a fine white shirt and trousers, with shiny black shoes. He was a friend of Uncle Ramesh, and his name was Suresh, and he worked as the driver in a house for a very wealthy family. My uncle informed us after he had left that he had found me a job. The family Suresh worked for were looking for a young girl to help with the housework, and it seemed they were willing to give me a three-month trial for which they would pay my mother. I remember thinking at this point that perhaps some of the money should have come to me, but I dared not say a word for fear of what would happen to me if I voiced such a rebellious thought.

Two days later, both evenings during which I massaged my aunt's feet, Suresh returned, again in the white shirt and trousers, looking even more polished and shiny. He waited while I put my meagre belongings into a plastic bag, and hugged Radhi close to me, kissing her on the top of her head tenderly, praying to the invisible goddess who existed somewhere to look after her. There were tears in my eyes as I said goodbye once again to this scrap of humanity who sat playing with her dress, utterly absorbed in the task of folding the hem of her dress into tiny pleats in a monotonous repetitive action. It was at that moment that it struck me that Radhi's behaviour reminded me of some of the less severe cases of the children I had looked after at the ashram, and I wondered if there was something wrong with her. My aunt and Selvi were not at home, having gone across to a neighbour's for a social visit, and I was grateful that I did not have to say goodbye to them. I thanked my Uncle Ramesh gratefully, and bent down to touch his feet in gratitude, as I had been instructed by my mother. But all thoughts of Radhi and my relatives went as quickly as they came, and I walked through the doorway out into the street where I saw a gleaming white car, long and smooth and shiny, with Suresh standing at attention beside it. I stopped in my tracks to stare at it in amazement. Local urchins had gathered around it and Suresh was busy flicking them away with his cap, making sure they did not get too close. I had only ever seen cars like this on the few occasions when I had travelled by auto, and now here was one waiting for me, to carry me to my new life, and I suddenly felt hopeful. My mother was even more awestruck than I was, and she hovered behind me nervously unsure of what to do next. Neither of us knew how to actually get into the car, and Suresh, after staring at us impatiently, opened the car door at the back and bade us get in. We got in cautiously, taking in the deep red velvety seats, the fragrance that filled the interiors, and the row of little deities who sat on the dashboard, smiling at us benevolently. Both my mother and I sat down gingerly in the back, feeling utterly intimidated and overwhelmed by this luxury and finery we were suddenly in the midst of. The windows were rolled up, and we looked out at the dirty street, and I was suddenly glad to be leaving all this behind. My new life could finally start and I hoped that this beautiful car was a good omen.

Suresh slid into the front behind the wheel and with a low rumble I took off into the unknown future, wishing that Selvi had been able to see me take this journey into a new horizon far beyond her.

I will remember that car journey my entire life, the smoothness of the ride, Suresh honking furiously at everything and everyone out on the road, as they scuttled out of our way, the coolness of the car itself which was such a pleasure after the intense heat outside, and the sights along the way … all of these burned into my memory. We drove through enormous busy roads with traffic so dense we barely seemed to move, and we went past bustling markets and shops with gleaming marble exteriors and colourful signages that proclaimed their wares. I tried to read some of them, but my reading skills were too slow, or the car was too fast, and everything went by in a blur of excitement and a cacophony of traffic. I glanced over at my mother and saw that she was sitting stiffly and was clutching the seat tightly, as if scared she would fall out of the car while she looked out of the window; I hoped she was as elated by this journey as I was. I did not give her too much thought though, as I wanted to savour every minute of this luxurious experience that was so much better than the battered van I had sat in on that memorable day out with Madam Judith. The journey seemed to last a very long time indeed, and eventually we came to an area with wide, tree-lined roads and huge houses that rose from the ground like benign monsters. Huge gates guarded the entrance to these palatial houses, and to my untutored eyes they did look like the palaces Madam Judith had told us of in some of the stories she had related. We eventually slowed down in front of one of these houses, and Suresh steered the car through the huge black and gold gates that were opened by a bent, old man wearing a white shirt and khaki trousers. The car rolled up along the side of the house, past a vast expanse of green garden, stopping under a porch. Suresh got out and came across to open the door for my mother and me and we slid out quickly to find ourselves standing on a marbled floor in front of a row of pots filled with fragrant flowers, and a compound wall, along which grew trailing green plants with little white flowers that gave off the most remarkable fragrance in the heat. But before we could so much as take a quick look at the whole place, Suresh shepherded us along to the back of the house, and through a small courtyard in which hung strand upon strand of washing.

Now you may think me stupid, but the washing fascinated me even more than the car or the trip to this house. Gay coloured sarees, beautiful shirts, embroidered blouses and fine skirts hung there fluttering every now and then as a hot waft of breeze blew across them. I had never seen so much finery in my life, and even I could tell I was looking at the most beautiful fabrics and clothes that money could buy. At least twenty people must live in this house, I thought, judging by the volume of washing that was hung out to dry. I dragged my eyes away from this splendiferous sight, and followed my mother and Suresh into the deep recesses of the biggest kitchen I had ever seen. Gleaming rows of pots and pans were lined up on all the shelves, and ornate cupboards and tables and drawers sat alongside gleaming white tiles and white painted walls, all of this lit by a row of tube lights that made everything sparkle even more. My mother and I stared at everything, unable to quite believe our eyes. A huge stainless steel stove stood on the glistening marble counter, on which a variety of fresh vegetables had been cut and laid out. In front of this riot of colour, a short, plump woman presided over two pots from which emanated the most delicious smells and it made my mouth water. She turned to look at my mother and me, and with a stiff nod, she dismissed us, and turned to smile at Suresh in the most benign manner.

"You've finally come back," she said, implying she had been waiting a long time for him.

Suresh smiled at her, and then filled a glass of water from the tap and drank heavily from it. I watched his Adam's apple bob up and down as he slurped down the drink and I could see that the plump woman was watching him too. He finished and put down his glass and took off through the door, and we started to shuffle after him, unsure of what to do.

"Stay here," barked the plump woman at us, her high-pitched voice, raised in annoyance.

We stopped in our tracks at her order and stood still … I could not get enough of this fascinating kitchen. A door opened off to one side, and through it I could see a small room stacked with shelves of food and condiments and all manner of boxes and tins. It looked like a treasure trove, and I longed to go in and peer in one of the tins to see what was inside. A long window ran along one side, and it looked out onto the length of the veranda that we had seen earlier. I could see the line of beautiful clothes and stared at them, wondering what would happen next. I soon found out.

The sharp tapping of shoes against the mottled marble floor brought my attention back to the kitchen; Suresh stood in the doorway and beckoned us to follow him. We stared at the woman's back as she stirred the pots vigorously, but she continued to ignore us, and we quickly ran after Suresh for what felt like miles through a long corridor with cupboards on either side until we reached an arched doorway and we walked through. I don't think I can ever describe the wonder of that first moment when I beheld the interiors of that house, but I shall try.

The room was enormous with huge glass cases that housed the most interesting manner of objects … beautiful teacups, stacks of china plates with floral pictures on them, glassware in different jewel hues, and at the centre of the room was a dining table with the most ornate wooden chairs I had ever seen. Even more ornate than the throne-like chairs Madam Nalini had sat on, on her wedding day. The walls were painted a glossy cream and a massive fan, from which hung light shades shaped like flowers, gave off cooling gusts of air. The most arresting of all these sights was the lady who sat at one of the chairs. She was tiny and dainty, and wrapped up in the most beautiful blue and yellow saree with a gold border. Her hair was swept up in an elegant bun and her lips and nails were painted a delicate shade of pink. Her golden skin gleamed under the lights and everything about her was so fine and elegant and beautiful that it took my breath away to see her. I could tell by the way my mother had stiffened up next to me that she was as awed as I was by this exquisite looking woman. Something about her jogged my memory, and I remembered the woman in the pink saree on that fateful day I entered the Anni Ashram. Only this woman was unsmiling. She looked up and my mother, Suresh and I bowed deferentially.

"Amma, this is the girl, Madhuri. I know her Uncle," he said, and looked down at his feet.

The lady looked at me and nodded, and gestured for me to come towards her. I shuffled towards her on anxious, nervous feet and came to a standstill about a foot away from her, and like Suresh looked at my feet.

"How old are you?" she asked in a clear, confident voice, enunciating each word clearly and carefully. I had no idea and so looked back helplessly, tongue-tied, at my mother.

"Sixteen, Amma!" my mother said in a hoarse whisper.

"Speak louder," snapped the lady irritably, and my heart sank at her tone of voice as there was something terrifying about the cold elegance of this woman, and I knew then she would be a harsh mistress. I realised she was talking to me again, and I turned my attention to what she was saying.

"Do you know how to clean floors and wash clothes and cut vegetables?" I nodded mutely.

"Well, that's all I really need to know. Suresh take her to Lakshmi and tell her to give her instructions and put her in one of the servant's rooms. And with a dismissive nod, she looked away, signalling that we were to leave. Suresh led us back to the kitchen and the fat plump lady we had met earlier looked at him enquiringly.

"She's hired," he said to her, "and you can start her on work right away." So this was Lakshmi, I guessed. She was looking at me assessing my capabilities, and with a dismissive nod, she spoke her mind.

"She's so tiny, how will she do anything? What's your name, girl?"

"Madhuri," I answered softly and politely.

"Wait in the veranda till I finish serving lunch, and then I will show you what you need to do." And with that she picked up the bowls of food lying on a tray, and waddled off towards the room we had just been in.

I went with my mother to the veranda and we stood looking at each other foolishly. Suresh, who had followed us, looked at my mother and handing her a wad of notes, said, "Count it." My mother took the sheaf of notes and, turning away from me and him, began to count them out under her breath. When she was done she turned back to him and gave a small nod of acceptance and then turned to me.

She turned around and gave me a few of those notes. I looked at them, and there was more money there than I had ever seen before. In fact, this was the first time in a long time I had held money in my hands and for some reason I was remembering the tangy sharpness of tamarind, but I could not understand why this association crossed my mind. I searched through my limited reservoir of thoughts to search for some meaning and was interrupted by my mother's sharp voice calling me back to attention.

"For emergencies. Keep it safe, and work hard" she said, and then with one last look, she folded her hands in a gesture of salute to Suresh and trotted away down the drive and towards the towering front gate. I stared after her retreating back in absolute disbelief. She had done it again, and for the first time in my life, I felt a surge of hatred for this woman who was my mother. The woman who had just sold me again into an unknown life and unknown fate.

I could feel Suresh looking at me and I ignored him as I tried to squash down the feelings that, years after that traumatic first day at the Anni Ashram, rose up again in me with the intensity of adolescent grief. I clenched my fists and bit down on my lower lip to stop from crying out loud at this renewed anguish of separation, as the fear of what lay ahead of me washed over me, yet again, in huge, overwhelming waves. I knew Suresh had left to get on with his day, and I just stood there in the sticky, Chennai heat, with the sun pouring down on me, reminding me that discomfort was never far away. I have no idea how long I stood in the veranda, staring sightlessly around me, when a sharp nudge alerted me to Lakshmi's presence.

"Come!" she said, and I turned to follow her, unquestioningly, in full knowledge that I had little choice other than to obey completely.

She led me around a cemented pathway to a huge backyard that was dotted with an assortment of trees that provided welcome shade from the relentless sun. A row of tiny shacks stood beyond the trees, and we walked across to these. They were crude constructions even to my untrained eyes… Rooms tacked on one to the other, with metal front doors and no windows. Lakshmi unbolted one of these and led me into a dark, musty room that was lit by a single naked bulb. There was a mattress on the floor and a small table at one corner.

"This is your room," she said hurriedly. "The lavatories and bathrooms are around the back. Don't use too much water, and always turn off the light when you leave your room. Have a bath now and come back to the kitchen when you are finished." And turning her back she marched out of the room.

I stared about me. The room was painted white and it was suffocatingly hot. There was a pillow on the mattress, and a sheet, and a couple of thin towels. I turned these over in my hands as it dawned on me that for the first time in my life I was on my own and would actually be living on my own. I put my little bag of things on the table and turned around abruptly as I heard Lakshmi re-enter. How quickly we get used to seeing a space as our own. She came bearing a toothbrush, tooth powder and a bar of soap. I took them from her wordlessly, and watched her wriggle out the door of my room. MY room. I could not believe it, and was not sure whether I liked the idea yet or not.

I took one of the towels and the soap and walked around the back of this little line of rooms. Behind them stood three doors and I opened each one and peered in. There were two toilets and one washroom, and entering the washroom I filled the big red bucket that stood under the brass tap and emerged five minutes later feeling only slightly refreshed. I went back to my room and putting away the soap and towel, I walked out, bolted the room shut and walked back to the huge kitchen to see what would happen next. Lakshmi was sitting outside in the veranda sipping tea from a large enamel tumbler. She beckoned me near her, and I went and sat down next to her and smiled at her diffidently. To my surprise she smiled back, a big wide smile that transformed her face, and reaching behind her she pulled out another tumbler, and poured out some of her tea into it and offered it to me. I took it gratefully and said thank you.

We sipped the tea together in silence for a minute and then she asked me,

"Do you know why you are here?"

"I have to work," I proffered as a way of answer.

She tutted at me in exasperation. "Yes, but do you know what your job is, and have you worked before."

I briefly told her about my duties at the Anni Ashram, and she nodded in understanding, when I had finished. "So you know nothing," she said rather cuttingly.

"You are here as the top servant for this house. It belongs to Mr. and Mrs. Srinivasan. You must call them Amma and Ayya. You are here to clean the ground floor of the house every day, do the washing and help me in the kitchen to cut and chop the vegetables. We start work every day at 5:30 in the morning and we finish in the evening after dinner has been served and the kitchen is clean."

This information was delivered in a rapid burst in an accent that was almost too quick for me to follow and I wondered why she spoke so strangely. I later learned everyone from her small village just outside Chennai spoke that way. I digested what she had said and looked at the kitchen door beyond which the house and its large interiors loomed most intimidatingly. I could not imagine cleaning that entire place by myself; it seemed so large. At least at the ashram I was never alone and the kitchen and cleaning duties had always been shared. This task seemed too big to take on by myself, but I did not say anything and nodded at Lakshmi as she looked at me enquiringly.

"Okay, good," she said, and getting up, she beckoned me to follow her. We rose and went back into the kitchen where there lay a pile of vegetables and various condiments and pulses (beans) on the table. Lakshmi opened a drawer which creaked noisily, and taking out a few knives she handed me one.

"Start peeling the onions and cutting them like this," she said, deftly slicing a pink round onion into thin slivers.

I had done this many, many times at the ashram, and gripping the knife firmly, I started working my way through the enormous bowl of onions. My eyes watered furiously, and I had to keep wiping my eyes on my sleeves, but I persevered and I could tell Lakshmi was pleased with the progress I was making. The very act of focussing on this familiar task helped alleviate some of the confusion and anxiety I was experiencing at being tossed into another strange environment. Lakshmi piled some of the onions into the pans that were simmering with oil on the stove, and threw in some garlic and different spices. A delicious smell of fried condiments rose up into the air and seared my taste buds, making me aware of how hungry I was. I sniffed appreciatively and Lakshmi turned to me with a big cheerful smile and said we could eat only after the family had eaten, as that was the rule. I nodded in assent and went back to chopping the onions, looking forward to that moment when I would be able to sit down and eat this delicious smelling food that this strange new person in my life was making. And she was strange.

Lakshmi was plump, with rolls of fat that hung out of the sleeves of her blouse and spilled out from under her saree and spread in layers of undulating dunes under her face. Her eyes were tiny and round and black and cheerful, and her hair was peppered with grey, with wisps that escaped the tight bun that she had tied it up in. She seemed very active and every bit of her seemed to crackle with nervous energy.

After the onions were done she showed me how to grate coconuts and chop tomatoes into small square pieces. And when I was done with that, she started me on washing up in the big shining stainless steel sink at one corner of the kitchen. I enjoyed the cleanliness and brightness of the kitchen, as it was such a pleasant change from the dank, dark one in Anni Ashram; Lakshmi Akka (I had called her that and she had not objected) and her matter-of-fact friendliness was infinitely preferable to Ramu's sullen temper and greasy hair. The meal took about two hours to prepare and by the time it was over, I was tired from the physical labour, the heat of the hot summer and the strangeness of a new life. Lakshmi saw I was tired and with a sympathetic cluck, gave me a bowl of rice with some curry in it, and told me to take it to my room and go and eat there. She said she would call me if I was needed, but to try and get some sleep for a few hours as it was just my first day.

I gratefully took the bowl of food and trotted off to my new one-roomed home and sitting on the mattress ate my food, When I had finished I took the bowl and went to wash up at the tap beside the bathrooms. While I was about it I cupped my hands and had a long drink of water and felt instantly refreshed. Going back to my room, I sat on the mattress once again, and looked around the bare room and realised with a sudden sickening emptiness that I was alone for the first time in my life. It was the most unpleasant sensation, and to ward it off, I lay back on the hard little pillow and closed my eyes to try and shut out the pain. It did not go away and I just lay there, a mass of jangled nerve endings, sending out a silent prayer to my uncaring goddess, wherever she was, to try to lift the loneliness of my life and very being. This was how I learned that being lonely was the worst thing that could happen to any human being. In later years, I realised that money, power, riches, friends, lovers ... all these are just things humans try to fill their lives with to smother this one acute affliction that fells every human no matter how low or high we are born. In this frantic exodus from loneliness we are all one.

I lay looking up unseeingly at the ceiling for a few minutes watching a gekko trace its upside-down path across it. And then in a swift movement, I got up and grabbing my plate, bolted out of the metal front door into the stifling humidity of the summer heat. In the minute it took me to scurry up the path to the little porch behind the kitchen, I was covered in moisture, my blouse sticking uncomfortably to my back. I entered the kitchen almost tripping over myself, and Lakshmi turned around as she heard me clatter in.

"Quiet," she said, sharply. "Amma is sleeping and in the afternoons there can be no noise in the house," she hissed.

I quietly put down my plate near a pile by the sink, and it caused another burst of annoyance from the plump Lakshmi.

"Not there! Those are for Amma and Ayya and Akhilama. Our plates go in here," she said in a muted scold, pointing at a shelf that lay opposite the sink.

I went across and placed my plate there, amidst a pile of bent and broken plates and glasses and mugs. A smattering of scratched plastic ware lay there and one of them I noticed had a colourful print of flowers across it. I picked it out and looked at it wonderingly, remembering Judith Madam's house and its colourful crockery. The memory brought a little smile to my face as I remembered that wonderful day out and the beach and the feel of Kalpa's hand in mine. The memory of her still hurt, but inside me a small voice of reason whispered that she had been spared this life of drudgery that was my everyday existence now, and in some ways she had been luckier than me.

I spent the rest of the evening cleaning the shelves in the kitchen as per Lakshmi's instructions and then later after another cup of very satisfying hot sweet tea, I set to work swabbing the floor and the verandah outside. When I was done with this, Lakshmi set me to cleaning the rice for the evening meal, and I settled down on the steps of the verandah with the wicker tray that held the rice and began to pick out the stones and dirt from the rice. It was peaceful work and the sun was finally starting to cool; leaning my head against the wall around the porch I sighed deeply and closed my eyes to rest a minute. I opened them and got a shock. A young girl was standing in front of me staring at me and I had no idea who she was. She was around six years old and had the most beautiful eyes and hair. As soon as she saw I was awake, she beamed at me and held her hand out and opening a grubby fist she offered me a sweet that she had been holding. I smiled back and took the sweet and popped it in my mouth; before I could swallow, Lakshmi had come out and put her arms around the girl. This was, as I discovered, Chinna, the adored daughter of Lakshmi and Saravana who worked as a peon in Mr. Srinivasan's office. Lakshmi sent Chinna away and told her to do her homework and nodded at me to get on with my work.

We prepared the food for the evening meal in silence as both Lakshmi and I were tired by now. She showed me how to lay the table, arranging the table mats, the napkins, the plates and glasses and flowers on the table and showed me where everything was kept in the dining room. I could not believe that human beings needed so many things just to be able to eat, and once again the starkness of my life hit me and I found myself wondering why I was who I was and why others seemed to have everything better than me. But I did not wonder for long… My attention was taken up with the arrival of the family. Mr. and Mrs. Srinivasan arrived for dinner and sat down at the sumptuously laid out table. Mr. Srinivasan was dressed in a suit and his wife was attired in a different saree from before. She wore glittering jewellery and her deep red saree shimmered with gold hues with every movement she made. She looked expensive and beautiful and I was in complete awe of her appearance. But the person who took up my real attention was the young lady accompanying them. She seemed to be my age, but there the resemblance ended. Her name was Akhila, as I discovered through her conversations with her mother and father, and she was a spitting image of her mother. She was dressed in a pair of dark blue trousers, that I later learned were called jeans, that I was to be very careful handling, and a sleeveless, blue and white checked blouse with dainty white shoes and a white headband. She had dark curls that tumbled down over her shoulders and her back in a way I had only seen on television. She had dark eyes and porcelain skin and her clothes hung on her slender frame most artistically. For a minute I thought she could not be real, that this kind of physical perfection could not possibly exist, so angelic did she look. I could not help staring at her and then realised she was staring back, unsmilingly. So I dropped my gaze, and following Lakshmi's lead proceeded to serve out the food and then retired to the kitchen to wait until they had finished eating. When I went back in, the dining room was empty except for an array of dirty dishes. and stacking them I carried them back. I spent the next couple of hours cleaning the dining room and kitchen and washing the used dishes, and re-arranging them in the kitchen. Laksmi sat at the door between the veranda and kitchen drinking more tea and giving instructions to me on where things went and how they were done. I worked quietly and slowly for I was very tired, and when I was done I trotted back to my room and with a grateful sigh fell on the little mattress and was sound asleep the moment my head touched the hard pillow.

Chapter Ten
THE PEOPLE

I was woken up the next morning by a soft hand patting my head. At first I thought, half awake, I must be sleeping, but then the patting became more insistent and I opened my eyes and Chinna's little face loomed into view, beaming at me.

"Amma sent me to wake you up. It's five o'clock and you have to be in the kitchen at five-thirty," she said.

I rose up and grabbing my towel and bath things, headed for the washroom at the back. I could hear raised voices next door and pointing at the sound, Chinna grinning at me again said, "My mother does not like waking up this early so every morning she shouts at my father because she is in a bad mood," she said cheekily. I couldn't help but smile at this, even though Lakshmi's bad mood probably did not bode well for my work day. As Chinna bounded out of the door and back into her own home, I walked under the tree-lined path to have a bath and start my first official day at work.

It was gruelling. I had to sweep and swab the entire lower floor of the house which was vast. There were two living rooms and the dining room, plus the office Mr. Srinivasan used occasionally. There were the wide stairs leading to the upstairs rooms, and an empty bedroom and bathroom, a veranda out front, and one at the back, as well as the entire compound we had driven through yesterday. After that backbreaking task was done with, I returned to the kitchen, hot and sweaty and after a quick cup of tea, I helped make the sambhar and chutney and idlis for the morning breakfast, lay the table and serve out the food. I stayed in the kitchen while the family had their breakfast, and I could hear their voices raised in argument. Akhila and her mother were fighting over something though it was unclear what the problem was. I wondered how anyone could fight or be unhappy surrounded by such wealth and comfort, but luckily there was too much work to be done and my philosophical train rolled into the station of chores and came to a quick halt.

After I had cleaned up after breakfast I was allowed to eat, and I wolfed down my idlis with gratitude. Lakshmi Akka and I then had a companionable fifteen minutes where she showered me with questions about my life and tutted in a suitably sympathetic manner over my miseries. I must admit the show of sympathy was new for me and I revelled in it. I hammed it up for her, especially painting Madam Shanthi in a particularly evil light. The short little session of gossip buoyed me considerably, to be replaced by dismay when Lakshmi Akka showed me where all the laundry was kept. There was a mountain of sheets and clothes to be washed and my heart sank. Thankfully the washing stone and tap were under a large neem tree, and the shade helped. I soaked the clothes in two buckets and then scrubbed and rinsed for the better part of two hours, and then strung out the beautiful fabrics to dry on the lines that were stretched out on poles in the backyard. I must admit feeling a glow of satisfaction as I surveyed the finished job. The air was redolent with the smell of washing powder and the beautiful clothes looked really pretty as they waved about in the warm breeze. I was exhausted, however, by the time I finished and went back into the kitchen where Lakshmi Akka had a pile of vessels waiting to be washed. I doggedly set about cleaning them to a silvery shine, and was rewarded by a smile from Akka who slipped a sweet into my hand, which I also wolfed down. Together we laid the table and served out the afternoon meal. Only Mrs. Srinivasan was there for lunch, and she stared at me coldly as I went about my work. I was glad to be away from her basilisk scrutiny, and after I had cleaned the dining room I sat down to a hearty lunch. Whatever else may have been the rigours of my daily life in that place, I could not complain about the food. There was plenty of it and Akka was a fine cook, who was clearly happy to teach and share cooking tips.

I discovered on this first day that afternoons, no matter how hot and sweaty, were the best time of day for me in this mansion. Akka went to sleep, Chinna was at school, Mrs. Srinivasan was either out or napping, Suresh was out and about with the master of the house, and Akhila was at school or tuitions. I had these two hours in the afternoon all to myself and that first afternoon I wandered around the huge compound, gingerly treading on the soft grass that lay to one side of the house. I sniffed at the vast beds of flowers that stood up in cheerful defiance to the angry sun, and when the burn of that orange globe got too intense for me, I went and stood under the shade of the huge mango tree in front of the porch and listened to the sounds of the birds who seemed oblivious to the scorching temperatures. Huge Ashoka trees lined the entire compound and flower pots stood in neat rows around edges of the house like colourful sentinels … the smell of greenery filled my senses and I breathed it all in heavily revelling in these news scents and surroundings. I decided to walk around the entire compound before making my way back to the kitchen, as I was unsure how much time I had and did not want to get into trouble for wandering off. So I trotted around the perimeter, almost skipping, and taking a corner, bumped into the old man who had opened the gate for us yesterday. He was still wearing khakhi pants and a white shirt and was watering the plants down that side of that house. He glared at me, slightly annoyed, and I quickly raised my hand in an apologetic namaste. He seemed a little mollified by this, and asked me where I was off to in such a rush.

"I'm going to see if Lakshmi Akka needs me," I said diffidently.

"No one will be around till 5 o'clock, so you have another hour to relax if you want," he said looking at a scratched, silver watch he was wearing. Then as an afterthought he asked, "What's your name?"

"Madhuri, Thatha," I said respectfully.

He nodded sagely. "I know your Uncle. I was the one that helped you get this job," he said, "and told him to send you here when I found out that he was looking to place his niece in employment."

This was news to me, as I thought Suresh was the mastermind behind my job, but I smiled at him shyly and said thank you. That seemed to touch a chord with him, and he smiled back, a great big beaming smile, and patted my head, and told me to go and rest for some time before I had to start work again.

"If you like, I can stay and help you water the plants," I asked him, and that made him smile even more.

"You see these flowers here," he said pointing to a big, deep green plant with clusters of orange flowers on them. If you pluck the flowers like this, and turn them over, you can suck out the nectar from the bottom. It's quite delicious." Saying that, he plucked a few and gave them to me. I turned them over and put the ends of the flowers into my mouth and drew in sharply. The sweet and gentle taste was heavenly and I almost ate the flowers, but Thatha stopped me with a laugh.

"You can't eat those, and make sure you don't pluck too many flowers or Amma will get very angry with you," he warned.

I nodded, still tasting the nectar on my tongue, and I could not stop smiling. The little encounter with Thatha that afternoon became a daily routine, and I would trail after him every afternoon from that time onwards, chattering to him about anything that took my fancy and helping him with watering the plants in the huge compound. My cue to leave was hearing the big white car honking furiously as it drove down the road to the gate. Thatha would drop his watering can and run to open the gate, and I would rush back to the kitchen where Lakshmi Akka was bustling about making tea and some savoury dish to serve to the returning Mr. Srinivasan and Akhila. I stayed in the kitchen and washed and chopped and cleaned and was rewarded with a big smile from Lakshmi Akka. All this was very new to me … Thatha's gentleness, Chinna's childish friendship, Akka's good cheer and approving smiles… for the first time in my life I felt that life held some joy and normalcy for me, and I went about my backbreaking work with a song in my heart.

One evening I learned how to make rasam and carrot poriyal and felt a thrill of pride when after dinner I saw that the bowl of poriyal was brought back empty. I went into the dining room to clear up the table and bring back the dirty dishes and halted when I saw Akhila still sitting at the table. She looked up at me as I came in and gave me such a look of dislike and loathing that I almost dropped the folded towel I was carrying to pick up the hot dishes. I nodded politely at her and went up to the table and started collecting the plates and glasses and dishes of food. As I went past Akhila to get her plate and glass, she reached out and pinched me on my arm. I looked at her in shock as I could not imagine what I had done to deserve that pinch.

She glared at me, "Ask before you take away something in front of me. Or are you too stupid to see I'm still sitting here," she said rudely.

I looked at her with my heart in my mouth. "Please, can I take the plate away," I asked humbly.

She glared at me again and then pushed the plate towards me and nodded condescendingly. I collected it and went back to the kitchen as fast as I could, my face hot and flushed from the encounter with the bad-tempered Akhila. She reminded me horribly of Revathi and the trauma of my experiences with her came crashing back to me, the joy of the day forgotten, and without realising it my eyes filled up with unshed tears. I didn't say a word to Lakshmi and put down the things next to the sink with my head bowed down.

Lakshmi continued to work and I went back out again to get the rest of the dishes. Luckily for me the table was now empty. The sounds of the television from the enormous living room came through the partially closed connecting door, and I could see Mr. and Mrs. Srinivas through the chink, sat on separate armchairs, looking at the screen. I could not see Akhila anywhere and for that I was extremely grateful.

It took a couple of hours to wind up our work and then Lakshmi and I sat down to a well-deserved dinner on the little porch at the back. Chinna came bounding up to us, and sat nestled next to me, occasionally demanding a mouthful of food. Thatha also joined us, and so did Lakshmi's husband, Saravana. We sat there, all of us, eating quietly and then with a sigh, Lakshmi got up, collected our plates and took them back to the kitchen where she and I washed them and put them away. And thus ended a day at work at the home of the Srinivasans, and as my eyes closed, I had to admit that on a balance it had been a good day.

Most weekdays passed with this undisturbed routine. Sometimes guests came home to dinner and the entire kitchen would be turned into an even busier beehive of activity. The house would have to be swabbed down with sweet smelling liquids, and the kolam that Laksmi drew everyday would be even more elaborate, greeting guests in a profusion of colour and intricacy. Vast quantities of food had to be produced and the amount of washing up afterwards beggared belief. Even Suresh was pressed into kitchen service and rushed about carrying beautiful china plates and fine glasses and ornate silverware into the dining room. The house would be redolent with incense sticks and the masses of flowers that Thatha brought in to be arranged in the huge vases that lay scattered about the rooms. In the evening cars would sweep up the drive and elegant ladies and men in fine shirts would arrive to spend the evening eating and drinking and making conversation. The sound of music and laughter would float across to us back in the kitchen where we worked feverishly to ensure plate upon plate of snacks were served up to the gay and perfumed throng in the living room.

Those were the only times we saw Mrs. Srinivasan in the kitchen on a regular basis. She came sweeping in to bark orders at us, and chivvy us to work faster and more efficiently. I could tell from Lakshmi Akka's pursed lips that she did not like being treated in this cavalier fashion, but she kept quiet and worked like a demon to ensure that all the orders were followed. After the last guest left, and the last spoon was cleaned and put away, we all sat in an exhausted slump on the kitchen porch, too tired to eat the leftovers. As soon as Thatha had finished his beedi, it was our cue to return to our respective rooms and sleep away our exhaustion. It would often be well past midnight when our work was done, and thankfully, we were all given the morning off the following day, which meant we could start work at eight in the morning instead of five-thirty.

The work was gruelling, and never seemed to stop. And other than the odd unpleasant encounter with Akhila, most weekdays went by in a blur of routine and rigour. The weekends were the time I dreaded the most. Mr and Mrs Srinivasan were home, as was Akhila, and she took it upon herself to be as unkind as she could possibly be to me at every chance she got. She would find fault with the plate I had placed before her, saying it was dirty and demanding a new one, or pinch me slyly when no one was looking. She constantly complained that I smelled, prompting Mrs Srinivasan to reprimand me and tell me to go and clean myself better. The problem was I had just two sets of clothes that were getting too small, and too frayed as I had to wash them every second day. Finally, Lakshmi Akka decided to speak to Mrs. Srinivasan about the state of my clothing. At first Mrs. Srinivasan was outraged that I had been sent to her without proper clothing and grumbled at how expensive new garments would be. After all, she had paid good money to get a cleanly attired maid. But then Lakshmi Akka pointed out that guests who came would see my clothes and it reflected badly on the family. This argument swayed the cold and elegant lady of the house, and the solution was found in some of Akhila's old clothes that she was no longer using. I was handed a deep maroon pavadai and blouse and scarf, and a dark green salwar with purple edging, and for more elegant occasions a blue saree with a deeper blue border and a matching blouse and petticoat. In addition, I was given some brown and cream cotton pajamas and tunics to wear when the better clothing was being washed, and suddenly for the first time in my life I owned more clothes than I had ever had in my life. With my own room and fine clothes and new friends, I felt quite rich and elegant. I took to wearing the green salwar in the afternoons during my time off, and I would walk around the garden preening like a particularly narcissistic peacock. Thatha played along and would pretend to bow and scrape as if I were a queen, and we would both end up laughing merrily at our own silly games. I grew to love Thatha very quickly. He was a gentle, shabby man, who possesses a quiet dignity, and always had a flower tucked away each evening for little Chinna. Lakshmi Akka's husband, Saravana was always very respectful of him and we got on marvellously, a little family, bound together in duty, labour and poverty to the Srinivasans.

I was happy enough in this new life, until the day that Akhila spied me, having come home early from school one afternoon, wearing her finery. She had obviously not been told that some of her castoffs had found their way to me. She stopped short when she saw me in the garden with a mouthful of flowers, busily sucking the nectar out. She stopped short as if she had been turned to stone and then rushing at me, started hitting me.

"Thief, thief. I'll tell my mother," she screamed at me pounding my arms and my sides with her clenched fists. She wasn't very strong, even though she and I were roughly the same size, but even so, I cowered down, and tried to shield myself from her blows. I had not realised she was talking about her clothes, and thought she was furious that I had plucked the flowers without her permission. Finally getting tired of assaulting me she ran into her home, and I ran to my room. Five minutes later Mrs. Srinivasan entered my room looking absolutely furious.

"What have you stolen from Akhila's room," she demanded angrily.

"Nothing," I said in a scared whisper. I had never been upstairs to the first floor ever as only Thatha was allowed to go upstairs to clean every morning. Her angry voice had brought

Lakshmi Akka to the door as well. Akhila was standing in the background flapping about in a rage still.

"What clothes have you stolen, you bad girl, I knew you were trouble the moment I saw you. I know your type only too well," said Mrs. Srinivasan nastily.

"Amma, I didn't take any clothes," I said, tearfully. "I only took a few flowers to taste the nectar. I'm so sorry, please forgive me."

From outside the room, Akhila shouted out shrilly, "Don't believe her. She's wearing the clothes and lying to you."

And then the penny dropped. Mrs. Srinivasan turned around heavily, and glared at Akhila over Lakshmi Akka's plump body.

"You stupid girl. I gave her those as you are not using them anymore. They were lying at the back of your closet for years. You've woken me up from my nap for nothing at all."

Stalking out of my room, she grabbed the complaining Akhila and headed back toward the house. We could hear Akhila's voice raised in protest over her clothes being given away to the likes of me. I caught the word 'urchin' and 'street child' and winced inwardly. Even in my unformed, uneducated mind, I knew what an insult that was.

Lakshmi looked at my distraught face and matter-of-factly told me to get into the kitchen and start working. And so, I followed her instructions silently and got on with my kitchen duties. Thatha came by a little later with a little daisy he had cut just for me. I smiled gratefully and later than evening put the flower under my mattress to press it dry. It didn't. It turned to mulch and left a bad stain on my mattress, and the memory of the event left a bad stain in my mind.

Morning after morning went by in unvarying monotony. I learned to cook enough to be able to cook a simple meal all by myself. My fondness for Chinna was extremely mutual and there were nights when she insisted on sleeping next to me. Feeling her little form curled up next to me, one arm and leg flung across me while she slept soundly, filled the sad space in my heart at being parted from my little sister, Radhi. I still wondered about her and hoped and prayed she was okay and well-looked after. Chinna was not Radhi, but she was a welcome substitute. Thatha was a surrogate grandparent for all of us. He would smuggle the odd fruit, or tender coconut, or mango from the many trees in the vast garden, and took unabashed pleasure in spoiling and petting Chinna and me. Saravana went to work in Mr. Srinivasan's office running and fetching cups of tea and papers for the important people who worked there. He never said much, even when his wife was shouting at him and carried on whatever he was doing as if he were deaf. Chinna would always come sneaking into my room when this happened in the mornings, and together we would giggle at the volley of insults that were issuing forth from Lakshmi Akka, most of which seemed to indicate complete scorn for his ancestors. Lakshmi Akka was fun. Her heart was as big as her temper, and she could go from gloom and doom, to anger, to gales of laughter in minutes. I learned, however, she never held a grudge and she took me under her wing in the most gratifying manner. She taught me how to tie the blue saree for the days we had a party and it was with her that I first got to visit a local market and a mall. The family had gone away for an entire weekend and we had a blissful 48 hours to ourselves, to do as we pleased.

Force of habit made us all wake up early, but we had a delicious breakfast of dosas and chutney that we ate out on the veranda, washed down with fresh coconut water. Gorged and listless in the summer heat, we sat silently for a few moments, when Lakshmi Akka decided she wanted to go to the market. She looked at me and Chinna, and smilingly told us to go wash and wear nice clothes. I wore the maroon salwar and Chinna donned her favourite skirt of bright red and blue flowers, and I thought we looked very fine indeed. Lakshmi Akka however outdazzled us both. She was resplendent in bright pink saree and matching blouse. She was bedecked with dangling earrings and bangles and a shiny new nose ring. She came up to us grinning widely, and holding out her clenched hands she asked us to pick a hand each. I chose left and Chinna chose right. She opened them and in her hands lay two gold and bead necklaces. She slipped one around Chinna's neck and then one around mine. Thatha who had been watching the spectacle with a grin as wide as Lakshmi Akka's gave me an oblong parcel wrapped in newspaper. I ripped it open wondering what it was … and my eyes widened in delight. A pair of black and gold slippers, brand new, and shiny and elegant stared at me. I looked up at Thatha in wonder and gratitude and he nodded at me to put them on. I slipped off my rubber slippers, castoffs from Lakshmi Akka, and put my feet nervously into these beautiful shoes. They fitted well, though one of the straps pinched into my ankle, but I did not care. Together the three of us said goodbye to Thatha, waved to Saravana Anna, and walked in single file out the side path and down to the big iron gate, and unlatching it, stepped out onto the lane that led to the busy street.

It was a glorious morning, heat and pinched ankle strap notwithstanding. We took a bus to a bustling marketplace and I revelled in the sights that I saw. Chinna excitedly pointed out her school to me, a big yellow building with a low red wall around it, and a big sandy compound around it. Some of the windows seemed to be broken, and the whole place looked like it had been standing too long and was tired and fed up now. But it was still better than the school I had attended as a child, as far as I could remember, so I nodded and patted Chinna on the head and told her she was a very clever girl. And that she was. Chinna always brought home excellent report cards from school and seemed to truly enjoy poring over her school books. Lakshmi Akka had once confessed she had high hopes for Chinna.

"I think we would like her to be a doctor or lawyer even, or perhaps get a good Government job," she confided to me one day. "She's very clever, even though she's a girl, and we are saving up money to send her to college someday."

This news was something of a revelation to me and I stared at the proud mother wonderingly. In my experience, girls from my world had no hopes of becoming anything beyond a housewife or maid.

But now, looking out at this world I was in, I wasn't so sure. I saw women driving cars, walking on the street wearing trousers and shirts like men, and haggling with auto drivers; I even saw one woman standing by the side of the road smoking a cigarette. I looked back in shock, but the bus went by too quickly for me to get a second glance. We arrived at the market in about half an hour and what a market it was! Stall upon stall of fresh vegetables and fruits were stacked in colourful rows. A man went by on a cycle with a box attached to the back. Lakshmi Akka waved him down and after some bargaining fed me my second ice-cream ever. This one was on a stick and had a brown exterior and a creamy-white interior. It was delicious and it was the start of my love affair with choc-o-bars.

We wandered past the fragrant flower stalls on which were hung garlands made from roses and marigolds. They reminded me of Madam Nalini's wedding, and I wondered if I would have big, heavy fine red and gold garlands at my own wedding. We wandered into a mall, a huge building with more shops than I could count. Some sold household ware, others clothes, some held racks of glittering jewellery – it was all overwhelming and bewildering and I stayed close to my friends, very silent, drinking in these new and elegant sights. Lakshmi Akka, Chinna and I spent a pleasant few hours looking at sarees and borders and blouses and then buying nothing, we scurried away from the angry faces of the salesman who had been serving us. I was shocked at how much some of the sarees cost, and realised what a fortune Mrs. Srinivasan spent on hers.

Lunch was back at the market, at a small restaurant, where Lakshmi Akka was obviously well-known. One of the waiters came rushing over to show us to a small table, and as we sat down he asked her how Saravana Anna was. I wondered how they knew this waiter, but I did not ask, because as I was about to, the young waiter whipped out banana leaves in front of us and another brought across a steel bucket from which he served us steaming hot rice. Another one brought us curry and vegetables and yet another pickles and curd rice. They kept plying us with food till we had eaten so much we thought we would all explode. We rose from the tables, Chinna groaning and clutching her stomach in mock agony to the amusement of the waiters who had served us. And then came my big shock. We had to pay at the cash counter on the way out and I realised I had no money. I had left the money my mother had given me all tied up in a piece of cloth in the folds of my favourite pavadai from childhood, back in the room. I looked miserably at Lakshmi Akka not knowing what to do or how to pay for my food, and too embarrassed and humiliated to even speak. Lakshmi Akka seemed not to notice anything wrong and paid the bill with cheerful smile and we were once again on our way, heading back in the stuffy, dirty bus and back to the house. I was grateful to Lakshmi Akka for the treat, but I'm not sure if she knew, for I never expressed it.

We stopped at a flower seller on our way back and bought some strands of marigold that we immediately wore in our hair, making a quick halt after this to buy a parcel of sweets from a vendor for Thatha and Saravana Anna on our way to the bus stop. It was a quiet journey home, my head filled with thoughts of this lovely day out, and I compared it to the wonderful adventure I had had with Madam Judith and her father. And despite the cinema and fine restaurant and glorious beach, I decided that this day was far, far better in my limited opinion. This time I was not going back to the ashram but to what was truly beginning to feel like a real home.

Thatha and Saravana Anna were indulging in a rare afternoon nap, and the three of us decided to do the same. Lakshmi Akka went off to her room, and Chinna trailed into mine after having changed out of her finery. I had slipped into my cream and brown pajama set and smiled as Chinna crawled next to me, flung an arm and leg over me and promptly fell asleep. I stroked her curly hair for a few moments thinking that this was the happiest I had ever been and fell asleep with a smile on my face, one hand protectively around Chinna, and the other around the chain Lakshmi Akka had given me which I had chosen to keep on.

I was woken by Chinna stirring, and we both rose sleepily looking wonderingly at the dark outside. We must have slept for hours. I took Chinna to the taps to wash the sleep from both our eyes and we made our way to the kitchen veranda. The others were there tucking into the sweet parcel we had bought earlier, and we joined them. And in the deepening darkness we chatted together like any normal family; about Chinna's naughtiness, the wealth of the world that never seemed to touch us, the heat of Chennai and its magnificent monsoons, and Saravana Anna regaled us with gossip from Mr. Srinivasan's office. By the end of the evening we knew all about the secretary who wore short skirts, the salesmen who drank secretly in the office, and the receptionist who hated everybody. It was most entertaining, this look at a life I had no concept of, and I had to wipe the tears from my eyes when Saravana Anna told us how a very important visitor had brought her dog into this place of business and how it decided to do its business on Mr. Srinivasan's brand new office carpet.

But as all good things come to a swift end, this glorious day also came to a close. Thatha stubbed out his beedi, and as the moon rose up from behind a tree to take her place in the inky sky we wended our way down the little path to our homes, and settled in to dream happy dreams and then welcome in a brand-new day that would bring back the Srinivasans into our merry fold.

Chapter Eleven

That Sunday was more peaceful than most others. We all managed to sleep in late and had a leisurely breakfast again. The Srinivasans were not expected until later that evening, so we still had a day of lounging about after the house was swept and cleaned. I helped Thatha clean the upstairs rooms today. He had a bad headache and asked Lakshmi Akka if it was okay for me to sweep and dust the upper story, and since no one would see, she nodded her approval. So armed with the broom and a few dusters, I headed upstairs with Thatha, rather tentatively, as I knew I was not really allowed to go into this upper sanctum. Nothing could have prepared me for the luxury I saw upstairs. There were five enormous bedrooms with glistening bathrooms attached to each one. The walls were lined with shiny, wooden closets and thick and heavy drapes fell to the floor from the ceiling, blocking out the heat and light. The beds, oh the beds … each was the size of the room I slept in with massive soft mattresses and soft sheets and pillows. Every room was colour-coordinated, and it was easy to see which rooms had occupants.

In Mr. and Mrs. Srinivasan's room there was a rich red brocade cover on the bed, and the curtains were of the same plush fabric. There were two arm chairs, and a little table, and a big table with a mirror upon which lay bottles of liquids, and lipsticks, and other kinds of make-up that I had no clue about. Mr. Srinivasan's ties were draped across a small stool and a bundle of clothes were lying in a basket by the door. A carved door led into a bathroom that took my breath away. It was gleaming white with blue tiles and a huge vat that Thatha said was a bathtub. I stared at it in wonder. Gilt taps sprang out from one side to fill up this tub with hot water and the whole thing was so decadent and so unusual that I could not stop staring. Thatha nudged me gently and then showed me where to sweep and dust, and how to fold the clothes and put them away, straighten out the bed covers and fluff up the pillows. I did this in quite a daze, the magnificence of seeing a sleeping abode done up like a palace stunning me into absolute silence.

Akhila's room was a slightly smaller version of her parents'. It was painted in pink and cream and had a light and airy feel to it. Her bed was a carved white affair with flowers and leaves framing the headboard. She had her own TV, and a table on which her school bag had been carelessly tossed, the contents spilling out onto the table. There were shelves with gay-looking books in English crammed into them, along with a collection of dolls and toys that took my breath away. I had never seen toys like this before, not even in the shops at the mall. Thatha saw me looking at them and told me that Mr. Srinivasan bought these for Akhila whenever he went abroad. The concept of abroad was a mystery to me so I did not ask any more questions, but I did wonder why Akhila, surrounded as she was by such wealth and privilege, was always in a bad temper. And, of course I wondered for the umpteenth time in my life, why she had the life she did and I had the life that I did. I cleaned her room carefully, and enviously folded her pretty clothes and put them away. The other three rooms were designated for guests, and had not been used so there was not that much to do there. I cleaned those quickly too, and finally Thatha swabbed the upstairs down with a sweet-smelling liquid, lit incense and we went back down.

Thatha smiled at me as we went down the stairs.

"Don't envy anyone who has more material things than you, Madhuri. Wealth does not always lead to happiness. Be happy in your own life. It is better to be poor and honest, and have real friends," he said softly.

His words made no sense whatsoever, but I nodded politely, for I loved and respected him and did not like contradicting him. Back in the kitchen reality returned, and I strangely found myself breathing easier. The opulence upstairs had been unsettling, and I realised the entire house reeked of loneliness and unhappiness, and I was happy to be back in the busy, comfortable kitchen in Lakshmi Akka's benign presence. She had made puliogare and tomato chutney and we all sat down in the little veranda eating an early lunch. A huge vat of biryani and various accompaniments had been prepared for the evening meal. Chinna read to us from one of her school texts, the story of a crow who managed to get water out of a deep dish by filling the dish with rocks. I felt that there was a lesson to be learned from it that could be applied to my own life, and I promised myself to try and find rocks every time I came across water that was out of reach. After lunch Thatha went on to water the garden, and I went back to my bare room and lay looking up the stained ceiling and then at the metal door that was open and framed a rectangular patch of sunshine that was so bright that it looked like a corridor of light leading to somewhere my imagination could not fathom. I slept again that afternoon … a delightful, unbroken sleep that was the ultimate in pure luxury for me that hot afternoon.

I was up as the sun began setting, and washing my face and tidying my hair and clothes, I scampered to the kitchen where Lakshmi Akka was cutting onions for a salad. A big jug of tea stood at the ready and she offered me some, and I drank it thirstily. Just as I was finishing it we heard the car horn blaring, and putting my tumbler of tea down, I turned around to find another knife and started to help cut the onions. The vapours hit my eyes pretty quickly, and as I heard the sounds of life inside the house as the Srinivasans came back home, the tears began to pour out of my eyes.

My new life was better than I could have expected. I had a sense of belonging and community that I never forgot. The pain of Kalpa's death dissolved into a numb ache in the recesses of my heart, and under Lakshmi Akka's firm, but benevolent tutelage I became an expert cleaner, and learned to cook a decent meal. In fact, she said my beans poriyal was the best she had ever tasted. Praise was so rare and so precious, that I worked extra hard in the kitchen just to hear these little nuggets of compliments come my way as often as possible. I learned to dust quickly and efficiently and to my credit I never broke a single thing … Thatha said I was a clever little girl, and that was especially sweet to my ears. Little Chinna was always in and out of my room recounting things she had seen and heard at school. Sometimes, if there was time, we did her homework together, and it always seemed to me that despite being so many years my junior, she always knew more than me. But it was good practice for me to remember the few things I had been taught at Anni Ashram, and I used those times diligently recalling the lessons from Madam Judith, Madam Shanthi and the faceless, rich ladies who came to teach us in spurts of charity. It occurred to me one hot evening that those rich ladies were probably like Mrs. Srinivasan and I wondered why most of them even bothered.

Mrs. Srinivasan was a beautiful woman, expensively dressed even early in the mornings, but her beauty was marred by a petulant, discontented droop that hung around her richly painted lips. Whenever she looked at me I felt I was being sized up as prey, and it always reminded me of the geckos in my room that fixed their eyes on some unsuspecting fly or moth. I avoided her gaze as much as possible and tried to be as unobtrusive as possible. But it seemed as long as I did my job and did not slack off, other than the sharp order or tersely delivered command, she did not really have much to say to me. The problem was her daughter. The joy and peace with my newfound family was frequently ruined by this young girl, who seemed to delight in tormenting me. And like Revathi, she was in a complete position of power to do so whenever she felt like it. One weekend she had a friend over, and they followed me around everywhere, even into the kitchen, giggling and whispering and pointing at me. Lakshmi Akka pursed her lips angrily and banged a few pots about loudly at this intrusion into her domain and at this treatment of me, but she too was powerless to do much to stop them. They followed me out when I went to help Thatha water the plants and between them made him pluck as many flowers as they could carry, and beckoning to me made me follow them to the front porch of the house.

This was a grand affair, with a huge veranda and porch that was marbled and laid out with chairs and tables while a massive mango tree provided a canopy of green off to one side, from where the kuyal called out its warbling song every day. A fan hung off the ceiling and wafted down streams of cooling air, and the entire veranda was filled with potted plants of every description … hibiscus and jasmine vied with dahlias and asters and the whole place was very pleasant indeed. I used to love watering the plants here as it always felt green and cool and welcoming. It was here Akhila and her friend sat down, cross legged on the long sofa, and told me to come and sit at the floor near them. I did as they asked and wondered why they had called me. Other than Thatha, who was weeding a bed in the distance and casting anxious glances in my direction, everyone else was fast asleep. Mr. and Mrs. Srinivasan were sound asleep after an irksome morning of watching television, Lakshmi and Chinna were indulging in a siesta as well, and Saravana Anna was out somewhere running errands as usual. The hazy afternoon cast a warm glow over the entire setting and the warbling of the birds lent a strangely lonely feel to the whole situation. I sat there not saying a word, and then suddenly Akhila asked me, "Why are you working here?"

I answered with as much bravery as I could muster, "My father died and I have nowhere to live so my mother sent me here."

Akhila didn't seem to be very moved by this and sharply asked, "How did your father die?"

"He had a heart attack," I said humbly.

"I suppose he drank a lot," said Akhila with unfaltering precision. "My mother always says that people like you drink a lot. And you steal."

This was unfair and I knew it, but what could I say, so I stayed silent and looked at the floor noting the intricate patterns the marble made against my hands that were resting on its cool surface. But my silence was not the answer these girls wanted, and Akhila prodded me with her delicately slippered foot.

"I bet your mother sent you here to steal from us," she said nastily.

I looked up in shock, and shook my head furiously. "No!" I said in a choked whisper. "I would never do something like that."

"You would if you saw my room and my things," she bit back vindictively.

It was on the tip of my tongue to tell her I had seen her room and cleaned it, and she had obviously found nothing missing, but I knew this would get Thatha into trouble, so once again I shook my head silently. And so it went on, this baiting, and then Akhila found my Achilles heel, and she knew it from the expression on my face.

"No one really wants you around. Even your mother sold you to mine, you know," she said in her high, pretty voice and as she said it my head flew up and my eyes met her, the rage and sorrow in my soul registering at this truth.

Akhila laughed spitefully as my eyes filled up with tears, and her friend muttered uncomfortably, "Akhi, enough. Don't make her cry."

Akhila looked at her friend scornfully and said, "These people don't have feelings, so stop feeling sorry for her," and prodding me with her foot again, she pointed at the bunch of flowers and said, "Go string them into a garland for me and my friend and bring it to me back here. And tell Lakshmi we're hungry and want something to eat."

I was only too glad for any opportunity to get away from them, and grabbing the flowers I ran back around the side of the house and woke Lakshmi up and delivered the order to her. She woke up grumbling but waddled off to the kitchen to make something for them, and I hunted for a needle and thread to make a garland out of the wilting blooms. It did not take me long and I soon had two strings of them fastened with a knot at each end and trotted back out to the front porch. To my dismay, I found Mr. Srinivasan was up from his nap and sitting with them. I walked up diffidently, and gave Akhila the two strands, who grabbed them and looking at them disdainfully tossed them on the floor.

Mr. Srinivasan looked up at this, and sharply reprimanded his daughter, "Behave yourself. Someone made you something, why are you treating it like this?"

Akhila looked sulky and answered him in surly tones. "I asked her to make it for me, but she used black thread instead of white."

"So what? And why could you not thread them yourself. I bought you that beautiful work basket, it's time you used it," Mr. Srinivasan said crossly.

Annoyed at being told off, Akhila grabbed her friend's hand and, getting up, flounced back into the house. I could hear her voice complaining to her friend as she disappeared up the stairs.

Mr. Srinivasan looked at me and grimaced, and mat-ter-of-factly said to me, "She's very spoilt. And just like her mother."

I did not know how to respond to such a confession and nodded politely waiting to be excused from his presence. Mr. Srinivasan looked at me and then it was as if he noticed me for the first time. His eyes swept up and down over me, in a way that left me feeling very uncomfortable. Luckily, Lakshmi appeared just then bearing a tray with tea, murkus and some golden fried potatoes. She took one look at me and Mr. Sri-nivasan, and putting the tray down quickly told me that Mrs. Srinivasan would be down soon, and I was to go to the kitchen and start preparing the things for dinner. Mr. Srinivasan looked at her, almost guiltily, and nodded his assent and I hurried away into the kitchen eager to be away from everyone at that minute. Lakshmi Akka came in a short while later, and she glared at me sternly as I looked up at her.

"Be careful." she said abruptly, "Don't let Mrs. Srinivasan find you talking to Mr Srinivasan." I was most surprised at this, and opened my mouth to ask her what I had done wrong, but something in her eyes warned me not to ask any more questions and I resumed peeling the pile of potatoes in front of me.

It was a while before I figured out what she meant, and her words came back to haunt me months after she had left and gone back to her village. And she left for the saddest of reasons.

The summer months faded into a humid and unusually wet monsoon. Huge, grey clouds scudded overhead, threatening a deluge, but only making our clothes stick to our backs even more. Flies buzzed around annoyingly and even the birds in the garden seemed more listless and did not sing as loudly as usual. There was a moist, stillness in the air and every breath seemed to choke us and make breathing a chore. It was unbearably hot in the kitchen and even the taps ran tepid water that was uncomfortable on the skin. But we plodded on and all of us relished the few moments we spent in the air-conditioned chill of the main house. But even those were few and far between, and often the power would shut down leaving us all to languish in the unbearable humidity. In our hot little rooms, we lay at night hoping for the rain to break, to release the much-needed cooling over this overheated house. Chinna especially hated the weather, and she slept very poorly, going to school sleepy and tired every day, her big bag of books borne on her small, drooping back, like an overworked pack horse. She was not the kind to complain however, but one day she returned from school with a raging headache, irritable and red-eyed and fussy and unable to bear any bright light. We kept her in my room, and out of Saravana Anna's sight who was exceptionally irritable himself.

I checked in on her the next day at regular intervals, for she was unable to go to class. Thatha popped in frequently too, to go and sit by her side and as always brought her a flower in the evening. By that night she was running a high temperature and it was obvious she was in a lot of pain. Saravana Anna and

Lakshmi Akka looked helpless and finally, just before dinner, Lakshmi Akka told Mrs. Srinivasan about Chinna. I was in the dining room and laying out the table so I overheard the conversation.

"Amma, Chinna is very sick. We need to take her to the doctor," she said quietly.

Mrs. Srinivasan's head flew up and her eyes narrowed as if she did not believe what she had heard. "What's the matter with her?" she snapped, "At that age they all pretend to fall sick to get out of going school." Akhila who was sitting at the table, reading a book glared at her mother as she said this.

"No Amma, she is running a fever and has a really bad headache and she has been vomiting," said Lakshmi Akka a little more forcefully.

"You know we have a big dinner tomorrow so we cannot have this disturbing our plans," said Mrs. Srinivasan, her annoyance coming through forcefully. "I'll give you some medicine to bring down her fever and if she's not better by day after tomorrow you can take leave and go to the doctor," she said dismissively.

After dinner she handed Lakshmi Akka a strip of Crocin and a bottle of cough syrup and told her to give it to Chinna. That evening we all sat around Chinna who was burning up with fever and bringing up even the water that was being given to her. Lakshmi Akka slept on the floor of my room that night, in order to get enough sleep, and as the morning broke it seemed that Chinna was not getting any better. She was muttering incoherently and waving her arms and legs about in jerky motions as she were running away from something. It was awful to watch her suffer and Lakshmi Akka kept me and Thatha on guard duty while she cooked dinner for the evening gathering and while Saravana Anna went to work.

That evening there was the usual assembly of glittering guests to dinner, and laughter and music flowed through the house, as Chinna writhed in immense pain and burned up with a fever, breathing laboriously to gasp in the sticky air around her. I fanned her gently, and Thatha sat by her side mopping her hot brow with a towel soaked in cool water and ice that had been stolen from the dinner party.

Lakshmi Akka and Saravana Anna reappeared when they had washed and cleaned up the house, it was well past midnight. Lakshmi Akka, taking one look at Chinna, gathered her up in her arms and strode out towards the front gate. Saravana Anna ran ahead of her to get an auto and they disappeared down the little lane carrying their daughter to what was hopefully help and sympathy.

I went to bed, having washed the sheets, and laid down on the damp sheets to get some relief from the heat. Thatha stroked my hair gently and told me not to worry and went to his little room to rest. But I did worry. The image of Chinna's pretty little chubby face, twisted in pain, her eyes wild and unseeing kept coming back to me. I prayed again, to my invisible goddess, to make her better soon, and I promised her that if Chinna would get better quickly I would never think a bad thought about Akhila ever again. I finally fell into a deep and exhausted sleep, even though I tried to stay awake to hear the sounds of them returning. But I heard nothing, not even the sound of the monsoon breaking sending down sheet upon sheet of torrential rain to the accompaniment of thunder and lightning.

I woke up to the deluge. Rushing out, I ran into the next room, but it was empty and silent. And then I heard it. The most awful keening that seemed to pierce my very soul. It seemed to come from the direction of the house and I ran dishevelled to the kitchen. The scene that met my eyes ripped my heart into a thousand pieces. Lakshmi Akka sat on the steps of the veranda rocking back and forth, wailing, a high-pitched sound that was being dragged out from the deepest part of her. Saravana Anna stood beside her, his expression blank, his head shaking from side to side, his hands twitching violently, and Thatha sat beside Lakshmi Akka staring at the old guava tree in silent sorrow. Mr. and Mrs. Srinivasan stood there together, awkwardly, and silently … and I knew. I knew Chinna had not survived and her absence was suddenly larger than the little life she had led. I let out a muffled sob, and rushed to Lakshmi Akka and fell to my knees next to her. She clutched me in blind agony and together we wept for the loving little soul that had brought us so much joy and had been ripped away from us without warning.

In the midst of this, Mrs. Srinivasan's voice cut through, "Madhuri, there's no need to make a bad situation worse. Go and start breakfast."

She then addressed the grieving parents. "Please make arrangements for Chinna's funeral. We will pay for it, of course."

And as if her duty was done she turned on her heel and went back into the house and all its luxurious trappings. Mr. Srinivasan paused for a second, and then he too followed his wife.

I made breakfast and served it to them, while the others went back to the hospital to organise the funeral. A priest was called, and Chinna was brought back home and then carried off the cremation ground dressed in finery. From Thatha I learned that Chinna had died of something called meningitis, and that had she got to a hospital earlier she could have been saved. He was bitter in his words and tone, "She died so these rich people would have their party. I hope God forgives them for murdering that poor child," he said putting a flower on Chinna's still form, his shoulders shaking from the muffled sobs that were emanating from his spare frame. I refused to look at the body. I could not bear to see Chinna still and silent and cold. I turned away as they carried her body off, and I went back to the kitchen and continued my duties like a machine. Lakshmi Akka stayed in her room and refused to see anybody. Saravan Anna got a day to grieve and then had to return to work. And Thatha and I, between us, managed to do all the work in order to give her some time to rest and recuperate. A week passed and the sadness we all felt became over-powering, and Lakshmi Akka refused to leave her room and we had to force her to eat a little. It seemed with Chinna's passing that the life had gone out of our little family unit and the gap she had left in our hearts would never be filled. My memories of Kalpa came flooding back and this new grief only compounded the old. Whoever said practice made perfect had clearly never experienced sorrow.

Mrs. Srinivasan eventually got tired of this disruption to her household. She came striding out to the back, to our rooms and entering Lakshmi Akka's room brusquely told her that she needed to pull herself together and return to work.

Lakshmi Akka turned to look at her gravely and said quietly, "Amma, you have a daughter too," and continued to stare steadily at her, her eyes bright with unshed tears.

Mrs. Srinivasan paled slightly at this, and then pulling herself up to her full height said curtly, "Of course I understand, but how long will you stay sitting here like this? It's time to get things back to normal."

And it seemed with those words she finally had placed the last straw on Lakshmi Akka's back.

"Nothing will ever be normal again for me, Amma. I am leaving this house, this work, and this terrible place that took away my only child. You took away my daughter, Amma. You could have called a doctor, you could have let us go to the hospital, but your dinner party was more important. I cannot work here any longer … I don't want to."

And with that she got up and turning her back on Mrs. Srinivasan she began to put away her few possessions into a battered old suitcase. Mrs. Srinivasan stared at her amazement, and then shrilly told her, "You can't leave just like that. You're overreacting. We did nothing wrong, and you're just upset because your daughter has passed away. Don't take it out on us."

But there was no point, and for all her bluster and Mr. Srinivasan's gruff rationalisations later that evening, Saravana Anna and Lakshmi Akka packed their bags, carefully putting away Chinna's things in a plastic bag, and the next morning they were gone.

Lakshmi Akka came to me early that morning and said goodbye. I was too stunned by all to react, and I nodded mutely at her as she told me they were returning to their village and would be living with her mother for some time. She pressed a little package into my hands as she was going and said, "This is for you. I no longer have a daughter, but I know you will someday get married. I was saving this for Chinna, but I want you to have it. Wear it the day you get married and think of Chinna and me. I nodded silently, my heart filling with pain and confusion again, for now I was to bear the loss not only of Chinna, but also this bustling, generous woman who had been the closest thing to family I had experienced in a very long time. She put her hand on my head, a gesture of blessing and I bent my head silently receiving it with gratitude and sorrow. She then told me softly, "Madhuri, be careful of Mr. Srinivasan. He will try to be very kind to you, and you must not let him. Stay far away from him, and keep out of his sight as much as possible." My head jerked up, and I looked at her questioningly, and for some reason the memory of his searching gaze on me swam into the forefront of my memory. I nodded, not entirely understanding, but realising that I had to grow up, and quickly, and that Mr. Srinivasan was a threat to my peace and security somehow. Lakshmi Akka looked at me for a few minutes, and then she rose up and left, and I watched her go out the door, a sad figure, and considerably less plump than two weeks ago. I watched her and Saravana Anna walk down the little side path taking with them their meagre possessions, the joy they had brought me and the dreams for their dead daughter who might have been a doctor someday.

PART II

Chapter Twelve
THE OTHER LIFE

What can I say of my life now?

I am grown up, a woman, with a husband and two children of my own, both a mere three years apart. I actually have three children, but I am not allowed to talk about that child for she is not mine anymore.

I could tell you about my wedding, but that should really come later in this story. Let me start with my time with the Srinivasans after Chinna died. Lakshmi Akka and her husband were never heard from again, and for a few months Thatha and I laboured over the cleaning of the house while everyone scoured around for a replacement for Lakshmi Akka, a task that was quite difficult. An old woman came for three days, but was found pilfering rations and promptly thrown out. Another couple came with two young boys but between the noise of the boys which Mrs. Srinivasan objected to, and the work for the parties which the couple found too onerous, their time in this grand house did not exceed a month.

Akhila, in the meantime, was sent away to a famous boarding school in some mountainous region. She proudly showed me the pictures of it before she left – imposing red brick buildings set amidst beautiful lawns and thick forests - a far cry from any educational establishment that I or Chinna had ever attended. Mrs. Srinivasan went to leave her in the new school, and that weekend, it was just Mr. Srinivasan, Thatha and myself in the big house. I cooked all the food and served it and that was the first time it happened. As I was serving the rice at the table, Mr. Srinivasan put his hand on my back and stroked it gently, and told me the food was very nice. I had never had a man touch me this familiarly, and I almost dropped the plate of rice I was carrying. I nodded quickly and politely and scurried away into the kitchen, and as I was washing up, Mr. Srinivasan came into the kitchen and stood very close to me. I tried moving away but he kept edging closer and closer and the large kitchen began to feel uncomfortably small.

In a soft voice, I told him I needed Thatha for something, and ducking under his arm I scurried off down the side path to find Thatha and get away from Mr. Srinivasan. Luckily he did not follow and that evening he was out. But the same thing happened at breakfast the next day, and this time he reached out to run his fingers down my wrist and hands. It felt like insects crawling over me, and for the first time I dropped a glass and it broke into sharp fragments. Whispering an apology, I ran back to fetch a broom to sweep up the pieces, and as I bent down I could feel his eyes boring into me.

Later that morning I told Thatha what had happened, and his eyes widened in shock. "Go to your room and stay there. Don't come out," he said, snapping at me in the most uncharacteristic manner. I scurried away hurt and upset at being scolded for this, and unsure of what was happening. Thatha went to Mr. Srinivasan and said I was very ill and vomiting and would need a couple of days to recover, and I stayed indoors and locked the room from inside to make sure only Thatha could come in. A fear had gripped my heart, far more basic than the fear that had held me in its sway at Anni Ashram. This was a basic fear, that of an animal that is cornered and is facing its own extinction, and I kept reliving Mr. Srinivasan's touch on my hand over and over again. I had no idea what his intentions were or why it felt so horrible, but some deep-seated feminine instinct told me it was all terribly wrong. I played over Lakshmi Akka's warning several times, and wished I had asked more questions. That evening Thatha brought me food in my room – it had been ordered from outside -- and I ate it voraciously as the stress of it all had made me ravenous.

And the next morning I had an unexpected visitor. I had not seen her in over a year, and once again it took me a minute or two to recognise her. She was even more bent and grey-haired than then the last time I saw her, and deep lines ran across her forehead and down her cheeks, marking a difficult life, spent in want. Thatha brought her around to my room and when I recognised her I could not bring myself to smile or greet her. The anger at what she had done to me repeatedly still burned in me and came to the fore again, and I glared at her in rage.

She nodded at me tersely, and told me to pack my things. I stared at her in shock, and wondered what she was going to do with me next. But years of conditioning and being dutiful stayed my tongue and I quietly began to put my things away into plastic carry bags. Thatha was waiting by the veranda when we emerged and I walked slowly towards him, carrying the bags in one hand, and clutching Chinna's old school bag with its tattered books in the other. As I approached him, he smiled at me sadly, and I put down the things I was carrying and knelt down to touch his feet.

"My daughter, I told Suresh to call your mother and take you away from this house before something bad happened to you," he said, gently. "Please be careful and look after yourself."

I wanted to cry but I couldn't. I knew I would never see him again and once again the changes in my life were sudden and not of my choosing. But I knew this was how life was by then, and I nodded mutely and quietly picked up my things and walked away with my mother out of those richly painted gates and away from the only real family I had ever known.

In later years I came to associate auto rides with my mother, and I must confess I never liked getting into one. This time we travelled to a collection of ramshackle buildings, and my mother got out and paid the driver. She silently bade me follow her and so I trailed after her through narrow, dusty, unpaved streets along which ran mud and crude cement buildings each one seeming to hunch and crouch over the other. It was incredibly dirty and crowded and filled with garbage and litter everywhere. Having experienced the peace and calm and finery of the Srinivasans' house, this was an assault on my senses, the stench and noise overwhelming me.

After what seemed like a very long walk past screaming children and women hanging washing up, and cooking outdoors on fires, and men hanging around smoking beedis, we arrived outside a crude. blue-painted dwelling. The brown iron door was rusting over, and loosely bolted. My mother unbolted this, and I followed her into the dark little room that lay inside. A single cot and a table lay to one side, and a small, upraised partition held two worn, plastic buckets and a mug. The table had an old-fashioned stove like those I had seen in Anni Ashram, and a few utensils stood around it, bent and twisted from age and use.

I put my bags on the cot and sat down on the edge with a thump.

My mother finally spoke to me, after she had finished washing her face from the buckets.

"You'll live here for some time now. There is no need for you to work." I could only shake my head in bewilderment, wondering what the future held for me.

"This house belongs to Kavitha Akka, a lady who works with me in the hospital as a senior ayah. She has two daughters and three sons. She will let us stay for a few weeks until we decide what to do with you."

I digested this information, and I asked her timidly, "Why did you take me away from that house?"

She answered tersely. "You are old enough to be married and we cannot risk anything, because then no one will marry you and you will end up on the streets."

I was surprised at this, and only vaguely understood what she was talking about … and settled back a little into the hard bed.

My mother left to go outside and told me to stay indoors and not let anyone except herself inside. "I'm going to see Kavitha Akka now," she said as she shut the door behind her.

I bolted the door from inside and slowly shook out my things. The pavadai from Madam Nalini's wedding, now too small for me, the beige sleeping salwar, and the pretty blue saree, my slippers, and the gold and bead necklace. I had also taken the little cotton towels and soap, toothpaste and toothbrush, and I laid all these out on the cot, caressing them and revelling in the familiarity. If the ache for Lakshmi Akka or the pain over Chinna or homesickness for Thatha started to encroach, I firmly pushed it back and concentrated on folding my possessions and then putting them back in the plastic bags. I drew out the pouch that Lakshmi Akka had given and lovingly caressed the gold bangle Lakshmi Akka had so generously given me. I had never worn it and was saving it up for my wedding as Lakshmi Akka had suggested. But looking at these treasures brought tears to my eyes, so I swiftly put them back in the red pouch they had been in and opened Chinna's school bag instead. I took out her English reading book and, ran my fingers down the lines, trying to remember what I had been taught. It wasn't easy, but it kept my mind busy and I studied the printed words by the light that came filtering through the latticed window on the far corner opposite the door. When I grew tired of this, I lay back on the cot, and using my clothing as a pillow, I looked up at the latticework watching the rays of sunshine stream in on narrow beams that were interrupted by dust motes that span and circled each other as if they were doing a lazy dance to music only they could hear. I must have fallen asleep because I awoke to the sound of banging on the door. I got up with a start, disoriented and wondering where I was and if I was dreaming, and then it all came back to me.

I leaped off the bed and went to the door and asked in a loud and nervous whisper, "Who is it?"

My mother's voice came back to me telling me to open the door. I slid back the bolt and my mother pushed the door open.

Bright sunlight flooded through the door and my mother was momentarily just a dark silhouette outlined in the door frame. Behind her a taller, fatter woman stood and she followed my mother in, and they came to stand before me looking at me searchingly.

"She's very small," she said accusingly. "And very dark." All my grandchildren will be dark."

I looked at her in some confusion, and then looked at my mother who just nodded her head at me and answered the lady in a surly voice, "She is hard-working and young enough to have many children. She has already worked in a big house and will easily find work and help with the family income."

The lady nodded disbelievingly, and I could already tell she did not like the look of me, and frankly I did not like the look of her. She reminded me of Madam Shanthi and I shrank away from her back towards the cot.

"Okay, I will talk to Selvam and see what he says. Take a picture of her by tomorrow, and we will show it to him." And saying goodbye to my mother she left without so much as looking at me again.

I had no idea what was happening, and what this conversation between this woman and my mother was all about. My mother in her usual silent way told me nothing, and her expression was worried and she looked unwell, so I forbore from asking her anything. After the lady left, I later learned this was Kavitha Akka. My mother told me this lady worked with her in the hospital as a housekeeping supervisor, and then she asked me if I needed the bathroom. I did – desperately. We left the cramped, stiflingly hot little room and wandered down the narrow alley till we came to some evil-smelling buildings. My mother asked me if I wanted to use the toilet and, even though I did, I shuddered at going onto the disgusting-looking building. But the call of nature was louder than the voice of my sensibilities and gathering up my courage and holding my breath I went into the dirty, smelly toilets and came out as fast I could. I was later surprised at how quickly I got used to this misery and used it every day for myself and my children without even thinking about it. After my mother had finished using the bathroom, we walked together to a couple of food vendors and she bought us some samosas and idlis, and we ate this from the plastic cup they had been served in, sitting on a wall near the food carts, side-by-side, in absolute silence. Behind us was a small field where grass struggled to grow in brave defiance to the dust and heat, and where a group of small boys were shouting and playing cricket. They seemed cheerful and happy, and looking at them the unbidden thought came to me – a hope that my children, if I ever had any, -- would be boys; girls' lives were just very difficult and I knew I would not want my daughter to endure my fate.

We went back to the room and going inside we lay down on the cot and my mother soon went to sleep. I stayed awake remembering random details from my life ... snapshots from the photo album of my life, pictures I had stored away to recall at moments such as these. I recalled my first day at Anni Ashram and the twisted children there. I remembered Ramu the cook and his short temper; I smiled as I remembered how shocked I had been by Madam Judith's short skirts and how commonplace they now seemed after seeing Akhila run around in gay dresses and skirts. I recalled Revathi's bullying and what I had seen between her and Madam Shanthi's office, and I lingered on that thought awhile, still trying to make some sense of it. I mostly remembered drawing patterns in the sand with Kalpa and our dreams for a seaside home, untroubled by the external world. I wondered where Radhi was when I remembered Chinna, and made a mental note to myself to ask my mother where she and my brothers were as I was suddenly seized with the urge to see them.

The little house was falling into darkness quickly as the sun shed the last of its light on this collection of humble homes, and as the voices of the city got louder in the darkness I felt myself give way to the bliss of ignorant sleep and nodded off, wondering about this new chapter in my life.

I awoke early the next morning while my mother continued to gently snore. I got up and opening the door as silently as I could, I made my way to the public toilets at the far end of this dilapidated colony. There was a long line of people waiting and I stood waiting in the queue till it was my turn to go. It was as dirty as I remembered from the previous night and as I was going back to the room, I dragged my chappals in the sand to try and get the wet and sticky sensation off them. My mother was awake and glared at me angrily, demanding to know where I had gone.

"I needed to use the toilet," I said meekly.

She gave me a smack around the side of my head and harshly said, "Tell me before you go out. Now wash up and wear your best clothes and comb your hair neatly. We have to take a photograph of you."

And with this exciting piece of news she departed from the room and I locked myself inside.

In the small, upraised corner, I fished water out of the bucket and poured it over myself sparingly, and then having wiped myself dry, I unplaited, combed and replaited my hair and put on the pretty blue saree. I put the gold and bead necklace on and even though I had no mirror, I knew I looked quite elegant and grown-up. My mother returned a few minutes later and I was gratified to see her look amazed at my appearance. She handed me a small strand of orange flowers to put through my hair, and thus attired we headed out into the heat of the Chennai morning.

We walked for what seemed like an age, and I took in the sights and sounds around me. The colony was enormous and stretched on forever it seemed. But we eventually came to a busy main road where buses and cars and autos and scooters belched out smoke at passers-by and blared their horns as loudly as they could to be on their way as fast as possible. Huge glass and steel buildings rose up on either side like giant sentinels guarding the road. My mother eventually went off a side-street which was lined with smaller stores and went into one with pictures of babies on the front window. We took my photo there, an elaborate affair, where I had to sit on a stool and pose in absolute stillness while the small, bald man who was the photographer ran around adjusting big silver umbrellas around me and flooding the room with massive lights, bigger than any I had ever seen before. After my picture was taken, my mother and I walked to a bus stop and took a bus to a temple. This was my first visit to a proper temple. Growing up in Thousand Lights we had only had the little picture of the goddess at home where we offered prayers. In Anni Ashram we were led in prayers in front of the little shrine in the compound by Madam Shanthi, and in the Srinivasans' house the elaborate cupboard which was the puja room, with its glittering gods and goddesses, were the closest I had come to divine instruction.

The temple was spectacularly beautiful. There was a massive pond next to its gaily painted exterior and going in we paid our respects to the deities and I prayed that my future would be a happy one, without the Akhilas or Revathis of this world crossing my path, even though I knew this was a futile prayer. We left to walk around the nearby market, which I recognised as being the same one that Lakshmi Akka had taken me to and it thrilled my soul to have been able to come back to it. My mother led me to a small shop where a man sat surrounded by colourful idols and figurines and some calendars and old textbooks. He was alone and walking up to him she nervously told him she needed to get my horoscope done. This came as yet another surprise, but for now I said nothing and sat nervously in front of this frowning, angry-looking man as my mother gave him my details. This was how I learned I was born on April 3rd and I was 17 years old.

The man told us to come back the following afternoon and so my mother and I left, and we returned to the little room having bought some more food from a vendor which we ate in the room. We slept again that afternoon, and in the evening Kavitha Akka was back, this time bringing with her a younger woman, just a few years older than me it seemed. She looked at me speculatively and I learned over the course of the conversation that her name was Janaki. I learned about her troubled marriage and how she could not have children and how her in-laws were harassing her, demanding she produce a child and heir for their only son whom she was married to. It occurred to me then to wonder why her childless state was solely her fault, for surely her husband must have some culpability for this too, but I was soon learning that I lived in a man's world where every blame could be laid at the feet of a woman. I felt sorry for Janaki at that moment, but if I had known then what was planned for me, I would not have spared this emotion on her.

They chatted for a long time, and every now and then stopped to ask me questions about what I could cook and what I had learned to do in the Srinivasans' house. It was a fairly entertaining evening except that I could not get rid of the niggling feeling that something about all of this wasn't quite right. There was something about the way Kavitha Akka and Janaki kept glancing at me that made me feel something was up that they weren't telling me about, and I later asked my mother about this, as we ate the dosas and chutney that our visitors had brought for us.

She nodded her head at me disapprovingly, and firmly told me to keep my curiosity in check. "There's no need for you to ask so many questions. When I was your age I only spoke when I was spoken to. You have been spoilt by your time away," she bit out curtly.

My next question was going to be about my sister and brothers but, at that I shut my mouth and obeyed her instructions, and lay down quietly next to her to sleep. But sleep eluded me that night as I was used to working hard and the lack of manual labour had made me restless. I lay tossing and turning in the heat, wide-awake, curious about what was happening around me and bored by the lack of any real activity. I finally fell into a fitful sleep and woke up to find my mother had beaten me to the trip to the toilet. I waited for her to return and then ambled across and back, dragging my feet wishing I was back in my little room with Chinna and Lakshmi Akka, feeling their loss even more keenly than usual, missing the familiarity of people who had treated me as an equal and who had extended a very real friendship and kindness to me.

We spent that morning picking up my horoscope and collecting my picture, I wasn't that interested in the horoscope but my own photograph fascinated me. I stared at the little shiny sheets of paper – I was sitting in one and standing in the other -- and the blue saree glowed against the pale background of the studio. I looked at myself over and over admiring the way my eyes were shining and entranced by the hint of the smile on my face, but my vanity did not last long in the face of my mother's irritation with it. She snatched the pictures back and stuffed them back into the crisp white envelope they had come in and walked away at a quick trot. I followed her, equally annoyed at having my pictures taken away from me.

We ate a hurried meal by the food carts again, and sitting on the wall I turned around to watch the young boys playing cricket. The sight made me wonder about Senthil and Mani again, and I turned to ask my mother about them.

"They're still working in the garage and living in a small house," she said proudly. "Mani has now even become a supervisor. They are earning well. I will get Senthil married next year if we can find bigger accommodation for them."

I was taken aback a little; I had last seen them as young boys and now suddenly we were talking about their weddings and it all seemed very strange. For a moment I had a sudden burst of nostalgia, for that little house at the top of the stairs in Thousand Lights, when the worst thing that could have happened to me was being sent out to the little grocery store more than twice a day. I realised I could not really remember my father's face either, and all that remained was a memory of the smell of beedis and hair oil and a remembrance of the vest that he wore. His face was indistinct, and I sat there in the humid heat on the wall trying to remember as much as I could from that time but could not. Unbidden, the vegetable seller's wife leaped into my mind with startling clarity and I was suddenly filled with an anger against her, my mother, my life, and this whole city that was carved up into the rich and poor in the most unfair way. I looked down at my feet, and seeing my black and gold slippers, I felt a bit better; after all a world that held people like Thatha could not be that bad.

We went back to the little room which felt like a furnace every afternoon, thanks to its asbestos sheeting and crude cement walls. We slept a few hours, having stayed in complete silence till we fell asleep. Flies buzzed in through the latticed window and the annoying humming finally lulled me into a state of half sleep.

That evening we had Kavitha Akka and Janaki visit again. My mother greeted them deferentially and sent me out to buy a few glasses of tea and a plate of onion bhajis from the tea-seller nearby. I came back and found my mother smiling in her tight-lipped, humourless way, while the other two ladies looked me up and down like I was a piece of merchandise they were assessing. And I was right. In the time it had taken me to get tea and come back, my horoscope and photographs had been given to Kavitha Akka and Kalyani, and they were deep in the transactions involving my marriage to Kavitha Akka's son, Selvam.

I learned the truth from Kavitha Akka who looked me over and brusquely and unsmilingly revealed their plans for me.

"So you will become my daughter-in-law and marry Selvam. It's a pity you are not fair, as he wanted a fair wife, but you will be useful in other ways and your mother has promised us that you are an obedient, dutiful girl. Which is why we are not going to take a dowry, but at least your mother will provide a mattress and cooker and utensils for this house where you can live with him."

She delivered the information as if she was doing me a big favour and the shock of the announcement stilled my tongue. I had always known I would get married, but the suddenness and speed with which events were transpiring threw even a seasoned warrior of life like me.

As my head jerked up in shock, she continued, "Of course, we will show Selvam your picture and if he approves and the horoscopes match, we will go ahead with the wedding."

I shook my head silently, and they mistook my disbelief for assent, for Kalyani said bitingly, "I hope she can produce boys, because I want a son."

While I was trying to make sense of this cryptic sentence, they got up to leave and my mother ushered them out of the door, and then turned around to face me. The look on my face must have warned her, for she held her hand up and firmly said to me, "This is a good match, they are asking for no dowry as long as you can have children." This was a little confusing, but I knew from my talks with Lakshmi Akka and the girls at Anni Ashram that a woman was expected to produce as many sons as possible to prove her worth, and this I understood only too well – who would want a girl? I mean, look at my life. I had so many questions, but my mother, as usual, was unwilling to part with even the slightest information, even one as life-altering as this. I did not question it further. I knew in my heart and from all I had learned with my limited contact with the outside world that women were supposed to do as they were told, speak little and demand nothing. So I held my tongue and hoped for an explanation and some clarity and prayed that it would come soon.

Two hot and monotonous days later, during which I mostly stayed listless and restless in turns, and slightly feverish from boredom, Kavitha Akka and Kalyani returned smiling and jubilant. They bore, in their hands, packages, and as soon as my mother saw the air of happiness about them, she too smiled more than I had ever seen before. Selvam had seen my pictures, and the match had been approved. Neighbours in the colony were informed, and people crowded around the little house and into it, to stare at me curiously. Most people knew Kalyani Akka, though now I was to call her Amma, as she owned two houses, as well as this little one-roomed affair and was known to be quite prosperous. This impressed me very much until I discovered that everyone in the colony knew everyone and everyone else's secrets and failings were everyone else's amusement and business. There were many remarks of how dark I was, and I overheard most of them, but a lifetime of hearing this sort of talk had inured me to it. I sat there in shock mostly wondering what Selvam was, and how he looked, and if anyone would show me a picture of him. I guessed from that fact that Kalyani called him 'anna' that he was older than her and I desperately hoped that he was not an old man. In Anni Ashram all the girls had stories of young girls who were married to elderly men, who became widowed before they were barely out of their teens themselves.

I sat quietly until the hubbub died down and the neighbours melted back into their own lives and hovels. Finally, Kalyani and Amma left too, having discussed some of the arrangements with my mother, and we were both left in the harsh light of the one naked bulb in the room. As my mother turned around and shut the door, she looked at me and saw the thousand questions in my eyes.

"You know you have to get married. You know I have no money. I know Kavitha Akka, and she has two sons. You will marry the younger one, Selvam. He works as a security guard in a big building and they will give you this house to live in," she said gesturing at the dank, dark, overheated room we were in, "so you're very lucky. He's only 24 years old." she added, looking quite pleased. "The only thing is, Kalyani's problems. She paused for a minute and then continued in a slightly gruffer tone. "Kalyani cannot have children. So you will give some of your children to her for her to raise as her child or else her in-laws will send her home in disgrace."

The news hit me like a bolt of monsoon lightning. A few days ago I was cleaning a huge mansion and making rasam for Mr. Srinivasan, and here I was, about to me married to a stranger whose face I had not seen, on the promise that in lieu of dowry I would become the baby-making machine for the whole family and gift away my children without demur to my sister-in-law.

Chapter Thirteen
THE MARRIAGE

And that was how I came to be married.

Within a month of my mother and Kavitha Akka -- no, Amma -- deciding the logistics of the marriage, I found myself in a deep maroon and gold saree, with a massive flower garland around my neck, and new slippers and a new pair of gold earrings provided by my mother, sweating into my gilt-edged blouse in the heat of the Chennai summer. The ceremony itself was not grand. A small, gaily coloured tent had been put up in a nearby field, and in this a fire was lit, and while a priest chanted prayers and verses, I married a complete stranger. I saw his face for the first time when we fed each other sweets after the ceremony. He was a small man, with a pinched face and narrow, closely set eyes. His moustache hung over his mouth like a caterpillar and his hair was slick, and oiled back, while about him hung the unmistakable aroma of stale alcohol. I looked away quickly, deeply disappointed in my first glance at this frail, sly-looking man. Any girlish, unformed dreams of romance that I may have had died instantly, and I knew that if I thought that life had been tough before, it would be even worse now. Unbidden thoughts of Mr. Srinivasan came to my mind, and I wished I had stayed back to suffer whatever fate that house might have held for me. But now it was too late, and I was a married woman, expected to conform to my new fate.

The only high point of my day was seeing my brothers and sister. They arrived at the little room the morning of the wedding and stood around looking about the place nervously and uncertainly. Radhi was a little taller, but I was still a complete stranger to her. She hung on to my mother's hand and stared at me curiously, clutching at her pavadai, pleating the fabric with her free hand in furious, stabbing motions. Mani and Senthil came in after her, and my eyes lit up when I saw them. I would have recognised them anywhere even after all these years. Mani had grown into a worried-looking man who was already losing his hair, and carried himself stiffly. He brought with him his wife – my eyes widened in shock, and then sorrow – and I looked sharply at my mother who shook her head and said matter-of-factly, "You were working."

I held down the anger at this, and smiled politely at Mani's wife who was a tall, severe looking woman, and by the look of her, in an advanced state of pregnancy. She smiled a tight smile at me, and then sat down heavily on the bed, a trickle of sweat on her brow the only indication of the discomfort she was in. Mani ignored her, as did my mother, and it was Senthil who came up to me, and smiled and asked me how I was.

I nodded at him self-consciously, and said, "I am fine. I'm happy to see you all again."

He grinned at me, and said, "You'll see a lot of us. We live in a small house quite near here."

The news made me enormously happy, and I broke out into a massive smile which prompted a sharp response from my mother who told me it was not proper for brides to be happy and laughing. The remark shut me up and I stayed quiet, while everyone fussed around getting cups of tea, remarking on my good fortune and Selvam's good job as a security guard with a reputed building company. A few neighbours popped in to look at me curiously, including Prema, the local fish-seller. She had the two-roomed hut next to my shack, and sold her fish just outside. The smell hung over the little lane like a foul-smelling canopy, and she herself reeked of stale fish and sweat, but it seemed she was unaware of the aroma she exuded. She was a hearty, loud and argumentative woman whom I was wary of.

But all the same she had become someone familiar, popping into the hut regularly to dispense fried fish and unsolicited advice. Today, she burst in cheerily, wagging her hands at my finery, and something about her reminded me of Lakshmi Akka, and then I remembered … I bent down and, reaching under for my things, I pulled out the plastic bag which held all the things from my days at the Srinivasans. I finally found the little pouch and opening it, pulled out the gold and bead necklace and put it around my neck. And then I gingerly opened the pouch I had been given by Lakshmi Akka for my wedding day, aware that everyone was watching me. Inside was a thin gold bangle with beautiful carvings – the start of the dowry that Lakshmi Akka had been saving for Chinna. I pulled it on where it settled with my glass bangles bought for my wedding, and I could sense my mother's curiosity as to how I had acquired this fine piece of jewellery. I refused to look at her, and swirled the bangle around my hand watching as the sunlight caught at it as it came though the cement grill window. This beautiful gift and the love that went with it comforted me on my wedding day, and clutching the memory of those few friends I went to the ceremony a little more cheered.

Mani and Senthil led the way, and my mother and Radhi and some neighbours walked with me to the tent, and escorted me to the little dais. Everyone, but myself, seemed merry and happy, and looking forward to the celebration, and I supposed this was how it was at every wedding. Even Madam Nalini did not seem excited at her wedding, but looked stern and grim, I recalled. I tried to remember every detail of her wedding and in doing so realised how shabby my own was, but somehow it seemed fitting to me that my wedding be a down-at-heel affair with no grand revelries to mark the occasion.

The wedding tent was hot and stuffy and at one end a huge table was laid with benches around it. People came and went having gorged down massive plates of biryani and raitha, and through it all I felt like an animal on display. I could hear the whispered comments about how my skin colour would affect any children I would produce, and I gritted my teeth and tried to quell the nausea that the smell of alcohol from Selvam was producing. We received a few gifts which were collected by my mother-in-law, and that I never saw again, but for the moment I did not care. All I wanted was to rest and get away from the heat, and from Selvam, and from this hot tent and the noise and crowd, and the smell of biryani that enveloped us in a rich and sticky scent. But I had to stay, and so I stayed and smiled politely at everyone who came to bless my union with Selvam, and tried not to scream out loud at this new turn of events in my life. The evening dragged on, and through the tent door I saw the moon rise into the sky as if it too wanted to get away from this cruel world. And then it was finally over and I was allowed to go back to the one-roomed shack that was to be the home that I would share with Selvam and that would be my home for the rest of my life.

And my home … it was a far cry from the beach shack I and Kalpa had dreamed of. But between my mother and Amma a few comforts had been added. We had two new shiny buckets and mugs, a kerosene stove, a radio, a small table fan, and some pots and pans for cooking. A thin mattress and two pillows covered the iron bed, and mosquito netting had been placed over the grilled window. I myself had three new sarees and petticoats and blouses and three new nighties -- my worldly wealth had definitely increased, but in contrast my happiness decreased with each day of married life with Selvam. I did not realise it at the time, but my mother, the woman I had no love left for, had worked hard to provide for me, but I only learned this when I was expecting my first child. For now, I had to be content with Selvam who owned me body, mind and soul, and every day was worse than the next.

Life with him was a misery from the word go. He drank all the time, and I never knew when he was going to be a happy drunk or a sullen one. We barely exchanged a word, and the most communication we had was when I had to ask him for money to buy groceries. Luckily for me he was at duty at the gates of the big building by eight every morning, and returned home late every evening, after a stop at the local Tasmac on his way back. He had a couple of friends from his work who would regularly return with him to our shack, and no matter how late they were, I would have to heat up food and serve them and then wash up. They would eat and then go outside again, while I cleaned and washed up, to drink and mutter about the tough life they had. And I had to admit it was a tough life. I used to walk to the building to give him his lunch every day and saw his daily existence was no better than mine. He stood for long hours in the heat waving in the various expensive-looking cars and their expensive-looking occupants, saluting them as they swept by. He and the other guards were rarely acknowledged and the drivers often shouted at them if the gate was not opened quickly enough. More than myself, he saw the lives of the rich who lived in this grand building, and it was a deep, unspoken wound in him, as it was in all of us, this raw pain that everyone else seemed to have so much while we struggled to get a decent night's sleep with the heat and mosquitoes and noise that surged around our poor lives.

I fell pregnant very soon after my wedding, much to the rejoicing of my in-laws and neighbours. The monsoons had spent their force on the city the last couple of months, and I was certain that the heat and humidity had been the result of my fatigue and nausea. But my mother dropped in one evening after her shift at the hospital – she still worked there - and looking at me critically, said I was looking fatter than usual, and suggested I go see a doctor. She set up the appointment herself, and with Prema in tow, we set off to see a lady doctor who had a small practice nearby and it turned out my mother's instincts were right. I was declared about three months pregnant and the news shook me. I sat there in the doctor's office, and as she examined me, all I could think was I hoped my children would not be born like those I had seen at Anni Ashram. I was terrified that my contact with them would mean their flaws would be carried over to my children, but as with most things, I kept my thoughts to myself, and pretended to smile and be overjoyed at the news.

We returned home, my mother and I quiet, while Prema chattered on about her children and relived her first pregnancy. She told us that her mother-in-law had gifted her a gold necklace because she had produced a son on her first try, and she hoped that I too would have a son, but I barely heard her. All I could think was how we would feed a new child as we barely had enough money to feed ourselves. Prema disappeared into her home, and we went into the shack together. I sat down on the bed and stared blankly at the wall opposite; I knew that children were a natural consequence of marriage, but this had come sooner than I expected.

My mother handed me a cup of water, and I drank it gratefully. "It's a good thing you've become pregnant so soon. Kavitha Akka will be pleased," she said matter-of-factly.

"I don't want this baby," I said suddenly, surprising even myself as I said it.

My mother gave me a sharp slap across my arm and said unfeelingly, "You have no choice. Better to get this over with as quickly as possible. This is your first child. Pray it is a boy. You'll get to keep this one."

And then I remembered the deal that had been struck between my mother and mother-in-law. I was to give away my children to my sister-in-law. And at this point I was glad of it. I told Selvam that evening and he looked at me blankly, and then nodding his head he went out, and returned home late at night, clattering as he fumbled around drunkenly trying to find his way around the cramped quarters. I woke up with a start when he entered, groggy from a pregnancy-induced sleep and the heat. I got up to help him and as I swung my legs down they got in his way and he stumbled and fell with a loud shout. He was up again in a flash and I saw his face lit up by the tube light outside, contorted with rage and liquor, and with another guttural sound of fury, he hit me across the head. Hard.

It caught me unawares and I stared at him in shock, saying nothing. My silence was not an acceptable response and he fell upon me like an animal and rained down blows on my arms and legs and head. I sat still and unmoving, too shocked and horrified to react, and only after he had stopped and flung himself across the bed did I get up. I shuffled across to the buckets which I had filled with water and washed my face with a precious mugful. By the time I had finished this simple task, Selvam was snoring, and I went and laid down on the floor next to the bed and tried to sleep. But I could not, and after about ten minutes the tears came pouring out, and my shoulders shook in a silent weeping that lasted all night. I rose at dawn and went to refill the buckets of water so Selvam could bathe before he left for work. The municipal taps were a fair walk away, close to the communal toilets and I dragged my feet, unwilling to go back to the shack and face my husband. I got back, dragging the heavy buckets wearily, to find him still sleeping and I quietly made breakfast and heated some water for his bath. His alcoholic slumber was a deep one, and I finally went to him and laid my hand on his shoulder and shook him awake as softly as I could, for fear of being hit again.

He woke up with a start and looked at me through bleary eyes.

"It's time for work," I said, almost whispering, fearing his reaction to my waking him up.

He merely grunted in response, and in a few minutes he got up, washed, ate his breakfast and disappeared out the door. I sighed heavily as the door clanged shut behind him and I laid down in the bed and, resting my head, got some much-needed sleep.

It was close to Selvam's lunch time by the time I woke up and I panicked because I had not prepared anything. I went to Prema's house and told her I had fallen asleep and needed to take food to my husband. She smiled sympathetically and told me that pregnancies made women very sleepy, and then packed me some food from her house, and I set off towards the fancy apartment complex that was my husband's place of work. I saw him standing at attention while a man in a purple shirt and black trousers was shouting at him. I knew this man. He lived in the building in one of the flats and he managed all the staff and various concerns of the building. Selvam was looking scared and small, and it gave me a vindictive thrill to see him being berated publicly. I walked up to stand nearby and over-hear what was being said.

"You're useless," the man barked at Selvam. "You come here every day smelling of sweat and alcohol, you sleep on the job, and you speak rudely to everyone. One more complaint and I will fire you, do you understand."

And turning on his heel he strode away into the plush, mar-bled interiors of the building. Smiling inwardly, I walked up to Selvam and handed him his lunch. He glared at me as if it were my fault he had been ticked off and snatched the tiffin carrier out of my hand. I looked down at my feet and tried hard not to smirk at his discomfiture, and saying a namaste to all the other guards who were watching, I turned around and left.

From that day onwards Selvam had no trouble beating me up. In fact, it became a habit. If his clothes were not neatly laid out, or if he was drunk and his friends were not there to divert him, I became an easy target. My life in this tiny hovel became the worst I had known, and even the Anni Ashram seemed like a picnic compared to this miserable existence. My first preg-nancy was difficult as I was nauseous all the way through, and for the first time my mother came through for me, coming on weekends to help me cook and clean. It was during those ses-sions that I learned more about my brothers and sisters. I hadn't seen them since the wedding, and I had often wondered why. Mani and his wife and Senthil shared a small, rented place – my mother proudly called it a two-roomed house. But apparently Mani had been caught stealing money from the garage that he had been placed in all those years ago, and had been summarily dismissed. His pregnant wife in the meantime had delivered a stillborn girl, and my mother harshly said, "It's a good thing they were not saddled with a girl child."

The old, unspoken hurt rose up again at this statement, and I quelled it, focussing instead on the tragedy that had befallen my brother. I asked after Radhi and received a shock when I was told that she was getting married too.

Horrified, I asked my mother why as she was so much younger than me.

"How long can I afford to keep feeding her? I am getting old and she needs to be kept somewhere safe," she responded in her usual flat monotone.

Something inside me burst at this injustice, and maybe my pregnancy gave me courage, I do not know, but I turned on her and hissed furiously, "You sold me to the Anni Ashram and then to be a servant at the Srinivasans, and then you gave me to a man who beats me. Will you do the same to Radhi?"

And as swiftly as my anger rose it fell away at her response.

"You think you've had it hard," she snapped back. "You think it's easy to be responsible for the lives and marriages for four children, without a husband or parents or in-laws to support you? All the money I got from the Ashram and from the Srinivasans, I saved to pay for your wedding. Who do you think paid for the things in this house, or for the wedding feast and the tent. Just because they did not take a real dowry does not mean they took you for free," she snarled. "The money I got as dowry from Mani's wedding paid the deposit on his flat, and for his wedding. All my savings from working in that hospital and cleaning toilets and vomit, that is now being used to get Radhi married. I have not bought anything new for myself since your father died. And you accuse me of selling you?" her voice faded away, and in the dim afternoon light of this stuffy room I could see her shoulders shaking as she busied herself lighting the stove to make some tea.

And in that moment the realisation hit me of how easy my life had been compared to hers, and I understood why she had done what she had done. I looked at her, and getting up slowly – my pregnancy was making things difficult – I went up to her, and asked her to sit down. She obeyed without a word and after a few minutes I handed her a cup of hot tea that she slurped gratefully. We sat together quietly, each of us lost in our own thoughts, and before she left, I reached under the bed and pulled out the bangle that Lakshmi Akka had given me.

"Take this for Radhi's wedding," I said gently.

She looked at me and a small smile appeared on her lined and worn face, and I noticed for the first time that her face and body were that of a bent, old worn-out woman.

"She is getting married in Gobichettipalyam which is where the groom lives. He is a widower as his wife died two years ago, so I will take her there next month. This bangle will help with the expenses," she said.

"Who is this man?" I asked curiously.

"He has his own small farm, and he is 45 years old."

I quaked inwardly, as Radhi was probably just a teenager, and I hoped that this man would be kind to her, but somehow I doubted it. I said nothing more as it was out of my hands, and shrugging I decided to not even think about it. I was due next month, in any case, and I would not be able to attend the wedding, and I doubted that Selvam or his family would allow me to go, in any case.

After my mother left and I had cooked the evening meal, I lay on the bed, my hands over my stomach, wondering whether my baby would be a boy or a girl. I hoped it would be a boy, as it seemed that girls just had a hard life. Not girls like Akhila, of course, I thought, remembering her pretty face and cruel nature with a shudder. But for girls like me, we were the lowest of the low, the most downtrodden, the most vulnerable and the most voiceless the most unseen, and I still could not understand why this was as it was. All I knew was this was the unchangeable truth and so I lay there praying my goddess to give me a son. For no other reason perhaps than a daughter would not be tolerated by Selvam or his family.

Strangely the greatest interest in my pregnancy came from my sister-in-law, Janaki. She was constantly popping around and checking on me, and it seemed to stem from curiosity rather than kindness. I knew that she was childless and as a result had many problems with her in-laws and husband, and at the time I thought she was just interested in the thought of a child coming into her family at least. I had by this time quite forgotten what my mother had told me, and then she said something one hot afternoon that brought back the words to me with shocking clarity. She had come in, sweating profusely and after having enquired about my health sat down waiting to be served her customary cup of tea.

"I hope you have a girl," she remarked pleasantly.

My back was turned to her, and I looked back now at this, and smiled, and said, "Why? Everyone else wants me to have a boy."

"Oh!" she answered evenly, "If it's a girl I will get to keep it. If it's a boy, Selvam will want it. I don't mind having a girl, and I can always have your next son, I suppose."

The cup of tea fell from my hand, and I whipped around in shock, staring at her, the horror showing clearly in every line of my body.

Kalyani looked slightly taken aback, and then her face hardened and she said, "You were told about this. This is why we did not take anything from you. Who would marry a dark-skinned woman like yourself without a big dowry?" Rising up she turned towards the door, saying harshly, "You had better get used to the idea and don't make a fuss as you have no choice." And with that, she was gone, only to return the day I delivered.

Yes, I knew. I had been told by my mother. But it had not registered with me fully until this moment, in my eighth month of pregnancy, feeling heavy and breathless and puffy, as I grew a life inside me, that I would be giving up my child. Feeling it kick inside me made me feel fiercely protective, and I put my hand over my tummy and tried to bite back the rising panic I was starting to feel. I realised anew the pain my mother may have felt when she left me at the Anni Ashram or consigned me to the mercy of the Srinivasans. I felt a surge of pity for her in that moment, one mother to another, but the dominant emotion once again was anger, and I thought that of all the things she had done to me, the others I could excuse, but not this.

One often sees pictures of mothers and children on advertisements and in movies, and I hear that scriptures are full of tales of devoted mothers who selflessly serve their children. I had no experience of this. All I knew from my mother was harshness and distance and cruel decisions, and while I understood she often had no choice, I was angry enough at my life to be unreasonable and uncharitable towards her. For after all, as my mother, was it not up to her to protect me and ensure my happiness? All my mother had done was ensure I had a roof over my head, and food in my mouth, and now feeling my baby move within me, I knew there was far more to motherhood than those basics. I hoped to be able to do better by my child than my mother had done by me. And yes, I prayed and prayed and hoped and wished that my child would be male, just so he would not be subjected to the cruelties that girls become victim to. And in thinking those thoughts, I did not even realise at the time until, years later, one far wiser than me pointed out, that I was becoming part of the problem of girls being unwanted and unloved. All I knew was I wanted the best for my child and the best thing for it would be for it to be a boy.

I went the next day to Prema and told her everything. To my surprise, she said she already knew. She nodded wisely and said, "That is how it is sometimes."

I wasn't quite sure I understood so Prema elaborated, "You are a daughter-in-law. You have to obey your in-laws and your husband and do as they say. If they want your child, give it gladly, or you will have even more trouble with them."

I saw the wisdom in this and tried to mentally prepare for my pregnancy, and the outcome of it if it was a female.

But it wasn't.

Early one morning, I went into labour, and as the pains grew worse, Kalyani and Prema took me to the local Government hospital, where, along with eight other women in the same room, I delivered my first child. And much to Janaki's disappointment, it was a boy.

I looked down at him as the ayah handed the boy to me, wrapped in the shawl Selvam's mother had prepared in advance, the only thoughtful thing she had ever done for me. They all arrived that evening at the hospital. Selvam peeped at his son and grinned sheepishly and disappeared half an hour later to celebrate with his friends. A celebration that would undoubtedly involve copious amounts of alcohol. Amma and my mother were jubilant that it was a boy, and Prema and some other friends from the slum came as well, bringing sweets and garlands and chattering excitedly about the births of their own children. I was exhausted after the long delivery and wanted some peace and quiet, but I knew better than to ask for it. I smiled politely at everyone and nodded affably when they praised me for my cleverness in producing a male heir. My mother-in-law scoffed at that, and said she always knew her son would produce a grandson for her on her first try. I looked at her wonderingly when she said this, resplendent in an orange saree and flowers in her hair, and wondered if she had forgotten the myriad times through my pregnancy that she had warned me not to produce a daughter, much to the annoyance of her own.

I breathed a sigh of relief when everyone was gone, and it was just my mother and myself sitting alone in the ward. The doctor came and checked me and pronounced me fit to return home the next day, and with that he was gone. There were several other women in the ward who had delivered as well. Some seemed jubilant, others less so. And as the evening wore on the congratulatory crowds faded back into their lives and it was just us women in the hospital, nursing our new children who gurgled and cried and moaned at their entry into this unforgiving world. Tired as I was I could not sleep, and I held Shyam, for that was the name given to him by his paternal grandmother,

and counted his toes and fingers and marvelled at his small-
ness and thanked the silent goddess that had given me a perfect,
healthy boy, with no sign of deformity. I looked at the downy
hair on his head and his smooth and perfect skin, his big dark
eyes that looked at me wonderingly and I realised that this was
what love felt like. Where you wanted someone else's happiness
and comfort more than your own. And it did not matter if I
had married a cruel, drunk man who beat me, or that I lived
in a small room where the monsoon's rains trickled through an
asbestos roof, or that I had lost friends to both life and death, or
that I lived in squalor and poverty. No, for this one night all was
perfect, and I was in love with my new baby.

Chapter Fourteen

Love is an amazing thing, and I honestly believe that no woman understands it until he or she has had a child. Shyam became the centre of my world, and hearing him cry even for the smallest thing twisted inside me like a knife in my very soul. I still cooked and cleaned and carried water from miles away, and walked in dust and grime to get to a filthy toilet, but somehow knowing that he was there made the world more radiant. Certainly, it was no picnic when he cried incessantly, or fell ill to stomach bugs, or when he stayed awake all night demanding my attention … and yes, I lost my temper and scolded him … but through it all I adored him and I would not do him harm for anything in the world. All I wanted was to find a way to school and educate him so that he would not grow up like his father, and that he would get a good job and have a happy life. I suppose it is the prayer of every mother. I had hung up a little bed for him from two nails and a suspended piece of fabric and on this he swung merrily, either crying, gurgling or asleep. My mother came to visit, as did Senthil and Mani; Radhi had been dispatched to her husband and his farm and we had not heard from her at all. My mother had tried to telephone the local STD booth where they could receive calls but there was no answer, so we assumed she was safe and that eventually she would get in touch with her family. Senthil and Mani and his wife brought with them baby clothes for Shyam, and when Mani held him I could see in his eyes the longing for a son of his own. His wife refused to carry my son and I could understand her reluctance in light of her recent experiences. Also, I did not want her to touch my child in case her bad luck and ill fortune rubbed off on my precious offspring. I promised to visit them the following week, and with that pleasant family visit I felt even happier.

I had, over the last year, got into a habit of sitting with Prema in her fish stall, to watch her haggle with customers over the price and freshness of her goods. I knew she kept the leftover fish on a big block of ice in her house, to try and sell the next day, and it stopped me from going to her house unless it was strictly necessary. The smell was unbearable but her husband and children did not seem to mind and, in fact, seemed to thrive on growing up surrounded by the smell of two-day old dead fish. She was a wonderful cook, however, and taught me how to make prawn curry, for which I was ever grateful, especially when she gave me a few pieces of leftover prawn from her daily sales. She would watch over Shyam for me, and all the women in the slum lent a hand to each other this way in the raising of children. We would share food, clothes, gift castoff clothes and furniture to each other, and share in the baby-sitting when others had to work. It was a dirty place, smelly and dusty and with barely any resources. Most of us stole electricity from nearby Government poles, and a new television in one home meant the whole neighbourhood could watch. I was warned of leaving my child unattended, of child snatchers who would steal my baby and cut off his hands and make him beg for money, or men who kidnapped and raped and sold young girls into prostitution. I had no idea how dangerous this world was, and over time it dawned on me how safe my mother had actually kept me, and there grew in me a grudging admiration for what she had done, replacing the old anger and hate that had formed during the years we had been apart.

I grew to love the sense of community that prevailed in this shabby little place, where the purchase of a motorcycle was cause for universal excitement, and the birth of a child reason for everyone to rejoice, where deaths were communally mourned, and weddings collectively celebrated, where friendships grew and fights broke out, where everyone pooled resources, if needed, to help out with unexpected expenses. I saw this incredible solidarity for myself when it came to Shyam's naming ceremony, and in later years for other events in my life. And the stench and squalor disappeared in the wake of friendly fights, neighbourhood politics and general camaraderie. For those who don't understand why poor people like me like to remain in this less-than-desirable slum lifestyle, this is why. We grow to love the community. It is our tribe and it protects us from the rest of the world which seems to want for nothing and yet never seems to stop wanting despite that. In our sameness, our poverty, our misery we band together to become one, and that is something the rich may never understand. Of course, we have our own competitiveness, and deceits and lies and vagaries like all humans, but we are united in a way no outsider will ever understand. We protect our young and we look after elderly and we do it side-by-side in a spirit of family and sharing that becomes the very pulse of these neighbourhoods.

One day, the police arrived in our slum searching for a young man who was wanted for theft. When they asked around, we all answered vaguely saying we had seen him a few days ago, and not since, even though we all knew exactly where he was and that he was, in fact, innocent of any crimes he had been accused of. We knew this because we knew him as a young boy who would run errands for us and fetch water and help us do our chores and we knew he was incapable of stealing. So we banded together, and even the mighty police force in their khakhi uniforms and lathis were no match for our combined armies of silence and false information.

The best thing that happened to me was that Selvam, while strutting about like a peacock about producing a son, could not bear to be around him, especially at night when he screamed and cried because of the terrible heat rashes that covered him. So he was gone most days and nights, opting for night shifts at his building, when his work and drinking would be less apparent and he would return to his mother's to sleep during his time off. However, when he drank he always came back to this one-roomed house for his mother had no problem raising her hand and disciplining her son for his drunken adventures. And so, for those evenings and nights, Shyam and I had to endure his cursing and I alone endured his violence.

But on most days I had this room to myself and Shyam and the friendships that were growing around me. So, for the most part I gritted my teeth and bore the beatings as well as I could, and nursed my sprains and bruises with Amrutanjan (pain balm) and ice provided by Prema. She knew, as did others, of the brutality that Selvam subjected me to, and while they all commiserated and felt sorry for me, they could do nothing to stop it. After all, most of them had husbands who got drunk and beat them up, and it was understood that this was just how it was. Men had dominion over women and there was precious little we could do about it. I later learned that this went on in the homes of the rich as well.

Asha, who lived three doors away from me, and who worked as a maid in a big house in Alwarpet, said that the master was always beating his wife and his daughter and there were always fights and upsets, and the lady of the house bore it just as we did. The only difference was she never told her friends and had to pretend that everything was okay and laugh and smile and praise her husband in public. This bit of information made us all feel a bit better about our own lives; at least in our slum we could share this common worry and confide in each other.

So between gossiping and fetching water, and watching my son grow every day and managing my in-laws, I had a full and busy life. My son and friendships provided enough joy to offset the misery of my married life and the harassment of my in-laws. I found some laughter every now and then, and once in a while we all watched TV programmes together. The TV belonged to Priya and her husband; her husband worked in a big factory and they were quite well-off compared to the rest of us. They were also utterly generous in letting all of us watch their black and white TV, so we gathered on many a hot dusty evening crowding into their small little two-roomed house, some of us standing squeezed into the narrow doorway to watch beautiful men and women dancing on screen and lifting us out of the squalid existence we all shared. We all brought around food and sweets and ate and bickered over portions, and most of us went home cheered and happy. Something told me these get-togethers in the slum generated more happiness for us than any pleasure that was experienced by the guests at the magnificent dinners the Srinivasans threw.

That life had faded for me quite completely now. I was so wrapped up in Shyam that the memories of that happy time faded into a deep recess in my memory, except for those rare occasions when I wished I could have shown Thatha my baby son. But the years had taught me well, and now I could block out the unhappy thoughts and focus most resolutely on the present, most of which revolved around avoiding Selvam and worrying about Shyam. Shyam did worry me. The constant mosquito bites and the heat left him with a terrible rash across his little body, and he kept having bouts of diarrhoea that distressed both him and me in equal measure. I told Selvam repeatedly that we needed to do something, but mostly he was too drunk to listen or care. His mother showed more concern, however, and she came over a couple of times, majestically insisting on taking Shyam to the doctor. She was, in her own way, very fond of him, and would come over as often as she could to straddle him on her hip and show him off to anyone who cared enough to listen to her prattle on about how beautiful and smart her grandson was.

"He'll be an engineer," she said, proudly one day, watching him tear apart a plastic mug. It reminded me of Lakshmi Akka's pride in Chinna, and I immediately refreshed the black mark Shyam always wore on his cheek to ward off the evil eye. For all I had gone through in my life, I know I would have died if anything happened to my baby, and my heart went out to Lakshmi Akka for only now I could understand the depth of her grief.

The trips to the doctor brought temporary relief to my son but falling ill was a permanent feature for all children in the slum, and as time went on I started to take it a little more in my stride. I was lucky that Amma was a hands-on grandmother who worked in a hospital, for this was how I learned that my son had to have some injections at regular intervals to protect him from illnesses. She personally came with me and when he was given these shots he cried and wailed for days afterwards. I found it hard to believe that any good could come from such suffering being inflicted on this tiny child of mine, but my mother and mother-in-law both insisted that this was the best way and that the doctors knew best. And so, I once again deferred to them and smiled and agreed to their plans for me and my son. My happiest moments were when he nestled against me at night and went to sleep. I would stay awake rocking him and fanning the flies off him and picturing a future when he would be grown-up and strong and get a good job and look after me; and on these pleasant fantasies I would fall asleep content with my life and the best thing that had ever happened to me.

When Shyam was around a year old, Prema came waddling up to me one afternoon, having pulled the sheet down in front of her smelly shop. She was quite a chubby woman, and as soon as she entered the door my small house filled up with the aroma of fish. I wrinkled my nose at it, and she good-naturedly wagged a plump finger at me, and said in a mock disapproving tone, "You don't mind the smell when I give you fish curry and free prawns," she said, and then grinned.

I knew she was right, so I smiled back wondering what had brought her here in the afternoon.

"I don't have long," she said, "but one of the ladies who buys fish from me came to me this morning, asking if I would be able to help find her neighbour a maid," she said, looking at me questioningly.

I wasn't sure what she meant by this, and why it was relevant to me, so I looked at her in surprise. She tutted at my stupidity, and said, slightly irritably, "You! Would you like to work for them? I think it involves cleaning the house, and watering the garden and washing the utensils. It's only in the mornings so you'll have the rest of the day free."

I digested this information slowly after she left. After all, there were many considerations, such as Shyam's care while I was at work. I would also need Selvam's permission and his mother's, both of which I was unsure of getting. My mother came to see me that evening and I told her about it. She mulled it over and then nodding her head slowly said she thought it was a good idea as long as my husband and mother-in-law agreed. I went to bed that night, wondering if I could get Prema to look after Shyam in the mornings and if Selvam would return home or not that evening. He didn't, so the next day, when I went to drop off his lunch, I told him about the job offer. He was standing with one of his security guard friends, and when I told him he said abruptly, "Why should I be the only one working, while you sit around the house. Yes, go work and try to bring some money into the house, instead of eating and doing nothing all day, like a maharani?" His friend guffawed loudly at this, then walked away to let us continue our conversation.

I wanted to snap back and tell him how hard it was to feed and look after a baby, and walk ages in the hot sun to fetch heavy buckets of water or to bring him his lunch on time every day, or wash his clothes and cook his food… but silence was the best answer when I did not want to provoke him further.

"You are right," I said demurely, looking at my feet, noting his pleased stance as I said that. He was an awful bully and show-off and he liked nothing better than proving his manhood in these petty ways. This pleased him even more, and he grandly said, "Start tomorrow, if you can."

I was thrilled at the outcome of the conversation. That evening Prema and I went to meet the lady she had spoken to and she in turn took us to meet her neighbour. Prema said she was very happy to watch over Shyam for me, especially as she had a little two-year-old girl and thought that the two would be able to play together and keep each other company. It seemed all the cards were falling in my favour. The next morning Prema took me to the house, about twenty minutes away from our slum. We rang the bell, and an old lady appeared at it, with a shock of white hair, wearing a deep brown saree. She had glasses perched at the end of her nose and her mouth and eyes were slits in a hard, bony face and she looked like a cruel taskmaster, I thought. But the house was much smaller than the Srinivasans and the garden was nothing more than a yard with half a dozen potted plants scattered about.

The old lady, whose name I did not have the courage to ask, grilled me for half an hour, and looked most disapproving when I said I was raised in an orphanage, but seemed slightly mollified by the fact that I was married and had a child. I realised then that despite the dreadful man I had married and the less-than-caring in-laws that I had, marriage conferred on me a certain respectability. It was necessary that girls get married as soon as possible to as they were viewed with more courtesy if they had a husband, no matter how poor in quality the husband was. My thoughts slipped to Radhi, and I hoped she too enjoyed this status as a married lady, and I hoped she was happy and safe as we still had not heard from her. My mother was talking about going to her village to check on her and was planning on taking my brother Senthil with her. I got lost in this train of thought and did not hear the rest of the conversation. I was brought back with a sharp nudge from Prema, as the lady was asking me a question and I only caught the tail end of that sentence.

"So after a year, if your work is good we will increase your salary," she said sharply, as if she knew I had not really been listening.

I nodded humbly, and agreed to come to start work the next morning and folding my hands respectfully I bowed my head and left the house with Prema. Luckily for me, Selvam had informed his mother that I was going to start working, and she agreed as he had pronounced that he needed the money I would bring in. She came that evening looking most cross that she had not been consulted in this decision, but after some hemming and hawing, and some suitable politeness and deference from me she nodded her approval as well, and I was free to go out and start earning money for the first time in my life. It was the most exciting thought, and I went to sleep that night, rocking my little boy, and feeling that life was finally turning around for me.

I left Shyam with Prema early that morning, having fetched water and cleaned my own house and trotted off in my freshest saree. Prema put some flowers in my hair and as I walked towards the home of my employers, I noticed things I had not before. I saw the incredible clear blue of the Chennai sky on a clear morning and the gaily painted carts of the food vendors that were parked by the side of the slum. I saw how a few houses had flowers growing in pots outside the door, and saw the women sweeping away the mud and throwing water before their front doors to settle the dust and cool the air. I saw washing hanging out to dry and heard the radios playing out the songs or news from open doors as I passed by. I nodded merrily at those neighbours I knew and told them proudly I was setting off to work. There were a few envious grimaces from some women, but mostly everyone wished me well, and I arrived cheery and happy at my new workplace.

The same old lady answered the door, without a smile and gestured me to follow her. I removed my slippers and followed her through a dark corridor into an even darker kitchen. She switched on a tube light and in the harsh white glare I saw, with dismay, that the sink was piled high with dirty vessels. She showed me the soap bar, and the buckets and the water tap in the small yard behind the kitchen and told me that I had to swab the whole house down every day, and then wash the vessels and clean the kitchen and water all the plants I had seen the day before. I had three hours to accomplish this task, and so I set to work immediately.

It was hard work, and the pile of dirty dishes seemed never-ending. I later learned this lady cooked for her son and daughter and sent them food every day, and in doing so she used up every vessel in the house to cook these meals. She insisted that the vessels be wiped dry as well, and if so much as the tiniest stain of grease remained she would make me wash everything all over again, convinced that I had been careless in everything. She followed my every move, watching me, and berating me as I swept, and peering into corners to make sure there was not the tiniest speck of dust. She complained about how much water I used up to mop the floors, and then complained I had used too much water to water the plants. All in all, she was an angry, grumpy woman, and her husband, older than herself, sat in a chair in the dank living room nodding to himself and watching television and drinking cups of tea all day. It was an unpleasant atmosphere and it did not get better with time. But I stuck to it faithfully for the little money it brought in enabled me to buy decent food for my son, and new clothes for him, and pay for the medicines for his constant rashes and upset stomachs. Earlier I had to ask Selvam or my mother-in-law for the money for these things, but now I could walk into shops and purchase things on my own and it was a good feeling. There was still a little to give to Selvam for his supply of alcohol, and so on the whole everyone was happy. I even managed to give Prema a little sum every now and then, and with that I realised the sweetness of returning generosity from one's own hard work and earnings.

And so life went on and my son grew every day, and started calling me Ma, which was the most beautiful sound I had ever heard, and filled me with love and pride every time I heard it.

I grew smug in my new life, and other than the altercations and violence from Selvam, I managed to carve out enough happiness for me to make the rest of the squalor and dirt and want seem bearable. But I should have known that my new-found happiness would not last. Two things happened that caused my life to spin out of control again, and as usual it was not due to circumstances of my making.

I fell pregnant again. And this time I recognised all the symptoms. I went back to the doctor on my way back from work, on my own and she confirmed it, and with a heavy heart I trudged home, feeling the weight of the world more heavily upon me than ever before. My in-laws had been pestering me for another child, and Kalyani had actually threatened to get Selvam married to someone else if I did not produce a child for her soon enough. And now here it was, inside me, and as I sat down on the bed in the afternoon, after settling Shyam into his makeshift cradle, I put my head down and wept. I wept all afternoon, silently, wondering how to protect this baby inside me and keep it with me, knowing the inevitable outcome of the pregnancy would be to part with this child. I kept the news to myself as long as I could, going to work and tying my saree as loosely as possible to hide my growing belly. But in the slum you cannot keep secrets from each other, and very soon my mother-in-law and Janaki found out. They arrived in the evening, agitated and irate that the news had been kept from them, and Janaki almost pounced on me, shaking my shoulders and crying out that I had tried to rob her.

I sat mute and still and when they left, with threats and warnings that I was to be careful and not lose the baby, or else…

I gathered up Shyam and held him close and tried not to think about the terrible day that was to come. I continued to work right up to the eighth month and then I got too tired and too weary to even walk anymore. When I told my employer I had to quit she shouted at me and accused me of being ungrateful and said she wished she had never laid eyes on me or employed me for I had let her down and failed her despite all her generosity towards me. In truth, the only time she had ever been generous to me was when she gave me an old thermos flask that she was going to throw away. Other than that, she seemed to have begrudged me even the tiny salary she paid me, and the promised raise never happened. I left her employ thankfully as her continual shouting and meanness were impossible to endure, and I pitied the person who would take my place.

And so the last months of my second pregnancy were spent quietly at home, and I sank deeper and deeper into a depression that engulfed me quite completely. I no longer wished to chat with Prema or any of the other ladies, and while they were concerned, they knew the situation and were helpless to help me. I sat clasping my arms around my stomach as if by doing so I would be able to keep my child safe inside me, and only ate when my in-laws came and force fed me to ensure the baby was born healthy. To them I was nothing more than a means to an end, and after a while they started talking about me like I was not even there, mostly accusing me of being uncooperative and a terrible daughter-in-law. I listened to them without retaliating as I knew it was pointless, and when I went into labour I heard them talking about me all the way to the hospital.

The labour was short and quick and easy this time, and the first night I held my beautiful baby daughter was also the last time. I kept her as close as possible, as long as possible, since I knew as soon as I was discharged from this ward with its peeling paint and stench of blood and illness, I would return home to Shyam and have to pretend my girl had died. It was the longest, most painful night of my life, and the next day I went home, broken, hurting, sore in body, mind and spirit. Kalyani triumphantly bore away 'her' daughter to her in-laws and I returned home to my shabby shack and to Shyam and holding him close I shed bitter tears of helplessness, rage and sorrow for my lost daughter.

I stayed indoors mostly, and only went out to fetch water and use the toilet, for I could not bear the pitying glances from everyone around who knew what had happened. No one dared question my mother-in-law or Selvam for their actions, and I alone faced the injustice in solitude and desolation. Prema, bought me food and vegetables and helped me with Shyam, for I did not see my mother-in-law or Kalyani for many months after. My mother visited regularly, and after a few visits she rebuked me sharply and said something that brought me back to my senses.

"Why are you moping about like this? All parents have to give up their daughters at some point. At least yours went to a home where she will be well-fed. Kalyani's husband is well-to-do and she will have a better life than with you and Selvam. You should be grateful for this," she bit out in her usual staccato, abrupt way.

I thought about what she said after she had gone, and for the first time in months I did not cry myself to sleep. I hugged Shyam closer than usual, and he tried to squirm away from me, as it was hot and sticky and he did not want me that close, but eventually he allowed me to hug him tight and we both slept peacefully, mother and son, comforted by each other's presence.

I woke up the next morning and my step was lighter, and I performed my morning chores with a less-heavy heart. Finishing up, I grabbed Shyam and we headed out to Prema's fish stall, who beamed gaily to see us out and about. I smiled at her, and went and sat down on the little stool next to her, the familiar and overpowering smell of fish assaulting me, and drowning out the sadness and suffering of the months before.

And so I learned the bitter lesson once again, that no matter how great the tragedy, life will carry on, and the world will carry on like your tragedy never happened. Prema had continued to sell her fish while I lay indoors too sad to move, her daughter had started school, someone else had bought a new motorcycle, and someone had run away with someone's wife. Life in this slum did not care that my daughter now belonged to my hateful sister-in-law and that my mother-in-law had forgotten that I existed. My husband I had not seen in weeks, and for that mercy, I was most grateful, because in that time since the birth I did not want to have anything to do with him and hoped that he would disappear and leave me and Shyam to figure out our lives for ourselves.

But he did return and of course, I got pregnant again, and my in-laws reappeared in my life like they had never left. The hope was this time I would produce a son for Kalyani, and that evening after they had gone, admonishing me to eat certain foods that would ensure a male child, I went with Shyam to the local temple and offering flowers to the goddess, I begged her to give me a girl, so I would not have to part with another child. This pregnancy was a difficult one, and I had to contend with Janaki's presence over me constantly. Her need for a son made her ruthless in her dealings with me, and she was constantly telling me to lie this way or that, or sit in a certain position, or eat the most revolting concoctions to ensure she got her wish. I acquiesced to everything quietly, and secretly plotted to run away somewhere before my next child was born.

I told Prema of my intentions, and Prema shrugged and said in even tones, "You can't run away. Who will you run to? And you might have another girl."

So I sat quietly through the hot summer months, dreading the monsoons that would bring another child into the world along with the torrential rains. There was a serious water shortage that summer and it seemed that I spent hours waiting by the taps for my turn to fill water. The corporation only supplied water twice a week during those dry, arid months and we had to ration ourselves most carefully. Even the cheerful Prema was cantankerous and snappy, and my mother even more silent and taciturn when she visited. She was very worried about Radhi as we had had no news from her, and she had approached my brothers to help her get to the village she was in. But both Mani and Senthil had grown up into men now, and had their own lives. They made it clear that they did not want to be involved in our lives: an aging mother and a sister who lived in a slum. Mani was a driver in a big house and his wife, still childless, did not like my mother or me. Since Senthil lived with them, he did as they did, and so our little family grew apart to a point where if one of us would have fallen ill, the others would not have known, and if they had known, would not have cared. So my bent and aged mother kept trying to call the phone booth in the village, and finally one day she got through. I was in my ninth month, and ready to burst, and terrified of what was about to happen to me again, when she came to me late one evening and told me she had spoken to someone in the village where Radhi was meant to have been all this time. My mother had been told that Radhi had been badly behaved and had run away from her marital home six months ago and no one knew where she was.

My mother said this quietly, but her voice trembled as she imparted the news, and she and I together went to the police station the next day to register a complaint for a missing person. We had a long wait, and eventually a rude and dismissive policeman with a big stomach and a bigger moustache took our complaint and details and said they would contact us if they found anything. But we knew they wouldn't, and we knew we would never see Radhi again or find out what had really happened to her.

I went into labour the next day, and to my joy delivered a baby girl, a beautiful baby girl with big dark eyes, and downy, dark hair, and the tiniest hands and feet I had ever seen. She was as perfect and beautiful as Shyam, but clearly this was not the opinion of my in-laws, and I heard that when they had been told the sex of the child, their faces had darkened in rage and they had turned around and walked out of the Government hospital, much to my relief. I named her Sandhya, and when I went home, I sat in my room with both my children, and breathed a sigh of relief, and thanked the goddess for granting my request. Unseen as she was, she seemed to occasionally hear my prayers. This child I would get to keep.

My mother-in-law arrived the next week, looking grim and determined, and with my husband in tow. This was unusual and my heart sank. I clutched Sandhya as close to myself as I could and kept Shyam firmly behind me, trying to hide him from their view. My mother-in-law glared at me and got to the point immediately.

"Your next child had better be a boy," she said sternly. "We did not take you in, asking for nothing, to be saddled with a daughter. Kalyani will have her son, and you will bear one for her, do you hear?"

Something in me broke and I spat back at her. "If you keep harassing me, I will go to the police and tell them what you are doing to me," I said, spiritedly.

My mother-in-law stopped in her tracks as if she had been shot. She stared as if she could not believe her ears, and then raising her hand she slapped me so hard that I fell back against the bed. Shyam burst into howls at this, and not to be outdone, Selvam gave a growl of rage and sprang towards me and brought his fist down on my head. I struggled to stay standing and keep Sandhya safe who strangely stayed silent through all of this.

"You'll produce a son," she said venomously, "and once you've done that, we'll see if we still want you around. Just remember this is my house you are living free in." And with that she turned around and stormed out of the room.

I sat down, and suddenly a conversation I had overheard in the hospital between two women came back to me and that's when I made a decision to finally take control of my life.

The aftermath was terrible. As I said, nothing in the slum stayed secret, and once one person knew it was not long before everyone knew and my in-laws and Selvam found out. They came armed with sticks and insults, and at one point Selvam rushed out and found a big stone and would have crushed my head with it, had it not been for Prema who, seeing the commotion, broke all the rules of non-interference and came rushing in and stopped him. The presence of a stranger halted them and seeing the crowd gathering around the open door, my mother-in-law, Kaylani and Selvam swept out, still hurling insults at me, and promising me dire consequences for my once big act of defiance.

And in that same spirit of defiance, I went to the police station that evening and lodged a complaint against my husband and had him arrested. He spent the night in jail and was released the next day on the promise of good behaviour and the assurance that no harm would come to me. And while I rarely saw my in-laws after this, Selvam came and went at will, and he still hit me when he was drunk, but he never got me pregnant again, and Janaki did not get her son, at least not from me. I must have been twenty-two or twenty-three years old at the time and you see, I finally took matters into my own hand.

I had arranged to leave my children with Prema for a few days, and went to the Government hospital where I had borne my children, and making my first independent decision as a grown woman, I got myself a hysterectomy, and freed myself from the anguish of bearing another child ever again.

And through this all, the unseen goddess I had prayed to my entire life, watched, and I believe, gave me her blessing,

Epilogue

I met Madhuri in 2006, when I moved to Chennai. I lived in a luxurious apartment building with a gym and swimming pool and carefully guarded gates. The flat was on the fifth floor, and I had a big car and driver, and managed to get a job with a big media house. I swanned about five-star hotels and expats who lived a similar lifestyle to mine, better actually, who moaned about their hardship postings to India. I hung about with Indians who loved being around these expats as it made them feel special. I must confess that I always felt out of place and a little uncomfortable with it all, because despite coming from a well-to-do family, I came from humble beginnings, having had no help other than a mediocre college education in a subject I had no real interest in. I myself had got into a deeply abusive marriage, and left India to escape the inevitable trauma that would come with being a divorcee. Recently, a girlfriend told me a mutual friend had referred to me as that 'girl who got divorced,' and this was twenty years later.

So when Madhuri came into my life, in Chennai, it was a breath of fresh air. I had just moved into the apartment and was looking around for a cleaner, and through the usual grapevine of neighbouring maids and drivers, she was bought to me by her husband, as she was looking for work.

Frankly, I was not sure if I wanted her around as she could provide no references and I was too lazy to keep my things locked up, and I had been warned over and over that 'these people' steal. But I was also too lazy to keep looking and so she was hired.

She arrived at my home the next morning and I remember it well. She was in a flowered maroon saree and a blue blouse, and her hair was neatly plaited and a little string of flowers tied artistically around it. She had on tiny gold earrings, a lovely gold bangle and smelt fresh and clean. She had the biggest smile on her face and I warmed to her that instant – it was cheery with a hint of mischief. She had a small pert nose, a lovely oval face, beautiful, big sparkling eyes. I thought she was really quite pretty and told her so, and she looked most surprised, and shook her head not agreeing with me, but not wanting to disagree openly.

I showed her where the brooms and brushes and cleaning things were kept, and how to use everything, and what cleaning powders and liquids were meant to be used on which surfaces. She picked it up from the first go, despite my appalling Tamil, and I saw her trying to hide a giggle or two when I made some particularly bad grammatical goof-up.

She set to work right away, and I settled down to my favourite pastime of the morning which was 'what to wear today?'

An hour later she was hard at work, and I wanted a cup of tea, so I went to her and asked her if she would like one too. She looked most surprised that I had even asked, and shyly nodded yes, and trotted off towards the kitchen to make it. I stopped her, puzzled.

"Where are you off to?" I asked

"To make tea for you, amma," she responded.

"You continue your work. I'll make it," I said firmly and I went off to the kitchen to brew up some tea for the both of us. A few minutes later, I went out onto the balcony, placed two cups of tea on the table and called to her and asked her to come and sit down with me. She looked positively horrified when I tried to give her the cup.

"No amma, I'll get another cup," she said hastily.

"Why?" I asked puzzled.

"No Ma, I'll get another cup," and I, thinking she did not like my cups, and feeling slightly offended, told her to go and get another mug.

She was out the door and back in five minutes with a cracked, battered plastic mug and proceeded to pour the tea into that.

I stared at her in horror and annoyance. Did she really prefer that nasty thing to my lovely bone china cups?

"How on earth is that cup better?" I asked as nastily as I could in my rubbish Tamil.

She looked even more surprised than me and answered softly and apologetically, "Ma, I live in a slum, how can I drink from your mugs, I will pollute them."

I snapped at her in exasperation. "Don't be silly. Pour the tea back into my mug. Throw that nasty plastic thing away and drink your tea."

Her fear of offending me was greater than her fear of polluting my cups so she did as she was told, and I saw her hand trembling as she lifted it to her mouth. And thus began our morning ritual for close to three years. A shared cup of tea every morning in which she related snippets of her life to me, never once complainingly, but matter-of-factly, and with such dignity that it left me humbled every time.

I learned about her son and daughter, and the daughter she sometimes saw playing in the slum who never knew who her birth mother was. I learned about the horrors of having to look after a large group of disabled children when she was just a child herself. I learned with dismay of her treatment at the hands of her employers and in-laws. I learned with shock that she still got beaten by her husband regularly.

But most of all I learned that poverty does not always mean suffering. I learned from her that honesty in small things was a great virtue. She would find a pin on the floor and return it to me. I learned that she was an excellent cook and made a mean vegetable fry. I learned I could leave my house keys with her and everything in my home was in safer hands with her rather than mine, for she broke not a single cup or saucer during her time with me. She kept my home spotless and never asked for a raise. And when I gifted her daughter Sandhya some money for a birthday, she spent half the money buying me, who had everything, the biggest bar of chocolate available in the market.

I saw her share the things I gave her like extra vegetables, or sweets, or clothes or other little things, freely with her friends and neighbours. I saw that her own home was as spotless as she kept mine, no mean feat given she had no access to running water or sanitation facilities. I saw her guard her children fiercely, and the only thing she ever asked was that I pay their school fees, something I did gladly. She never let her daughter go anywhere alone, and she made sure they were neatly clothed and well-presented and well-spoken at all times.

I never saw her frown or be irritable. Given the life that she told me about over our morning tea sessions, I was amazed at her good cheer and compassion and gentle humour. In fact, she always found something to laugh at, especially when she related tales of how she had outwitted her husband. Her face grew sad when she spoke about being abandoned by her mother, but she admitted her mother had done the best she could, and I saw her care for her mother quite tenderly and give her money as and when it was needed.

She saw me through the death of my beloved pet, and while she could not understand why the death of a dog could affect me so profoundly, she understood loss better than others and stood by me like a rock through that dark time. She rubbed my feet and shoulders endlessly through my many illnesses and no task was too little or too big for her.

I was her defense in some small way, I suppose. I visited her in her home and met her friends. I took her out in my car and we went for dosas together. I took her husband aside and told him in no uncertain terms that if he ever hit her again, I would personally see to it he never made it out of jail. And at least for a few years she had some respite from his relentless violence. But then I had to leave Chennai and leave Madhuri, for I could not take her with me. I tried to find her work, but she was not ready to work for anyone else she said. And so, I drove away and tried not to cry as I left her behind to her life in the slum.

I saw her face in the rear-view mirror as we pulled away. A forlorn figure standing at the gates watching the car turn into the busy road and be swallowed up by the teeming traffic on the dusty roads of Chennai.

You can see her too. She is one of the many faces you will pass on the streets of India, sweeping them, or hurrying on to clean the homes of others, or standing by the wayside, bent and worn before her time. She is, to me, the embodiment of human courage, testament to what a human being can endure, to what the spirit can survive and still emerge proud and unsullied.

I stayed in touch with her for a few years. She went to work as a maid in another house, and said they were not very nice to her. She said she missed me, and this was mutual. The daughter that was taken away from her was unceremoniously returned to her as she was a girl, and therefore too much responsibility and expense. Thankfully, I could still hear the laughter in her voice on the occasions I phoned her, as she told me of the trials visited upon her by her children, stories not dissimilar to those that I hear from mothers from all walks of life, from all around the world. When I put down the phone I was, as always, humbled by her affection for me, and I picture her in her little room in Mandaveli, in Alwarpet, recalling her sweetness of nature and her simple authenticity and her strong spirit. I truly believe that she, and others like her, make the world a better place with their service and humility and courage. Madhuri was the embodiment of the feminine divine; strong yet gentle, resilient yet vulnerable, authentic yet so adaptable, timid and yet so very courageous. She is, to me, The Unseen Goddess.

Acknowledgements

This book is the result of so many people who believed in me.

Firstly, and as always, my beloved Carol Bujeau who still remains all I aspire to be.

A big thank you to my family… David, mum, dad, Sanjay, and Sujatha for… well… everything.

My gratitude to my non-genetic family from around the world… Karel Dobbels, Judith Ellis, Jude Angelo, Benton David, Susan Timothy, Flossie Jayakaran, Marie Longserre, Meghan Vozila, Harry Tee, Shagufta Patel, Gamze Tonoglu, Nalin Parikh, Hana Sadiq… how I hate that my heart lies scattered in so many different parts of the world.

Love and thanks to my rocks, my raakhee brothers Navroze Sethna and Meherzad Mehta - I am so blessed to count you as one of my own.

My incredible students at Izmir Institute of Higher Technology - you are my hope for a better world. Thank you for filling my heart as you have done.

I bow my head to Shreekumar Varma, writer extraordinaire, mentor and friend.

To the many friends and loved ones I have failed to mention here… I apologise. The list is long but you know who you are…

And of course, my dogs, past and present, who have been my proof that there is a loving God somewhere in this universe. Or a loving dog at the very least.

To Serif, Noel Hagman and Starla Keith - this book happened because of you. You, more than me, have been the voice for those whose journeys would otherwise go unnoticed. May

Villa Magna Publishing always be the beacon that guides readers to stories that matter. You have my heartfelt appreciation and thanks.

Glossary

Word	Meaning
Akka	Sister
Amma	Mother, madam
Ammachi	Grandmother
Anna	Elder brother
Ashram	Sanctuary
Auto	Three wheeled public transport
Ayah	Maid
Ayya	Sir
Beedi	Local cigarette
Bhaji	vegetable dish or pancake
Bindi	Coloured dot on forehead
Biryani	Spicy Indian risotto
Chappati	Flat bread
Curd rice	Yoghurt and rice dish
Dosa	Lentil and rice pancakes
Dupatta	Shoulder scarf
Idli	Rice and lentil dumpling
Jubba	Long shirt
Kala jamun	Deep fried milk dessert
Kolam	patterns made from chalk powder
Lungi	wraparound cloth worn by men
Madras	Chennai

Maharani	Queen
Murkus	Deep fried savoury snack
Namaste	Form of greeting
Pallu	End of a saree that hangs over the shoulderlong
Pavadai	Long skirt
Peon	Office clerk
Poriyal	Stir fry vegetables
Prasadam	Sweet offered at temples
Puja	Prayer ceremony
Puliogare	Tamarind rice
Raitha	Curd with onions or other vegetables chopped in..
Rasam	Spicy soup
Saheb	Sir, master
Salai	Road
Salwar	Long tunic with loose trousers for women
Sambhar	Lentil based curry
Samosa	Filled pastry snack
Savitri	Indian name, from legend of a virtuous Indian wife
Sundal	vegetable made from beans or chickpeas
Tasmac	Local liquor store
Thatha	Grandfather
Upma	Spiced Semolina dish
Vanniyar	A caste of South India
Vermillion	Red Powder applied at hairline

www.ingramcontent.com/pod-product-compliance
Lightning Source LLC
Chambersburg PA
CBHW040930050726
47507CB00022B/300